EN

SERIAL KILLER

A totally addictive psychological thriller
with a shocking twist

STEENA HOLMES

Bervie Springs Book 1

Originally published as *The Perfect Secret*

JOFFE BOOKS

Revised edition 2024
Joffe Books, London
www.joffebooks.com

First published as *The Perfect Secret* in 2020

Cover art by Nick Castle

ISBN: 978-1-83526-419-5

Some books I write because I 'need' to, some I write because I 'have' to, but this book I wrote because it was 'fun' to. A lot of that fun came with the help of one special friend, a woman who leads with a smile, a joy in her eyes and has the heart of a true Mama Bear . . . Alexius Karns. Thank you for being the inspiration for two characters, for your devious mind and for encouraging the handmade keychain idea!

1: THE ENDING OF THE PERFECT LIFE

Monday 6:49 p.m.

Premonition. Pay attention to that nudge of warning, and it can save your life.

I ignored that shiver, ignored the advice Mom told me oh-so-long ago. Ignored it even when I knew better.

Every time I don't listen, I tend to end up in jail.

After one of the worst days working at Soil and Springs Landscaping, I'm finally home, curled up on my second-hand, used-to-be-beige couch, in leggings and my favorite sweater, doing the one thing I've wanted to do all day.

Nothing.

Nothing means bliss, me-time. Nothing means a big bowl of cereal while watching the news followed by a long hot bath. Nothing means for the first time today, I have no one to be accountable to.

My cell rings and after being on the phone all day at work, I'm talked out. When it starts ringing again, I know it's Mom and I should answer, but texting is faster. A quick connect and I'm done.

Me: *Just got home. Call you later?*

She hates when I text instead of talk.

Mom: *Turn on the news.*

Me: *Why?*

Mom: *Tell me you're not involved.*

Me: *Involved? What?*

I have the news on; I always do at this time. What's her problem?

Mom: *Starla Bishop, stop playing games with me! Please tell me you are safe.*

Me: *Relax. I'm home. Involved in nothing. Playing it safe for thirteen months now.*

She knows this. She calls every single night to make sure. I'm a jailed bird without the prison bars.

Mom: *Then why did they say staff?*

I re-read her texts and feel a headache forming.

Why am I not surprised tonight mirrors how my day began? First, I poured hot coffee into my bowl of cereal. Later, I dropped my phone in the toilet after receiving a panicked text from my boss telling me to stay at the office and not answer any calls. Then I lost one of the diamonds on my new engagement ring after hitting it on the corner of my desk, and if that wasn't bad enough, while on my hands and knees, looking for it, I accidentally hit the panic button at the office and set off all the alarms, which of course, had the phones ringing off the hook.

My finger rubs the empty area on my ring. Nothing went my way today.

Premonition. It yells louder than inmates in a cell block with no heat. And while I'm doing everything right, it screams in my ear.

My phone goes off again.

Mom: *Starla, tell me what is going on. Do I need to come down?*

Curled up on the couch, legs tucked under, I unmute Sassy Sedona, the news anchor joking with Tyler, the weather guy. Normally I like their fun, sarcastic, grin-provoking interaction.

Not tonight. Tonight, their banter is aggravating. Annoying. Angering.

Mom blows up my phone with her texts, demanding more information.

Me: *Give me a minute. I have no idea what's going on. I'll call you when I do.*

The camera does a close-up pan on Sedona and her wide, welcoming, window-dressing smile disappears. In its place is her this-is-serious-pay-attention look.

"In breaking news, a local landscaper has been arrested with three charges of first degree murder. Here is Danai with more news."

My heart thumps to a disco beat. Thump. Thump. Thump. A bruising bass that drowns out every thought but one.

Local landscaper?

Shit. Shit-shit-shit-shit. Nothing else. Just shit.

A video plays on the television.

I recognize the company.

My legs hit the floor. I'm on my feet, chest constricting, and I wait, the milliseconds taking forever, before the headline flashing across the screen confirms what I don't want to admit.

Councilman Donald Dixon suspected of multiple murders. I'm not breathing, and my lungs do a one-two punch.

So many thoughts, so many questions, so many worries. So many fears.

Breathe. My fiancé's voice is in my ear. *Just . . . breathe.*

In. Out. No breath. Lungs hitch. Vision funnels. Black spots dance. Breathe . . . in.

My boss is being led away by the cops.

Not me and yet . . . me. My hair falling forward, my face hidden, my shoulders slouched, my wrists cuffed. Not me and yet . . . me, surrounded by flashing lights, police, cameras, being hauled away . . . again.

Not me. Not me. My boss.

My phone rings. I jerk, dropping it to the floor. Bang-bang-bang on my door.

I stumble back. Fall onto the couch.

"Open up. Police."

Boom-boom-boom. The knock is harder, louder. My front door sounds like it's about to break.

I know that force, I've heard it before.

My gaze switches from the television to the door and back to the television.

"I'm here on the grounds of Soil and Springs Landscaping—" Danai, the reporter, begins.

Another figure appears on the screen, being led away.

My heart thuds to a stop.

"—where Donald Dixon, finance director and councilor for Bervie Springs, along with his ex-wife Alexius Dixon, joint-owners of Soil and Springs Landscaping, have been arrested on three charges of first degree murder and accessory to murder for the co-defendant."

Shit. Shit-shit-double-shit.

I was just there. At the office. Planted that garden being dug up. Got a text message saying I could leave for the night.

That man in handcuffs. My fiancé. Donny. Donald Dixon. That woman in handcuffs. My boss. Alexius.

Thwack. My door bounces. I fumble forward, jerk the handle, swing it open. A man stands there with his mouth open, speaking words I can't hear.

The man, he seems familiar. It's the sharpness of his expression. I know that look. I've seen it too many times. On faces like his. Cops.

More men stand behind him with similar expressions. Men with guns.

I back up. The first cop is talking, but I hear nothing. No words. No sounds. Everything is muted. Every. Single. Thing.

They all step forward, but all I see are their holstered guns. Not pointed at me, but they could be. They have been.

I raise my hands.

Thirteen months ago, I had a sense something like this would happen.

Damn premonition. I knew better.

2: PROMISES ARE MEANT TO BE BROKEN

8:55 p.m.

I made myself a promise thirteen months ago.

I would not find myself back in this situation, back in a room like this, back where I've been detained. Again. And yet, here I am.

A prisoner of my own making, by my past, but not by my actions.

I'm here voluntarily, able and willing to answer any questions they may have, but that fact changes nothing. Not for me.

My lips are chapped, my hands clammy and cold, and my right calf is spasming, but I refuse to let my anxiety show. I've been in rooms like this before and I know even one small emotional slip could have devastating consequences.

This room is the same as all the other interrogation rooms I've been in. One metal desk. Four cold chairs. A large one-way mirror facing me. A camera up in the corner recording my every word and movement. Bottle of water on the table.

A warm air blows on the back of my neck, but it's not to keep me warm. The goal is to make me tired, make me slip up, say too much.

I don't know what they're hoping to find out from me.

I play with the ring on my finger, still not used to the weight. My finger covers the missing diamond from this morning.

I can't believe I'm here. That Donny is here. I will repeat to every single officer who asks that Donny is the type to help college students finance a new vehicle, to buy a sleeping bag and tent for the homeless man who sleeps in the alley next to his dealership and to create a program to help freed inmates start over. Ask me if he's a killer and I'll say no.

They'll believe me, too, for one simple fact. I know killers.

But Alexius? Nothing she does surprises me. She probably bathes in all that blood she had me order six months ago. She says it's for her soil experiments, but I can sniff out a lie every time, and she reeks of it.

"Any way a girl can get a hall pass? Bathroom break?" I speak directly into the mirror. I know I'm being watched.

I've sat here over an hour. Staring back at the woman in the mirror. I see the woman who used to sit in these rooms, rooms that meant I'd chosen the wrong path.

Again.

Same face but more wrinkles. Same scar on my chin from a knife fight. Same piggy nose I used to get beat up for. Same, but different.

Donny tells me to look for the good, to see the beauty he sees when he looks at me. I'm only seeing the ugly, the shame. Shame has a way of flaunting what the dye job, makeup, and new clothes try to conceal. Shame shows the years prison has added. That mirror I'm staring into holds the power to make me feel naked.

This room holds more power over me than it should. I hate myself a little for that.

He says there's more to me than I recognize, that it's always been there, beneath the surface. I need every inch of the good person he thinks I am right now.

Thirteen months ago, Donny saved me. A few months ago, I decided it was my turn to save him.

The dipshits-with-a-stick-up-their-ass cops are making me wait before they show up with questions and accusations. But this time, I have the upper hand. I've done nothing wrong.

A muted cough comes from the other side of the door. I turn, hiding my shaking hands. I remind myself this time is different.

I'm not guilty. And I haven't been arrested. Yet.

Remain calm. Sit up straight. Speak clearly. Show them I'm a changed woman.

"Starla Bishop?"

The moment I feel my lips move into a grin, I squash them. "Starla, I'm Detective Leon Spikes." He drops a file, my file, on the table and pulls out the chair opposite me. The attempted smile doesn't change his expression, which tells me the attempt was just that — an attempt.

He looks as old as I feel. The lines on his face reveal more to me than he knows. He's seen a lot. Too much. What's he like? Stone cold hard? Indifferent? Rigid? Dangerous?

I stay silent. Show no fear. It's the only way to survive.

"My partner is waiting to take you to the bathroom," he says.

I stand, shoulders straight, hands relaxed. I wait for him to open the door.

A female officer stands in the opening. Her face is blank, eyes emotionless. She nods and moves one step back.

I step out and stare down the corridor. Will she walk me past the room where Donny sits, watching his life be destroyed?

The woman points to a door across the hall. Five steps. Five steps from my door to the bathroom. She holds it open and follows me in.

It's a small room. Two stalls, two sinks, one large ass mirror. "You need to go too?" My voice barely cracks. I step past her and close the door to the first stall.

I don't need to use it. I just had to get out of that room.

She's still there when I exit. She has that look that says more than it should. I wash my hands, taking my time to lather the soap, rinse under the warm water. She hands me a paper towel, opens the door.

Detective Leon Spikes is still there. Sitting in that chair. Reading through his notes.

Leon Spikes. Do I call him Leon or Spikes? Leon was the chaplain during my first prison sentence.

Spikes it is.

"Are you aware of why you are here?" he asks after I sit.

I want to remain silent. I want to have a staring contest. I want to let the Old Starla out and issue a challenge no cop would dare to ignore. But this is the New Starla, the innocent Starla.

"You arrested my fiancé and his ex-wife." My voice doesn't fluctuate, making me appear cold, composed, and completely calm. I hope. "I'm here because I work for them and you think I'm an accomplice." The breath I let out releases all the stress I'd been trying to hide.

I'm good at lying to myself. I've been doing it for years.

3: THREE TIMES THE CHARM?

9:43 p.m.

My file sits between us on the table, stuffed with pages filled with every detail of my sordid past. A past Spikes will use against me.

"I want to thank you for coming in."

"Didn't really seem like I had much of a choice."

"There's always choices, Ms. Bishop. You of all people must know that." Spikes opens my file and rifles through the pages, looking for . . . what exactly?

You can't tell me he hasn't gone through those sheets a half dozen times now. He knows about every arrest. Every incarceration. Every . . . thing.

"Were you aware of your employers' extra-curricular activities?"

Of all the questions he could be asking, that wasn't on my list of top ten.

"Aware that Alexius likes to play in dirt? She's a pedologist. They own a landscaping company." My sarcasm runs thick.

"You like to play in the dirt too?" he asks me, his tone bordering on mockery.

I hold up my fingers so he can see my bright pink manicure.

"Looks new." He inspects them more than a man should. "No nicks or chips, so I'd say you got them done yesterday. Mimi's Nail Boutique?"

I snort. Can't help it. What? Does he have my bank records too? I bet the receipt was on the coffee table and his snoops picked it up along with whatever else they deemed important.

My house is going to be a disaster zone when I get home.

"Do you get yours done at Mimi's too?" I look at his nails and sit back, surprised to find his nail beds in good shape. They look clean, no dirt to be found; he either takes care of his nails or doesn't like to get his hands dirty.

"I've never been able to trust a man with clean hands."

"Who says I'm not trustworthy?"

Damn it, I said that out loud.

"There's something about a man who works with his hands. Says a lot about their nature, don't you think?" Most cop hands I've seen have a few calluses, knuckles roughed up from fist fights, but for the most part they're soft, smooth; sit behind a desk, drive behind a wheel kind of hands.

Spikes takes a look at his palms and gives a shrug before picking up his pen.

"Donny has real man hands," I say. "Rough skin, chipped nails. He's not afraid to do what needs to be . . ." I don't finish my sentence because I know how it sounds. "He has to, you know? Owning a car dealership means he has a lot of used vehicles to take care of." Even I hear how weak that sounds.

I scratch the side of my neck, then pull my hand down back to my lap. Everyone has tells, and the people behind that glass, they're trying to read me like a well-read childhood classic.

I know better.

I'm straddled on a wobbly fence, not sure what side I belong on. I'm innocent, but also guilty in their eyes. In their eyes, I'll always be guilty.

"Were you aware?" Spikes asks me again.

"No." Simple. To the point. The truth.

"To be clear, you were not aware that your employers were hiding bodies in gardens they landscaped for the town?"

I rub at a spot beneath my eyebrow. I think I over-tweezed it last night before bed.

"I was not aware that Alexius hid bodies, no."

The look on Spikes' face reminds me of Mom's when I'm trying to get around being one hundred percent honest with her.

"Do you know how many victims we've found so far?" he asks me.

I shake my head. I don't want to know. I've been avoiding rolling that question around in my head, not wanting to dwell on how many people have died.

"Do you think Donald knows?"

I shake my head, not able to answer thanks to the golf-ball-sized wad of words mixed with emotions currently lodged in my throat. *I will not cry. I will not cry. I will not cry.* I look away, focus on a penny-sized scuff on the wall and empty my mind of everything that may make me cry.

"You have kids?" The question jumps off my tongue the moment I return my attention to Spikes.

His brows scrunch together. He has no idea where I'm going with this.

Neither do I.

"Teenagers," he says.

That explains it. He gives off that father vibe I'd always wished I'd known. Don't get sucked in. Don't get played. "Whatever you are hinting at, can we lay it out? Speak plain?"

He nods.

"The Donny I know isn't a killer."

His head bobs. He's actively listening. Good.

"You believe that?"

"With all my heart. Donny . . . he's different. He pushes me to be different, to be better." I don't hide the warmth in my voice, the smile.

"Trying to turn your life around?" He glances up in surprise.

"I have turned my life around." There's no lie in my voice because it's one hundred percent the truth. Well . . . maybe more like 79 percent but isn't life all about a work in progress? I'll get there.

The point is, I want to get there and that's all he needs to know.

"Yeah? Why this time? According to your file, you're a regular at the Thompson Hopper Female Correctional Facility." There was no censure in his voice, no accusation. He said it with the same intensity as if he were reading out my home address.

"Third time's the charm, maybe?" I say, lifting my shoulder in an indifferent shrug, but we both know it's not. Why this time? Good question. Looking back, I wish I had done this sooner. It's a lot of hard work, but I'm a better person for it.

"I never thought I could do anything different until I met Donny. He showed me a different way to live. A better way that doesn't have to include breaking the law."

Detective Spikes nods, writes something down on his notepad. "Must have been an adjustment."

It wasn't really a question, more like a statement and I must admit, I'm almost liking this guy.

"Keep in touch with any of your old contacts?"

"No."

"Sure about that?"

That part about almost liking him? Gone.

"We've got time," he says. "Don't feel you need to rush your answers or anything." Spikes leans back in his chair, crosses his arms and waits, as if he isn't in the middle of an active crime scene where time is of the essence.

"Who's rushing? You asked a question, I answered. I severed all ties the day I walked out of prison." And yet, something niggles at the back of my mind, something that tells me I'm not being as honest as I could be.

Could be, should be, does it matter? There's only one goal here — to walk out on my own, without cuffs wrapped around my wrists or ankles.

"Listen, Starla, I'm not your enemy." His piercing gaze, almost hypnotic, has me wanting to believe him. "I get how you'd think so, from foster care to jail . . . how can you trust me, right? But who else can you trust right now? I'm the only one on your side." He says this like it matters, like it holds weight when it actually doesn't. I'm used to it.

Cops have never been on my side.

"I'm only here for answers. I'm not your enemy." His voice lowers as he repeats himself. "But I could be your best friend, if you work with me."

Like I haven't heard this line before.

My skepticism is written all over me in invisible ink and he's the decoder. I don't like it. He leans forward, hands clasped on the table and for the first time since opening the door, gives me a mask-off, blinds-open, honest smile.

"The first cop who said that sent me to juvie for shoplifting." I've been fed this line too many times as well. "Do you know what I lifted?"

Spikes says nothing. He taps his pen against the metal table, giving me the space, the room I need to talk.

I lace my fingers together and tap my thumbs. One. Two. Three. Three heart beats. Three blinks. Three breaths.

"A sandwich."

He blinks.

"I have a hard time believing cops want to help." The truth tumbles out before I can shut my mouth. Damn it.

"Rough foster life?" The tapping stops. His left brow lifts as if he just realized something.

"Same story, different kid." I heard enough horror stories in prison to know foster care came with its own scars.

His head dips in a slight nod. "I've been in the system. I get it."

That surprises me. Never have I had a cop be that honest like that. Never.

"Mrs. Cranberry, the foster mom, held a strict routine. Dinner at five on the dot. Miss it, and you get nothing. I was always late," I explain, as if it matters.

His brows curl inward until they resemble a giant grey caterpillar. "Seems harsh," he says.

Seems harsh? It was harsh. One small mistake and my future disappeared; my path written in cement.

"The shop owner made me an example. Said I'd threatened her with physical violence. What a joke. All anyone had to do was look at my scrawny body and they'd know."

I look away. So many years ago, the catalyst for all the paths taken since. The pain is still there. Still gnawing, still aching. Like a phantom pain, it'll always be there.

This stupid sandwich memory has cost me. Stolen sleep, time and money.

The pain is still fresh from recent counseling sessions.

"I'm sorry."

Two words. Yet, how he says them, the honest softness of his face, leaves me believing him.

I'm tossed around like a volleyball between wanting to believe him and knowing I shouldn't. I need barriers to be erected. I need my mask in place.

"Why apologize for something you didn't do?" Thank God my voice doesn't betray how much this means to me. It's the first real apology I've gotten from a cop. That sinks in, and I'm not sure how I feel about it. "But thank you." I give a very small I-know-I-need-to-be-polite kind of smile. "My counselor would be proud."

"Your counselor?" There's a look on Spikes' face, a look that says I just gave him some information he'd been unaware of, information that could come in handy, information I could have kept as a bargaining tool.

Damn it. I need to stop speaking my thoughts.

"Therapy." I once would have spat the word out, but not anymore. "I'm broken, go figure. Repeated prison sentences can do that. Donny found her for me."

"Have a name for this therapist?" Spikes pen is poised above his notepad.

"She's not going to tell you anything."

"She will if I have a warrant," he says. "Do I need one?"

Does he? "I've nothing to hide."

He tears out a piece of paper from his notebook and pushes it toward me. He doesn't ask me anything, doesn't say what he wants, but he doesn't need to either.

I grab his pen, write down her name. Leigh Kits. "If I had my phone, I'd give you her number too." I'm trying to be polite.

"I know Leigh. She's good." He looks at the name, gives me a nod and folds the paper in half.

He doesn't say anything. Why isn't he? Why isn't he bombarding me with questions? My stomach is a cauldron of mixed emotions, anxiety, fear, worry, anger . . . I'm not in control and I hate that.

"Is Donny going to be okay?" I ask, turning the conversation away from me. "He's innocent."

"So you've said." Something crosses Detective Spikes' face that bothers me, but I can't pinpoint the expression. His shoulders push back and he taps his finger on the file in front of him.

My file. I've never liked having a closed file in front of me.

"How exactly is it you'd know he's innocent, Starla? I have multiple bodies being dug out of flower beds that tell me a different story."

Good question. Even though I feel gut-punched with that knowledge, I'm not sure I'm ready to answer.

4: COCKROACHES ALWAYS SURVIVE

10:15 p.m.

"Tell me Donny is okay." I sound calm, much to my surprise. Tension builds inside me until I'm about to erupt.

Old Starla would have. New Starla can't.

Spikes' left eye squints, a nerve in his cheek twitches, but he remains silent.

That silence weighs about as much as a rock. A rock the size of Mount Everest.

"Okay isn't the word I'd use to explain the predicament he's in." There's a tone to his voice; I can't quite make it out. Sarcasm mixed with . . . something. Irony?

I want to ask more, figure out what he's trying to tell me, but I stop myself.

"Will I get introduced to your partner?" I ask instead. Eventually she'll join us. They always do.

"Kaarns? She does the heavy lifting while I'm in here." He lifts his right shoulder and rolls it. Despite his calm facade, he feels the unease between us.

Glad it's not just me.

"Are you going to arrest me?" It's the question I've wanted to ask but haven't.

Spikes leans back, pushes his shoulders until the crack doubles, then triples, until his whole spine sounds like a xylophone.

"If I need to, yes. If evidence shows you're more involved than we've been told, yes. But for now, your cooperation is appreciated."

My cooperation, which means I have a choice. Force the issue, demand to leave and have them arrest me, detain me and make my life hell, or play nice, answer their questions, play the game. Win the game and walk out of here a free woman.

"There's things about Donny you don't know."

"Like what?" Spikes seems patient, ready to wait as long as it takes for me to tell him everything.

"He won't give up his ex-wife, for one. He'll do what he can to protect her. But he doesn't know that this—" I lift my hands and point to the mirror behind him — "this whole experience will destroy him, his career . . . he has no idea."

"But you do."

I nod.

"I can promise you he's fine." Spikes must read my face, understand my thoughts. Didn't need the sarcasm, though.

"How do you know? You're in here with me. Unless—" I lean to the side to see if he has an earpiece in — "someone just gave you a check-in?" Yep, it was there. Good to know. He'll be fed information as it comes.

"I know Donald Dixon. We . . . go way back. He'll survive, always does, always will, the man's a . . ." Spikes clears his throat but doesn't finish the sentence.

"A what? A cockroach, that's what you were going to say, wasn't it?"

Spikes shrugs. "Like I said, I know the man."

Every hair on my body bristles at his tone. "I know the man too." I rush to defend him.

Spikes shakes his head. "You know the man he wants you to know. I've known him since we were kids. Men like him, they don't change."

"Or women like me?" I take exception to this because I did, I am . . . changed, changing.

Spikes pulls back with a knee-jerk reaction.

"I believe you."

I'm stunned. First an apology and now belief. Two things I've never experienced from a cop. Until now. There's a hint of sincerity in his voice that surprises me.

"Him on the other hand . . ." Spikes doesn't finish, but I get it. I can read between the lines.

This isn't a first for me, meeting someone with a different opinion of Donny. Truth be told, I once felt the same way. Until I got to know him. But to hear it so matter-of-fact, without the hint of a past between them, but as if it is what it is, I'm on the edge of a ledge crumbling beneath my feet.

"He's a man who's been through shit and came out looking like a diamond," I say. "Just because he's into politics and sells used cars doesn't mean he's a sleaze bag."

"I've always thought of him more like a fungus," Spikes says, something between a sneer and a snort in his voice.

I play with my ring, twirling it around my cold finger.

"Fungus that grows in shit. There's no diamond quality about that." Spike looks at my ring. "Look, it's plain you worship the guy. How about you tell me why?"

Worship Donny? I'm not that naive. I believe in him, which is what he needs right now. I'm probably the only one who does.

5: MORE NEWS ISN'T GOOD NEWS

10:47 p.m.
DETECTIVE LEXI KAARNS

A low buzzing vibrates in my pocket. I pull out my phone and scroll through the messages lighting up my home screen.

"We found another one." I swallow the mixture of excitement and dread as I turn from the mirror and face my team. "Add the Kincaid property to the map. Corner of Cedars and Pike. Find the contract date for that one, add it to the list."

My stomach coils, winding tighter and tighter until it resembles an unopened jack-in-the-box.

I count, even though I don't need to, how many locations are on the map now.

Four.

Four unearthed gardens with multiple bodies. How many in each grave, we have yet to determine. But it makes me nauseous. One body is too many, as Spikes said earlier.

My fingers are solid bricks of ice. I rub them together, needing some heat. It's shock, that's why I'm so cold. Not to mention the hours spent outside, standing over the mounds of dirt at our first location as the crew carefully repositioned each bone found from the garden bed to the blue tarp.

Bodies were expected. What I hadn't expected, though, was how I'd process finding them.

Spikes had pulled me aside to walk me through the next few hours. Nothing he said, nothing I'd seen, could have prepared me. What they show you on television, those detective shows where Forensics finds and catalogs bones, that sure as hell didn't prepare me.

"Found another site," I say to Spikes through the earpiece. "Kincaid house."

He rolls his shoulders, leans back in his chair and I picture the look on his face. Deep brown eyes that almost look black. A muscle twitch in his right cheek. A slight lowering of his eyelids as he processes the news.

Reading him hasn't always been easy. He's not an open book, more like a locked vault with decades of dust and dirt gummed in any tiny crevice.

"Stop being so nice to her. She's playing you." I know he knows this. Why play good cop when it's not needed?

We don't know much but what we do know has helped in making the arrests. We know she's involved, that she was brought in to run the office so the Dixons could keep their hands clean. She's a decoy but no less guilty.

Spikes thinks she's an unwilling partner.

I think she's playing us.

"Anyone see that ring? It's massive."

I glance behind me and catch the nods, but that's it. We're all engrossed in the conversation Spikes is having with Bishop in there.

I argued with Spikes to arrest her, but he wouldn't listen to me.

This has been the year of murders for Bervie Springs. In the past six months, three bodies have been discovered, buried in various locations around town. The first had been attributed to hitchhiking gone bad, the body dumped in a shallow grave just outside the town limits. The second body had been found by the new owners of a home and their dog. The third was a university student.

These were my first murders, but not Spikes'. He had transferred back home from New York, to get away from this, wanting a quiet life where he could retire.

I'm lucky to be partnered with him. I know this. He knows this. Hell, everyone in the squad knows this. Especially now.

I bounce on my toes, nervous energy flowing through me. "When did he buy that ring?"

No response.

I shift and look at the group sitting behind me. "Come on, folks, we've got Dixon's bank records and boxed receipts. Who found the ring?" I look specifically at Danvers, the new kid tasked with going through those receipts.

We hit the jackpot when we found a shelf full of shoeboxes with receipts going back five years. The crap he kept from shops hours away — the guy was hiding something and we were going to find it.

"Nothing," Danvers' voice squeaks as he steals a look at me. "I flagged all the big purchases but there's been no jewelry."

Odd. That ring is huge.

"Keep looking. Look for insurance too. There has to be something."

I turn my focus back to the room with Spikes. I hit my earpiece.

"We're looking for info on the ring. Maybe it's an heirloom?"

My voice is lowered, not enough that I'm not overheard, but enough that Bishop can't hear from the earpiece in Spikes' ear. We learned the hard way. "How long has she been wearing it? Alexius still wears hers; did you notice?"

What ex-wife wears a ring from a ruined marriage? He taps his pen. Our signal that he's on it.

6: HOW DIRTY ARE YOUR HANDS?

10:59 p.m.

"How long do you plan on keeping me here?" I look around the cold room and shiver slightly, despite the warm air still caressing the back of my neck.

"As long as it takes. I'm not going to lie to you, Starla. We've got multiple bodies right now being dug up in various garden beds throughout town." Spikes pulls out a few printed images and lays them out in front of me, exactly like what you'd see on television. I glance away, not wanting to see the gory mass graves.

"Do you recognize any of these locations?" His voice is insistent, his tone resolute.

Locations. I might be okay to do that, to look. As long as there's no blood or dismembered body parts of . . .

I give a sweeping glance over the photos again, to see if anything stands out.

"That one." I point to the third photo. "That's Brown's Pond, one of the new development areas. Alexius had that contract set up before I came on board."

Detective Spikes pushes the photo closer to me. "How can you be sure?"

I jab my finger onto a bench that's off to the side of the photo. "We just had the plaques added to the benches. Donny and I went out and took care of that ourselves a few weeks ago."

"When exactly?"

"A few weeks ago. I don't know. I'd need my calendar and notebook to give you anything more specific." How do they expect people to remember dates and times at the snap of a finger? It's ridiculous.

"Can you tell me everything you did when you were there? Don't leave a deal or conversation out, please."

I look behind Spikes, to the glass. "No chance fresh coffee's been made, is there? It's already past my bedtime."

Spikes yanks his neck from side to side, loud crick-crack-cricks happening as he does. "Good idea. What do you take in yours? I'll see if I can scrounge up something to snack on too. It's been a long night and I missed dinner." Spikes pushes his chair back and stands.

He's going to get me the coffee? Not send a lackey out instead?

"Just cream, thank you."

Spikes nods, places all the photos and random papers back in the file and takes it with him as he leaves.

I lean back in my chair, a little caught off guard. More than a little, actually. Just as I'm about to tell him about Brown's Pond, he gets up and leaves?

My gaze goes from the mirror to the camera back to the mirror.

How many people are watching me? How many do they have working this case, the largest mass murder case in Bervie Springs since . . . never?

In the year I've been here, there's been a few questionable deaths, but nothing like this.

There's a small knock before Spikes pushes the door open with his shoulder. He sets the coffee cups down on the table, one for each of us, and drops a container he'd carried under his arm. It hits the table on an angle, rolls almost to the edge before it stops.

"Wife packed me some homemade cookies. Figured I'd share." Spikes rights the container and opens the lid. A delicious waft of chocolate floats toward me and my stomach growls in response.

I haven't eaten since earlier this afternoon.

I sip my coffee, enjoy a cookie and wait for him to make the next move.

"It's going to be a long night," Leon Spikes says. "More bones were discovered at a different property."

More bones? Not bodies? There's a difference. This I learned from a cellmate once. Bones means the deaths are far from recent, may be dismembered or there may be multiple bodies in one grave. If he'd said they'd found another body, that's one person, one location . . .

My insides do a set of jumps and twirls, and I'm about to throw up the cookie I just ate.

He must see it on my face too because one second Detective Spikes is about to raise his cup to his lips and the next, he's lurching to the side to grab the garbage can left close to the door.

I remain in my seat, stomach contents intact, but I appreciate the gesture.

"Brown's Pond." I push the words out of my mouth and swallow the bile that chases after them. "Donny and I were there. If there's evidence, that's why."

"Interesting you'd say that. What kind of evidence should we expect from you there?"

"Fingerprints, hair samples, basic DNA stuff," I say. "We were there for a solid three hours attaching the plaques to different park benches. We petted a few dogs, had a picnic, watched the sunset before we headed back to my place."

"Did you work in any of the gardens?"

"Then or anytime?" I want to be clear I understand what I'm being asked.

Detective Spikes doesn't reply. Nothing on his face changes. Not a flicker of a lash, not a quirk of his lips, not a pulsing vein in his cheek. He's a rock; solid, firm, just as cold.

I can't seem to get a good read on him.

"We did not carry shovels with us to bury bodies, if that is what you are attempting to pull out of me." My sarcasm is real, and I've no doubt my eyes did roll right then.

"Do you always deflect when you're asked a question?"

"Do I . . ." I halt the rest of the words about to tumble out. "If they were understaffed or late on a project, there were times Donny or Alexius would ask me to put in some extra hours to help."

"Did you at Brown's Pond?"

I scramble in haste as I go through my memories. "Sure, I think . . ." I say, trying to remember distinctly if I had or not. I probably had.

"You don't remember?" I can hear the "are you kidding me?" in his voice.

"If I'm hands deep in dirt, it's usually after a full day in the office and it's usually not just one location I visit, but a few at a time. Alexius doesn't trust me much when it comes to her plants, so she doesn't have me doing much beyond digging and filling."

He writes this down. "Filling what? Holes?"

"The beds with mulch or stone. I don't dig much either, for the record. She'll leave potted plants in sections she wants a hole dug. I dig the size of the container and drop it in, water and leave. That's it."

He's still writing the information down. "Ever fill in a hole where a dead body had been left?"

"No."

"How would you know?"

"Never seen a dead body, human or animal, in any hole I've filled with a plant or shrub."

Detective Spikes pauses for a moment. "Correct me if I'm wrong, but you've done landscaping before, haven't you?"

I nod. I was on the grounds team at the prison. I always figured that came into play when Donny first hired me.

"Ever killed anyone before?"

I snort. "You've read my file." Not quite the answer he's looking for but . . . oh well.

Spikes' gaze remains on the paper in front of him. "But you would know how to dispose of a body if it became necessary, correct?"

I lean back in my chair and plop my hands down on the table, my palms creating a slight slapping sound.

"Spend as much time as I have in prison" — sarcasm tumbles out of my mouth with truth I know I shouldn't be admitting to — "with roommates full of interesting histories and you can figure out just about anything." Even as the words leave my mouth, I realize I'm painting myself into a corner.

I push my lips tightly together and swallow. What have I done?

7: IT'LL BE DIFFERENT THIS TIME . . . PROMISE

Thirteen Months Ago

The electronic whirl of the closing gates sent a shudder that tiptoed along my entire body, and when those gates clicked, an electric jolt of energy pushed me forward, away from the steel barriers, from the place I'd called home for the past four years.

To a home I never wanted to return.

I couldn't get away fast enough. The push was everything I needed to leave my past behind.

I was determined to never return. Life would be different. I would be different.

The day was gorgeous. Brilliant sun with a gentle breeze that teased my split ends. The exit process hadn't taken too long and this time, my exit counselor was there to say goodbye, a first for me.

The long road ahead of me was busy. I wasn't the only inmate being released. A few trees lined the pavement, but not many. To the right was a parking lot full of old Fords and Chevys. A few new ones were in the mix, probably belonging to lawyers. It felt . . . surreal to be out here, looking back at the gate, the yard, the bar-covered windows. Surreal and almost . . . wrong.

It only felt that way because I normally looked out the other way, through the window, past the bars, the yard, to the gate and vehicles beyond.

To the left of where I stood was a guard post. A crowd was gathered there, but I only cared about one person who waited for me.

Mom.

"Starla, baby," Mom gushed as she pulled me in for a long mama-bear hug. She smelled of vanilla and rosemary, fresh baked bread and Lysol wipes. She smelled of home and my eyes filled with tears I didn't want to shed.

They fell anyway.

She leaned away, her own eyes sparkling and gave me a full-body stare down, shaking her head. "Too skinny, like always. Let's go eat," she said, "you need a good meal, a long shower and a soft bed."

We had a release day routine. Meal at a local diner with the best milkshakes, followed by some me time. Mom and I would spend the evening curled up on her couch and caught up on movies before I headed to bed.

I didn't say anything as we walked to her truck, I just reached out and held her hand, tight, like a small child in need of reassurance.

She squeezed back, letting me know I wasn't alone anymore.

Mom filled the void of silence between us during the drive with small talk, filling me in on the latest gossip around town.

It wasn't until we were seated in the seen-better-days diner, our butts in the cracked vinyl booth, milkshakes in front of us both, that she heaved a very long, tiresome sigh that told me more than I'd wanted to know.

"It'll be different this time," I said before she opened her mouth.

I read the disappointment on her face. It was in the lines around her eyes, the way her smile faltered, the sudden drop of her shoulders as she leaned forward.

"You said that last time, Starla."

It was all there in her tone.

She didn't owe me a thing, but I owed her everything.

Everything and more. My incarceration had taken a toll on her. She looked older, more tired, more . . . just more. It hurt, the knowledge I was the cause of all those lines, the weariness, the grey hair.

"How long will it take this time for you to be mixed up with the wrong crowd? To be lured in? You never could turn away from a promising target."

She might as well have inserted a knife into my heart with a twist. Damn, that hurt. But she was right . . . I always got lured right back in. The idea of risk and reward was something I never seemed able to resist.

"I'm clean. I'm making changes. I swear." I needed her to believe me. I wasn't going back to prison. I wasn't going to be played again. I wasn't going to take another job that promised rainbows and instead offered concrete. I'd been promised a lot of money and a contract list, but what I ended up with was slops and prison wear.

I had a whole list of 'I wasn't going to do this again' and I meant it all too.

"Starla, you had a year added on for dealing inside prison." Mom's voice had that let's-not-play-this-game kind of tone to it.

"I was framed. I wasn't playing by the rules of another inmate and that was the price." I knew the consequences for my actions but at the time, it didn't matter.

Her lips went pencil-thin. "It's never simple with you, is it?"

I pulled my gaze from hers. No, nothing was ever simple with me. That was the problem. Simple equaled boredom. I preferred the thrill, the chase, the knowledge that any wrong move could crumble the house-made-from-cards I'd so carefully created.

"This time will be different." I repeated the mantra. This time, it was more for me than her. It was a reminder that I had to be different this time around if I wanted a different outcome to occur.

Mom didn't say a word, which made me nervous. I hid the shaking of my hands by playing with my hair, pulling the elastic out and redoing my messy bun. I needed her to believe me.

I needed to believe me.

"I know I'm a strong person, but I can't handle you going back in, Starla, I just can't." She pushed her strawberry milkshake to the side and picked at the fries on her plate.

"You won't have to handle it again. I promise." I took a bite of my chicken wrap that was half gone and chewed. God, it tasted so good. Like fresh cotton candy good. "I have a plan," I said, once my mouth wasn't so full.

"Finish your food, please." Mom looked away.

I quickly swallowed, wiped my hands on my pants and placed my elbows on the table.

The southern-belle-turned-northerner gave me one of her 'I raised you better' frowns, the one where her lips became pencil-thin while maintaining a semblance of a smile since we were in public.

I hated that look — all I felt was guilt, knowing I'd disappointed her yet again.

I pulled my arms back, dropped them to the side and sat up straighter. She was right; she had raised me better. From the age of fifteen to now, she'd been the only mother figure in my life, my last foster mom, the first foster parent to believe in me.

"Have you been to Bervie Springs lately?" I asked.

Her brows knitted together, the wrinkles on her forehead more pronounced. "Bervie Springs? Not really. There's not much there, why?"

"They've partnered with the prison to host a work program. One of the council members there interviewed me last week and offered me a job."

"A job?" Mom leaned forward, interest spreading across her features. Gone was the parental display of disappointment and in its place was interest.

That gave me hope. I didn't want her to give up on me. Not when I had just started to believe in myself.

"Doing what?"

"Administrative work for a landscaping company. Guess they're busy and the pay is decent. They'll provide a company vehicle for me after three months if I agree to help in the field if things get busy."

Her brows shot up to her hairline. "A vehicle and decent pay? Anything is better than working at a fast food place again," she said as she reached for another fry. "I'm assuming you said yes? It's not every day you have a job land in your lap like that."

I nodded. She was right. Doing administrative work, even if it's boring work just answering phones and scheduling projects, had to be better than flipping burgers or dishing out ice cream. My options were limited.

"How did you apply? Why didn't you tell me about this before?"

"It just kind of happened," I said in between sips of my shake. "Melanie, the counselor assigned to get me ready for my release, mentioned they'd been approached about this program. My name was on the list they'd given out. This company was the only one who requested an interview with me."

"At least they sought you out, that's positive." Mom relaxed then, I saw it in the way she leaned back against her seat. "So now what?"

"I need to head there, the day after tomorrow, for the official interview." I hated to ask to borrow her vehicle, but . . .

"I'll take you."

"Are you sure?"

The smile, her smile, said everything I needed.

She reached across the table, grabbed onto my hand and squeezed tight. "Love, if it means helping you onto a different path, I will do everything in my power to make it happen. Don't let this opportunity slip by, okay? God landed it in your lap, he's finally answering my prayers and . . ."

"Mom." I lost my belief in God a long time ago.

She waved her hand in the air, dismissing the warning in my voice. "Believe what you want, and I'll believe what I want, okay?"

I shrugged, stealing a fry from her plate.

"You need clothes." Mom pulled out her notebook she always kept on hand. "Clothes, shoes, probably some undergarments too." She looked up at me. "There's stuff in your closet, but your wardrobe needs to be updated if you're working in an office."

The level of excitement in her voice as she planned for my future warmed my heart. I'd been so afraid she'd given up on me. She'd told me the last time I'd been arrested that there were no more chances.

"Just pants and shoes. They'll provide tops for me to wear."

"You'll wear a dress for your interview, though. I have a few you can try."

I wasn't going to argue. If she was there, supporting me through this, I'd do anything she wanted. I was not going to disappoint her again.

8: WELCOME TO OZ

I was an imposter dressed in a red print cotton dress with a relaxed waist, wearing discounted flats that pinched my toes. Why had I agreed to wear a dress? I was more of a slacks and blouse type of girl, and I had a few outfits left in the closet that might not have shown their age.

The drive to Bervie Springs took forty-five minutes. Forty-five excruciating, long minutes along a two-lane highway where Mom spoke non-stop about nothing. It was a struggle to keep a friendly look on my face whenever I turned to acknowledge a point in her story. Didn't she see how nervous I felt? How inadequate? This stage of my release didn't normally hit for a week, yet here it was, two days after I left prison.

Why, out of everyone, had I been picked for a job I wasn't qualified for? Manual labor working in dirt, sure. But office work, dealing with computers and invoices and clients? Didn't they realize once word got out I was an ex-con, they'd lose business?

"Nervous?" Mom's chattering finally stopped.

"A little."

"I can tell. You've hardly said two words and I know you haven't been listening, despite that oh-so-polite smile you keep giving me."

I rubbed my nose with the palm of my hand. "Sorry. What if this isn't real? What if it's all a mistake? What if I get there and they realize it's not going to work? I mean, the program is new and apparently, I'd be the first hire. What if they realize how sketchy it looks with an ex-con working for them?" I couldn't keep my fears to myself, even if I'd wanted to.

"Starla Bishop." Mom let one hand off the wheel and reached over to grasp mine. "You stop that nonsense right now. Negative talk isn't going to help you get anywhere in life. I taught you better than that."

"Out of your mouth, your heart will speak," I repeated, my voice blending in with Mom's as we recite together advice she always gave me. Time and time again.

"Be positive," she said, a motherly attempt to encourage me that I desperately needed. "Speak it out and it'll come true. Look for the positive and you'll be surprised at what you find." She squeezed my hand before returning hers to the wheel.

We were getting closer. The welcome sign to Bervie Springs, New York, was just up ahead. It was known as the garden town and even before you passed the welcome sign, you could see why. Rather than fields of grass along the side of the highway, old wooden fences covered in climbing vines and flowers invited you to come and stay for a while.

I'd be more than happy to stay as long as they would have me.

"This just might be what you need," Mom said, "a fresh start in a town where nothing happens."

"You know small towns are just as bad as cities, right?" I snuffed out the sarcasm as best I could.

The look on her face said I didn't do a very good job.

"Less opportunity, how about that?"

I shrugged. My plan, if this all worked out the way I needed it to, was to spend my days at work, then lock myself in my room at night. No bars. No shopping trips. No walking the streets where I'd meet those I shouldn't. Keep my nose clean. My hands spotless. My feet planted.

"Do you need to check in with the local department here?" There was a smile in her voice, but I caught the slight tremble too. She needed me to remain safe just as much as I did.

"It's probably a good idea." I wasn't sure if it would be a requirement for employment or what, but the drop of Mom's shoulders told me I'd said the right thing.

"Did we leave ourselves enough time for coffee? Maybe walk around a bit? Unless it's too hot. If it's too hot, you don't want to start sweating. Maybe we should just find a cafe and have a coffee." Mom's nervous energy was about to make me go crazy.

I reached a hand across and grabbed hold of hers.

"I did a Google search on your laptop last night. There's a bakery close by which claims to have the best coffee in town and there's an outdoor sitting area too. Let's go there."

She nods and lets out a deep breath. "I'm not sure who's more nervous. Me or you?"

I give a small laugh, the kind that answers the question without having to say the words.

"That's what I thought," she said, giving my hand a soft squeeze.

We remained silent as we coasted into town, her slowing down to match the speed limit. The town should have been called Bervie Gardens. From one flower bed to the next, it was like living in the Land of Oz but instead of a yellow brick road to walk on, this town offered a flower-lined street to drive down.

There were flower baskets as far as the eye could see, hanging from street lights. The bridge we'd just driven across had been covered in trailing ferns and geraniums. Every single lawn in front of every single house had a garden either beneath the front windows, beside the front porch or along the front walkway.

"I'm thinking you might be a little busy," Mom mumbled.

"Is this the garden capital of New York state?" The window was down on my side and it was too much for me to keep my head inside the vehicle. I was like a golden lab in a truck, head sticking out, tongue flapping in the wind. Except, my tongue wasn't flapping, but my mouth was gaping.

After being in prison for four years, this was heaven. Instead of steel bars, steel fences and grey walls, I had a mirage of colors, textures and smells and I loved it.

Even before knowing the job was mine, I'd fallen in love with the town.

It wasn't long before we pulled up into a parking spot.

Bervie Springs was one of those towns with two main roads that met up in the middle. The street we were on was covered in shops, restaurants, bars and a grocery store. The crossroads led to the hospital, police station and chicken farms, or so the signage said.

A quick glance at my watch said I had fifteen minutes until my scheduled appointment. I was to meet Donald Dixon in his office at the town hall.

"It's right there, on the corner, across from us." Mom must have caught me looking for the building.

"You should go early. It looks better if you do," Mom said, her purse slung over her shoulder. "I'll be here, waiting." She indicated to the outdoor patio of Springs Bakery.

The bakery itself carried that small-town curbside appeal the reviews I'd read talked about. Quaint, family-run, homemade baked goods, welcoming from the moment you approached. The signage outside invited customers with books to read to join them, receiving a ten-percent discount on coffee if they showed their book. That should make Mom happy. She never went anywhere without a novel to read.

Mom looked from me to the building across the street, then back to me. Her smile faltered somewhat before it became a full-fledged Mom's-got-your-back type of smile. With a heartfelt hug, meant more for her than me, I was pushed toward the building where my life was about to change. Possibly. Hopefully for the better.

9: MEET YOUR FAIRY GODFATHER

I was shown into a corner office where the windows stood wide open.

No bars. No barbed wire. No armed guards.

Must be nice to have a view where the only thing you see are dozens of garden beds along a stone-lined walkway.

I'd take it any day.

"Starla Bishop, I can't tell you how happy we are to have you here," a voice boomed behind me. I jumped, turned and raised my hands, palms out, ready to block whatever came at me.

"Nice view, isn't it?"

If he noticed my reaction, he didn't say anything.

"I had a hand in designing the garden space," he continued, standing by my side at the window.

His size dwarfed me. His stature intimidated me. His voice soothed me.

I didn't know how to feel or what to think as I stood there.

I liked to measure up my opponents, discover their weaknesses, see where I could needle them, push them, work them.

I couldn't do that here.

I expected him to invade my space, put his hand on my shoulder or even on my back, in an attempt to display dominance right from the beginning.

He did none of those things. He stood beside me, leaving space between us, hands clasped behind his back, his gaze straight ahead.

"Know what I love about Bervie Springs? It's a safe place for reinvention." He looked at me then, the full force of his dark brown eyes peering into mine. "Of all the applications we received, I figured you could use that chance."

"So you decide my fate?" The words came out before I could stuff them in.

He chuckled, hand reached out in greeting.

"We haven't been properly introduced. I'm Donald Dixon. Consider me your . . ." He glanced outside for a moment. "Your fairy godfather."

He didn't smile. Neither did I. This wasn't a joke. It wasn't a gab session. It sure as hell wasn't a casual get-to-know-me session either.

There were two possible ways to handle this conversation. The Old Starla or the New Starla way.

Mom's way meant I smiled, remained polite, showed how thankful I was for the opportunity and did everything possible not to screw it up.

My way meant being real, using the smarts curated in prison and not kowtowing to anyone, not even my fairy godfather.

Especially not a man who calls himself that. What am I? Twelve?

"What if I don't want a fairy godfather?"

The way he sized me up just then, like a guard choosing his next victim, I knew I'd made the right choice.

"Starla, I'll be honest. You need one and I can promise you won't find anything better." He lifted his shoulder in a shrug. "The offer is there. If you don't want that second chance, if Bervie Springs isn't for you, go back home. But I bet you'll end up back in prison in less than a year."

I bristled at his words.

"You know me so well, don't you?" I tried to add a semblance of a smile to my tone, but it didn't happen.

His gaze, the way it poked through the poorly constructed walls around my heart, had me looking away.

I couldn't take it.

I didn't want to read the truth in his eyes.

I didn't know the man from Adam and yet, the way he looked at me, really looked at me, there was a sense of recognition. Damn it. I knew this would be too good to be true. He was everything I was trying not to be. He knew it too.

One imposter always recognized another.

"Why me?" I said to break the silence. It became uncomfortable. I'd rather uncomfortable words than silence. Words, I can fake. It was truth in silence I couldn't face.

"Why not you?" He turned his charm on me right then, a charm I figured he must own by being on the town council.

"Our program is meant to give someone like you a second chance. I read your file, Starla. I looked you up. The life you've been given hasn't been an easy one."

I backed up, two steps of distance between us, but it was enough.

"I'm not a charity case," I said, chin raised, fingers curled, ready for a fight. "Thanks for the opportunity, but no thanks."

"Who said anything about a charity case? You think I'm doing all this out of the goodness of my heart?" He laughed, sinister, dark, a foreboding kind of laughter that had spiders crawling all over my skin.

"This won't be an easy gig. You'll have to prove yourself. You'll work hard and earn every cent too. And I have rules. Strict rules. Break them, you are out." He turned his back on me, almost as if on purpose, pulled out his desk chair and sat. "If that sounds like a charity case, then by all means, there's the door." He motioned to it with his finger.

I didn't respond. The choice was mine, it seemed. Did I leave or stay?

Mom would be more than disappointed if I left. It might be the breaking point for her. I couldn't handle if I broke her.

"I'd like it if you stayed, however," Donald said. "There's a fire inside of you I like. I can use that."

I caught what he said, even if it was a slip of the tongue. There was more to this offer than he'd let on.

"What do you—" I looked at a framed certificate on the wall — "Mr. Councilman, get out of this?" Everyone always had a motive behind their good deed. Always. Nothing ever came free.

"Dixon," he said. "Donald, if you prefer. Close friends call me Donny. What do I get?" He had the decency to blush just then. "If this goes well, maybe one day I'll end up mayor. But call me a Boy Scout if you need to. I like to help others. I'm in a position of power where I can. To not would be to abuse that power."

I pulled out the chair closest to his desk, set my small cross-body purse on my lap and smiled for the first time since I walked into his office.

"Dixon, I think you have a different idea of what abuse of power means than most people." My back remained rigid, I didn't sit back in my chair, not like Dixon. I didn't want to give off the appearance of ease, of being relaxed.

Even though I knew his was a position of power and mine gave off a show of weakness.

"Maybe," he said, "but my idea is what counts right now, isn't it?"

The smugness on his face had me itching to wipe it off, but that would for sure get me fired, reported to the cops and the first in a short line of steps leading back to prison.

"You mentioned rules?" Better to be clear and upfront. The more information I had, the quicker I'd decide if I stayed or not.

Let's face it. While this might be the best gift an ex-con like me could receive, even the best gifts came with consequences.

Dixon pulled out a sheet of paper and slid it across his desk.

That sheet was full of numbers, of words, of rules I wasn't sure I wanted to live by. I'd had enough of people running my life with their rules, beliefs and laws, thank you very much.

The first two were no-brainers: Weekly visits to Officer Burnard. Random drug tests. I might have sold drugs once upon a time, but I've never been one to imbibe, so random tests didn't bother me. Officer Burnard, hopefully he was a lazy-ass, donut-eating, alcohol-drinking, waiting-for-retirement cop who wouldn't be all up in my business.

The further I read though, the more bothered I became.

"Attend Bible study? Volunteer at the food bank? Be a tour guide during the garden festival? Who the hell are you—" I lifted my gaze — "a freakin' pastor in disguise?"

His hand went to his throat, as if fingering the collar that wasn't there. "Just a good citizen trying to be a mentor. Anything I'm asking you to do, I'll be doing myself."

"I don't need a mentor. Or fairy godfather." If anyone needed a mentor, it was this dude. Who the hell called himself a freaking fairy godfather?

"I think you do, but we've already covered that. Are you in or out?" Dixon leaned forward, hands clasped on top of his spotless desk. From his tone, it didn't seem to matter what I decided. But I had learned early in life never to trust words or the way they were spoken.

Read the body. Watch the muscles. Listen to what's not being said.

His death-grip-whitened knuckles, along with the pounding vein on the side of his neck told me my decision mattered.

I leaned back in my chair, relaxed the grip on my purse, and smiled.

I gave him that canary grin the guards never wanted to see. The one that said I knew. I knew I had the upper hand and now that he knew I knew, I was the one in control.

My favorite position when it came to social interactions.

I pulled the sheet with his rules onto my lap and looked it over again.

It was a wish list. A how-to guide to remodel a convicted criminal. A guide Donald Dixon was going to use to become mayor.

Did I want to help him?

The answer seemed obvious. I really didn't have any other options.

"I'm in."

10: ON THE HUNT

Tuesday 12:09 a.m.
DETECTIVE KAARNS

We are fools. Every single one of us. Bishop should be locked up, behind bars already.

Officer Burnard, Bishop's probation officer, sits across from me, leg bouncing a mile a minute, sweat pooling on his forehead. I'm tempted to offer the sucker a tissue, but he's a grown man and I'm not his mother.

I don't know Burnard all that well, even though we've worked together for a few years now. I've probably said a few words in passing, acknowledged him at the bar, that kind of thing.

I have a feeling I'm not missing out by not knowing him all that well. There's something about him that has me on edge.

"You've got to give me something," I say to him, for the third time. We've sat here for close to fifteen minutes while he rifled through Bishop's file.

"I've got nothing," he says, his voice on a level that would have my dog's ears perk up. "She's been clean. All her drug tests came back negative."

I lean my head back, scrunch my shoulders and groan as the crack-crack-crack of my spine dances up my vertebrae.

"How did you get assigned to her? When did you first meet with her? Let's start at the beginning." I want to bash my head against the desk. I want to reach across the table and strangle the guy. I want, I want, I want. There's so much I want to do right now and yet, here I sit, babysitting a man who should know better.

He'd better not be dirty. The rumors are there, the suspicions, but nothing's been proven.

I sure as hell don't want to be the one to dig this guy's grave.

"Dixon asked me to do him a favor," Burnard's Adam's apple bobbed.

Things aren't looking good.

"Why would you owe him a favor?"

"Who said I owed him one?"

Did I need to reply? One brow raise along with a cock of my head should do the trick. It does.

He swallows again, hard. "He helped my kid out with a car, you know?"

"One of his famous Dixon Deals?"

Burnard nods.

"They really that good? What's the trick?"

Burnard's ping-pong gaze bounces across the room.

Everyone knew about the Dixon Deals. Donald Dixon wasn't just a council member, he owned Dixon's Used Cars and Rentals, just on the edge of downtown. He did everything to beat city prices and usually threw in a few bonuses too.

Hell, I'd even bought my Civic off him. Got one of his famous handmade leather keychains too. I didn't get a Dixon Deal, though.

"I can't really say . . ." Burnard's gaze is now on his boots.

Seriously. If I were to write my reports with one hundred percent accuracy, this is where I'd be inserting my eye roll.

"Signed a contract and all that, you understand."

I lean forward. "Come on, dude, you know what's happening. I don't need to spell it out for you."

Seconds turn into a freakin-waste-of-my-time minute while he considers whether to play ball or not.

I hope he does, for both our sakes. Not just play ball but strike it out of the park with a whack so loud and clear there will be no doubt whether he was dirty or clean.

Burnard's hand goes up to his ear and tugs on the lobe, something I've noticed him doing a few times since we've sat here.

"I'm not the only one who's taken a Dixon Deal," he says.

I blink. And wait. Then sigh. This is ridiculous.

"What do you want me to do? Pull in the chief? Get you a deal?"

The moment he nods, I slap the table hard with the palm of my hand and stand.

There's so much I want to say. So, so much. Spikes would be proud of me for not opening my mouth.

I fling open the door, the knob banging into the wall with a loud thud, and storm out.

"Freaking five bodies, who knows how many more graves and the asshole wants a deal. A freakin' deal," I mutter loud enough and hope everyone around me hears. There's more here than what we're seeing.

I head back to the observation room, a thundercloud of anger and frustration, and stick the earpiece back in.

"Burnard wants a deal. He's covering something." I barely get the words past my clenched jaw.

Spikes isn't even there. What the hell?

"Where is he? Why did he leave?" I turn to face the group at the table, all their heads bowed, pretending to be invisible.

"I can hear you," my partner says, his voice disturbingly calm. The complete opposite of what I feel. "Join me in the hall."

I'm so tense, every breath I release feels like I'm spitting toothpicks.

Spikes is there, relaxing against the wall, a file in his hands.

"Burnard is spooked, huh? Wonder why."

It takes me a moment to reply. In that moment, I let the million thoughts running through my head filter out until I'm focused only on this case and nothing else. Thoughts like why he's so relaxed, and doesn't appear as stressed as I feel, or why he looks like he could run a marathon where I'm ready to curl into a ball and weep like a little kid.

"Things are going to get worse before they get better." He gives me that fatherly look I both hate and appreciate. "I know it feels like a sprint, but that's when mistakes happen. We focus on one thing at a time, don't jump ahead, and wait for the clues to reveal themselves."

I sink against the opposite wall and groan.

"We have multiple bodies, Spikes. When will it stop?"

"This ain't no Chicago PD television show, Kaarns. Nothing is going to get solved within the hour. Relax. Steady yourself." Steady yourself. I hate those two words.

"Tell me what happened with Burnard." He lowers the file he's holding and gives me his full attention.

"Dixon was owed a favor. Burnard got one of the Dixon Deals when he bought his son a car. The minute I tried to squeeze more information out of him, he clammed up. Says he's not the only one on the force to get a Dixon Deal and wants the chief."

Even as I say it, I know everything about this will go south. Everything.

The chief and Dixon are friends. Pals. The kind of buddies found tossing back drinks, throwing darts, walking downtown throwing candy to kids kind of buddies.

"Want me to talk to him?"

I shake my head. Him talking to Burnard is the same thing as my dad fighting my battles with my roommate over a missing dress.

"How's it going in there?" I ask instead.

He shrugs. "The kids are pulling up information as I need it. You've trained them well."

By kids, he means the group back in the observation room.

I try not to stand as tall as I feel. Praise from Spikes is always good for my ego.

"See what you can get out of Burnard before getting the chief involved. We're not on the hunt for dirty cops, just answers."

"He's not stupid, Spikes. He knows what telling the truth means. If he's wrapped up in this somehow . . ."

The look on Spikes' face has my face glowing like a scolded child. I know better and without telling me so, he got the message across.

"We follow the clues, Kaarns. That's all you'll do. Follow the clues."

11: HOW DEEP IS THE HOLE?

1:09 a.m.

I breathe deep. In. Out. In. Out. My stomach is rolling, churning, heaving as the images of those upturned gardens play with my mind.

Dead. Another body. Dead.

I swallow the acid clawing its way up my throat.

Mom used to tell me she broke into a million scattered shards when the cops would arrive on her doorstep for me. A million scattered fragments that couldn't be put back together.

I never understood until now.

I'm here, not because of something I'd done, but because I'm the perfect scapegoat. I did the one thing I knew I shouldn't have done, stepped directly in the middle of something I should have left alone, and now I'm paying the price.

Donny and Alexius are partners in every sense of the word; both life and business have become so intertwined, so connected, that it sometimes feels impossible to sense where I belong.

It's taken some getting used to, having to share him with her.

"Wanna call your boss back in? Either that or provide a cot?" I talk to the window where I've no doubt others are staring at me right now, watching me, measuring my worth.

I could save them the trouble. I'm not worth much. I know the truth. I'm a realist, not an optimist like Donny.

My currency here is information. I'll give them anything and everything they could possibly want if it means walking out of here free.

I stand and crack my back, bending one way then the other. Stretching feels amazing after sitting for so long.

I joined a yoga class in prison a few years ago. The instructor once owned a studio in the city, with rich clients who also requested personal hands-on sessions. Nothing wrong with that until a spouse found out and called the cops. Came out she'd also been skimming, stealing money in the process.

Ballsy, blonde and one hell of a yoga instructor.

She got out three months ago and got hold of me. We had quite the . . . enlightening conversation. I don't think I told Officer Burnard about that. My bad.

The door finally nudges open. A black shoe appears at the bottom, holding it in place and . . . then nothing.

Just the open door and shoe.

Is it Spikes? Someone else?

I want to look, walk around the table, pull the door and see who's standing there.

Instead, I return to my place at the table, pull the chair in and wait for whomever is standing there to deign to grace me with their presence.

If it weren't for the obvious male shoe, I'd almost hope to have a chat with Spikes' partner. She looks feisty. Interesting. Someone who might tell me more than Spikes.

A cop I haven't seen yet steps into the room, lays down a pad of paper and pen, refusing to look at me.

"What's this for?" I say to his retreating back.

His response is a closed door.

"I'm willing to be helpful," I say to the mirror. "You need to give me more than this." I hold up the supplies laid out in front of me. "What do you want me to do? Draw? Write something down? Confess something that isn't true? Work with me, Spikes."

I have to assume he's behind the mirror, studying me.

That or he's with Donny.

My mind whirls with so many thoughts, so many questions, that it's physically painful. This is going to be a long night, I know it, but I wish there was something I could do to speed up the process.

The door opens again and I jerk. Spikes finally appears. He's left me in here for over an hour.

"Oh good, they brought it," he says as he takes his seat and plops down a file folder.

"Is it for me to doodle? Keep me awake?" I smother a pretend yawn. I'm not tired. Not yet.

He opens the file and pulls out a printed map of Bervie Springs. There are five red circles he's drawn with a marker on the paper.

Those must be where the bodies were buried. Found. Are.

"We have records dating back years of projects Soil and Springs has worked on, but I'm wondering if you could help us pinpoint locations that were important to Alexius and Donald."

He doesn't look at me, keeping his gaze down on the print-out.

I lean forward and angle it more toward me.

"Important, how?"

Spikes raises his gaze then.

"Any spots they checked over and over, or spent longer than anticipated, had you work at . . . anything that seemed overtly suspicious to you."

I lean back in my chair. "Everything Alexius does is suspicious. And no, nothing jumps out at me. Every project we've had since I joined has been within the normal range of things. Not everything runs as smooth as you'd expect and quite often, they miss their deadlines, but when that happens, the client is always compensated."

Spikes straightens.

"Compensated, how?"

Why is this so important? "Alexius always gives them a discount, a deep one, actually, and then she adds on extra shrubs and fill."

He scrawls some things down on his pad. "How deep?"

"The discount? More than half off sometimes. Depends on how badly things have been screwed up or how late they are."

Spikes cocks his head a little to the left. Someone is speaking into his ear and if he thinks he's fooling me, he's crazy.

"They've got ads all over the place about being the best in the business and always meeting deadlines."

I want to laugh. I know this man isn't naive.

"Anything to beat out the competition," I say. Donny stresses this a lot. Give the customers what they want, over-promise, do anything to keep the sale.

"He's in charge of the marketing. Not sure if you've noticed but every commercial for his used car sales is followed by an ad for Soil and Springs. He evens gets their logo, a sign, their flowers into his ads and vice versa. Every Soil and Springs vehicle advertises his car lot."

"Must make for difficult accounting."

"More like inventive."

His brows perk up to his hairline and I catch a slight movement with his fingers.

"I'm sure you've already got your team looking into his accounting." I look past his shoulder into the mirror. "You won't find much. He prides himself on being aboveboard."

"You don't believe that," Spikes says. He shakes his head like a father about to have a serious talk with their child. "Nothing Donald Dixon does is aboveboard."

"You're wrong." My chin juts out and a fire blazes inside me. "People change. The man you think you know, he's dead. Donny said I brought something new to his life, had him rethink everything and made him want to live differently."

Spikes scratches his forehead and I can see him trying to find words to prove me wrong.

But he can't.

Donny isn't the same man he used to be, the man I was first introduced to.

We both changed. We both sparked an implosion into the lives we used to live and created something new.

Spikes is rubbing his face with the palms of his hands and I can see how tired he is. Lines form beneath his eyes as we sit, staring at one another. He massages his temple, the pad of his finger turning white from pressure.

"You need to drink more water," I tell him. "It's the only thing that will help at the first sign of a headache."

"Water won't help this one." His voice is lowered, a little gruffer than I expect to hear from him. "I came here for peace and quiet. I dealt with enough murders in the city. I came back home to focus on my family, to retire, to grow old," he mumbles, loud enough for me to hear, but not for those listening in from the mirror to catch.

Interesting.

"Have you ever seen a dead body?" he asks, his voice louder now.

I shake my head, then waffle. "In prison." He nods, understanding. I think.

I've seen more dead bodies than a normal person should.

I've watched as they were killed. I've held them as they died. It's hard to escape death in prison.

"The first dead body I saw stayed with me for weeks. I had nightmares, swore I smelled death every time I turned my head. There's a scent that never goes away, no matter how many times you wash," Spikes says.

I'm not sure where he's going with this. What is he trying to say? What message am I missing?

"Seeing a photo of a decomposed body; it's horrific, but nothing compared to being there in person as it's exposed." He pulls out a print-out and every bit of liquid in my stomach rolls into a slow boil until I'm seconds away from upchucking. I look away, breathe in deep, swallow and force my throat to open wide enough to stop this from happening.

Small bone fragments reach through soil my fingers had touched. Two eye sockets, filled with nests of worms and other bugs, call out to me. A swatch of red fabric covered in dirt draws my attention and I swear I can feel the fabric beneath my fingers, see things moving in the oozing . . .

I bend over, my face falling toward the floor when the small garbage pail beneath the table is pushed my way. I throw up and I swear I can smell the rotten carcass even now.

"This was the first body we found," Spikes tells me as I raise myself up and take the napkin he's holding out to wipe my mouth. He pours water from the jug into my glass and I drink half of it before I can't taste my vomit anymore.

"The slime is what gets me every time," he continues and I wish he'd shut up. "You can't get it out of your clothing once it's there."

"Why are you telling me this?"

"Better to be informed, don't you think?"

This is information I don't need, thank you very much.

"Why are you here? With me? You should be spending your time with Alexius, nailing the evidence to her ass, instead of squatting here, unless you're doing it to make her sweat?"

Spikes tilts his head to the side and I'm pretty sure he's measuring my words, if they're worth the breath it takes to answer.

I pass muster because he leans toward me; his shoulders push back, chest out, palms cupping the edge of the table.

"Starla, we have enough with the five bodies as evidence right now that ties Soil and Springs to the murders. What I need is to tie everything together. That's where you come in."

He wants me to be the glue on the envelope that seals all of this up tight, help them tie their knots, fill in the blanks, get that mark of approval for doing a great job.

I'm not sure who he thinks I am, but that person isn't me.

When it comes to assigning roles for this crime, my part is insignificant.

"You know more than you're letting on," Spikes says. "We'll sit here all night and then some if we have to."

I'm not sure if that is a warning or a promise.

I pull the notepad closer, pick up the pen, look at the city map laid to the side and begin to think. He wants to know locations important to Alexius, but he's only focused on Bervie Springs.

That's a mistake.

12: THE MOST IMPORTANT PERSON IN HIS WORLD

Twelve Months Ago

My life was a fairy tale. I just needed the glass slippers and the shimmering ball gown, and I'd almost believe it wasn't a dream.

Almost.

Two days after agreeing to take the job, Dixon met me at the bakery and handed me a set of keys. Mom's jaw dropped as he told me he found an apartment, rent free for the first three months.

"Who do I have to sleep with?" I asked. "Is there a roommate? What's the catch?"

"Starla." Mom's tone felt like a slap on the hand.

Donald Dixon laughed, raised his coffee and took a long sip. "I think you and I will get along just fine, Starla Bishop."

Donald set his cup down with a clink. "The apartment is yours, free and clear. Fully furnished as well. The last person to live in the apartment died, but the rent was paid in full for a year. If you don't like the place, feel free to look around."

I wasn't sure what I thought of the idea. I mean, who wants to sleep in a dead person's bed, live in their house, or use their stuff as if their ghost didn't linger?

Every free gift comes with a cost. Every. Single. Time.

"No catches?" Doubt filled my voice as well as my gaze. Dixon looked up and I could see him work through something.

"How about this . . . ?" He stopped as someone approached our table.

The man was of medium build, a bit round in the stomach area, and waddled as he walked. He was bald with an overgrown beard and if he wore overalls, I'd swear he was a redneck.

"Dixon, how you are? Been meaning to come by the lot so we could have that chat about your Dixon Deals."

"Hey Jack, good to see you. Let me introduce Starla Bishop, she's going to be helping Alexius and I out at the Shed."

Mom and I gave each other a quick look. The Shed?

"Yeah? Business that good, huh? Surprised she's not a piece of skirt for your lot, though." He coughed that last word out before bending over to rub his knee. "Sorry, that was rude."

"Damn right it was. We're better than that here." Dixon's look said something like 'what can you do?'. Did he think I'd be offended?

"Wasn't thinking, Dixon. That's all." Jack's voice rumbled before he cleared it.

"Come on by later this afternoon," Dixon said. "I'll be at the dealership around three. We'll see what we can do for you then, that work?"

Jack gave his watch a glance; his shoulders heaved in a long sigh.

To watch the dynamic between the two, Dixon had the upper hand and Jack knew it.

"What kind of deals do you give?" Mom waited for Jack to leave before she asked.

"You looking for a newer truck?" He twisted in his seat and looked over Mom's vehicle. "I could give you a decent trade-in value."

"I've a few years left on this one, but would love to have no payments, if that's something you could do."

Dixon's brows dropped until his eyebrows became one straight line.

"Tell you what, before you leave, come by the lot. I'll take your VIN, give it a good look over and then get in touch when I have an offer, sound good?"

Mom nodded, but I could see the smile in her eyes.

"Don't you worry, you are part of the family too," he told her.

I leaned back and crossed my arms. Something just didn't sit right with me, not when it came to Donald Dixon.

"Family? First you were my fairy godfather and now we're family? This sounds like a con job to me." I knew con artists, I was a con artist, and I refused to be pulled in by another. I'd made myself a promise I fully intended to keep. If it meant bolstering myself with steel walls so I didn't misstep again, then that's what I'll do.

Again with the chuckle. Dixon's face lit up brighter than a sparkler at sunset. "And you would know, wouldn't you?" His eyes twinkled. "Starla Bishop, what is it going to take for you to trust me?" His huge-ass grin grew wider. "Since the moment we've met, you've had it in your head that I'm not to be trusted, and yet, I haven't done a single thing to prove that. I've given you a job, an advance and now an apartment, so your mom doesn't have to drive you here every day. I know I promised a vehicle after three months, but I'm working on getting it to you sooner. I'm here to help you, that's it."

Mom nudged the side of my thigh with her finger. It was one of those 'take notice' nudges.

"You'll have to forgive her," Mom spoke up. "She's not used to trusting people right off the bat."

I coughed, my way of telling Mom I didn't need her to speak for me. I wasn't sure she got the hint though.

Dixon leaned forward, his hands fisted on the table. "I get that. But things are different now, and your life is going to be different here on out. Stop letting your past dictate your present. It's the only way to ensure your future doesn't repeat the past."

I wanted to roll my eyes. This guy was a motivational speaker along with being a council member and used car salesman. If he wanted me to start believing him, his words needed to be followed by action.

I wanted to believe him. I'd never had a man want to help or take care of me, especially when there weren't strings attached. I hated that I was waiting for the other shoe to drop. I wanted to have faith that Dixon was who he claimed to be, but I couldn't afford another mistake.

Sure, Dixon had done everything to make me believe he could be trusted: He did give me an advance, handed me keys to an apartment that came rent-free for three months and was working with Mom on getting a new truck.

"I appreciate all you've done for me, Dixon, I really do. Be patient with me, okay? Anyone who ever told me they had my back ended up stabbing me in it." I reached over and patted Mom's hand. "Other than Mom. She's the only one who has even watched out for me."

"Well," Dixon said, "now you've got two sets of eyes watching out for you."

Mom teared up, raised the napkin from her coffee to her lips and struggled not to cry. I could see it. The edges of her lips twitched, one of her many tells.

"Why don't I grab us all another coffee to go and we can head out? I'm sure you're wanting to see your apartment, but I'd like to introduce you first to my partner in crime. Alexius Dixon is another woman who will be by your side, Starla, I guarantee it."

He pushed his chair back, the metal screeching on the patio tiles.

"Alexius Dixon," Mom said. "Is she your wife?"

Dixon shook his head. "Used to be until we realized we were better off friends than spouses. Alexius and I are partners. She runs Soil and Springs, where Starla is going to be working.

I'm a silent partner, there to help as needed, but she's the queen of green thumbs. That woman can do wonders with soil." The pride in his voice, in his eyes, on his face, spoke volumes.

"It's not often you hear of divorced couples remaining friends," Mom said.

"I'm of the mindset that anything can be done, if done right. Divorce doesn't mean disaster, it's just a new path to take in life. I'd be lost without Alexius. She's the most important person in my world, always will be." He held out his hand, showing off a wedding band. "We still wear them, to show how connected we are."

"How long have you been divorced?" Wearing rings just seemed downright creepy.

"Give or take ten years." He shrugged. "I know it seems weird, but once you meet her, you'll understand. Trust me."

He left to gather more coffee for us and I turned to Mom and realized we were probably thinking the same thing.

"That poor sod is still in love with her." Mom tsked. She gathered her purse, slinging it over her shoulder and stood. "You be careful with that, Starla," Mom warned. "No need to get involved in history like that. It'll never end up well for you, take my word for it."

13: SAY HELLO TO THE ICE QUEEN

I've worked for landscapers before. Pushed a mower, dug holes, did grunt work only ex-cons can get. The companies were always small, their rent-a-trailer office grimy and smelling like week-old coffee.

I've never worked for a company like Soil and Springs Landscaping.

Mom followed Dixon as he pulled into the circular driveway and whistled.

"They must cater to the rich and famous," she said in an awe-filled whisper. "I heard some big names live around here but never believed it."

When we parked, I almost didn't get out of the vehicle. Self-doubt was playing havoc with my belief system — the first time in a long time I've experienced this. Who was I to work at a place like this? Maybe Dixon had it wrong. Maybe I was to be on a crew, digging holes again and not in the office.

For some reason, I could stomach that better than working inside an office. I wasn't sure why and didn't want to know.

Dixon stood on the steps, his focus on his phone as we walked up to him. It didn't take long for him to pocket the phone and throw his arms out wide, welcoming us to . . . his home?

"This is home base. I know it looks monstrous, but don't let that scare you." He eyed it like candy. "I live in one half and Alexius lives in the other. Neither one of us wanted to give it up and the market was just as bad when we divorced as when I bought it."

Mom nudged me in the side.

"We converted the back half into an office," Dixon continued, ignorant of the looks between Mom and I. "There are a few greenhouses where Alexius plays with her plants and then her own special . . . well, we call it the Shed. It's where she hides most of the time."

"Hides?" My spidey sense went haywire.

Dixon shrugged. "Maybe not the right word for it. My wife, sorry, my ex-wife is a pedologist. She is working toward her doctorate and often heads into the city to teach."

He must have caught our blank looks.

"She studies soil."

Mom and I nod in unison as if that made all these sense in the world.

Studies soil? Like a scientist?

"That's just great. I barely got my high school diploma and you want me working with a bloody scientist," I said. Any self-worth I had disappeared. Just hand me coveralls and send me out for heavy labor. That's where I belonged, not working side by side with some brainiac.

"Come on, I want you two to meet. You'll love her. And don't worry . . . she's more interested in what's happening in the soil she's playing with than anything else."

Every step we climbed, the muscles in my body tightened as I realized just how out of my element I was. We veered off to the right, following a stone pathway that took us behind the house.

Dixon stopped just around the bend, turned and smiled with a broadness the size of the dump truck. He didn't say anything, but he obviously wanted a reaction.

Mom gasped when she saw the backyard.

My chest pinched; fingers of dread worked their way up the skin of my arms. I swallowed what felt like glass shards as I took in the grounds.

I'd seen photos of the big castles in France, with the gardens fit for queens to parade around, but never did I ever dream I'd see one in person.

That's what this felt like.

"We've been photographed by various gardening magazines both in North America and in Europe." Dixon's peacock-puffed chest deserved a snarky reply but I reined myself in.

"This is amazing," Mom gushed appropriately.

I didn't respond.

"Starla? What do you think?"

It took me a moment or two to answer. I was too focused on the gardens, the fountains, the bushes shaped as animals. What did I think? I couldn't. I was too overwhelmed.

"One thing you'll be responsible for," Dixon filled in the silence, "is booking events and even some weddings here. From May to October, our weekends are booked solid."

Weddings? Events? Did they expect me to work those?

"You didn't mention anything about event planning." It surprised me how strong my voice was because I felt anything but.

"We have someone who handles all those details. You'll just take the bookings. They're mainly done online. Alexius will explain it all to you, don't worry." He stepped toward me and placed both hands on my arms. "You look overwhelmed and that's my fault. Listen, I won't let you fail, I promise."

"Dixon?"

Off to the side, a woman appeared, wearing grey yoga pants, and what looked like a purple plaid shirt, arms rolled to her elbows. Her hands were covered in dirt, which left smear marks as she wiped them on the apron wrapped around her waist.

"Alexius, come meet Starla," Dixon called out. His hands dropped and from the way he moved, I would have sworn he was about to put his arm around my shoulders.

I stepped closer to Mom.

I was face to face with the most important woman in Dixon's world and I recognized her instantly.

Not her, per se. But her demeanor. Attitude. Dominance. She was the rightful queen, conqueror and she knew it. Not just knew it, but expected everyone else to know it too.

I reached my hand out.

She didn't say a word. Neither did I. Dixon shuffled his feet and Mom stood by my side as I waited.

She grabbed hold of mine. Her fingernails were caked in dirt. The lines of her hand were outlined with soil. Her grip was gritty, grungy, grimy.

"Donald says you're the perfect fit for us." Her soft, cultured voice held a hint of warmth.

"I think he oversold me, to tell you the truth. Just like he might have undersold this job."

Something like a smile played with the edges of her lips. She wore no makeup, her hair was pulled into a messy bun, and she had streaks of dirt along her cheek, chin and down her neck.

"He's a salesman at heart," Alexius said, her gaze leaving mine and going toward Dixon's. Her eyes softened for a moment, from ice queen blue to a soft greenish hue, the color warming the longer she looked at him.

If Dixon was still in love with his ex-wife, the feeling was mutual.

"Don't believe half of what he tells you. He believes everything he says, whether it's the truth or not." She laughed, and something passed between the two that told me the inside joke wasn't a new one.

"He gave you the keys to the apartment? When can you start? I expect your wardrobe is somewhat limited, so I took the liberty of ordering you a few tops with our logo you can wear." Without time to reply, Alexius turned and headed toward the double French doors surrounded by potted ferns.

Dixon walked past us, then beckoned us to follow.

"She seems . . . nice," Mom whispered to me.

I wasn't sure. Nice wasn't the right word to give Alexius. There was a word for her, I just didn't know it right then.

The office we walked into was huge. A giant cavern with a few desks, couches and chairs, large screens on the walls and a corner table. Everything was white and clean, with hints of green mixed in through throw pillows, figurines and potted plants.

At the back of the room, to the left when we entered, was a desk with a computer, a large whiteboard on the wall, and a gift bag sitting beside the computer screen.

"I guessed at the sizes, but I'm pretty good at measurements. They should fit." She eyed me again. "Even with some decent meals in you, they'll look good."

Mom nudged me again. "See, I said you were too skinny," she said without keeping her voice down.

Dixon chuckled. "I think you look just fine."

The quick dart of a glance from Alexius told me she didn't like his comment.

The last thing I wanted was to get between the two. Mom was right. I'd have to be careful.

14: WHEN SECRETS RUIN MEMORIES

Tuesday 1:15 a.m.

I'm busy scribbling on the pad of paper, writing things that flash into my head when Spikes clears his throat, an obvious attempt for my attention.

I look up. He's got a look that reminds me of a child trying to do a puzzle.

"What's up?"

He scratches the back of his neck, taps his pen on the desk and gives his head a slight shake.

I really need to figure out what's being said to him.

"While you're doing that, why don't we talk about your mom a little bit."

I raise the pen off the paper and swallow back the anxiety that ricochets through me.

Mom. She's got to be frantic by now. I'd tried to send her a message, but the cops took my phone and refused to give it back. I even asked them to send it on my behalf.

"Why?"

I search his gaze, look for clues, see what I'm missing but he's a blank slate.

That damn one-way mirror stares at me over his shoulder. Who's sitting back there? What was said that would make my mom a subject of interest?

"You guys seem to talk an awful lot." He says this like it's a bad thing. "Must have a close relationship?"

Don't most mothers and daughters? I want to ask, but don't because I know the answer.

I know more than enough women who either have no relationship with their mother or wished they didn't. I've always counted myself fortunate to have Mom not only in my life but at my side.

I've seen what it's like not to have a mom like that.

I put the pen down and lean back in my seat, trying hard not to let my anxiety show.

Every time her face comes to mind, every time my thoughts go in her direction, I push them away. We've gotten so close the past year, she's immediately going to assume the worst and I don't want that to happen.

"You're confusing me, Spikes," I say, thankful my voice doesn't jump to a high note. "I'm getting mixed messages here. First you tell me to write things down, now you're asking me questions. I can't do both . . . so which is more important?"

He glances down at the paper, pulls it to him and reads over what I've written.

There's an address or two on there.

Directions to a camp ground I know Alexius likes to hike to on her weekends off.

A secret cabin I found one day while filing.

He looks at me, tears the sheet off the pad and raises his hand.

I start counting . . . one, two, three . . . I hear the dull thud of a door slamming shut . . . four, five, the knob on our door turns and opens.

Someone is watching. Always watching. What signals is he giving them, other than raising his hand?

I'll have to start paying better attention.

Detective Kaarns, his partner, steps in. She looks fresh, crisp and wide awake. Meanwhile, I'm sure I look disheveled, messy and nearing that black-craters-beneath-the-eyes exhausted.

"Starla here has given us some new tips. Look into them, will you?"

Kaarns reaches for the paper, never once looking my way.

While she looks over what I wrote, I tap my fingers along my thigh, anything to keep me alert. I, for one, am not a night owl.

"You see this?" she says, focusing on Spikes and pointing to a line on the paper.

He nods and nudges his head toward me.

"You want me to look for a file named—" Kaarns glances down at the paper — "*Honeymoon*?"

I smile. Not one that's full of positivity. More like one that carries a pure hatred for the word, the file, and everything it represents.

"You've got everything from the office, right? Files, notebooks, drawings, contracts." I wait for her to confirm with a nod. "That's the one you'll want."

Alexius is a master at hiding the obvious.

"What's so important about this file?" Spikes asks, pushing or pulling his chair, I wasn't sure. It squeaked, like wet rubber on plastic.

"A cabin." I've been there, slept there, got engaged there. I thought it had been a rental.

Sometimes the best kept secrets are hidden in plain sight.

"That's obvious, but what else?" His voice pushes me into a zone I'm not comfortable with.

I had good memories of that cabin. Once. But I've since pushed all those memories into a box wrapped in an unbreakable chain. There was no key. No secret code. No way in hell I'm going to open that box.

"It's a cabin that's not supposed to exist."

Kaarns straightens. Spikes leans forward. Guess that got their attention.

"Find the file, you'll find the cabin."

"Why is it such a secret?" Kaarns asks me. She's measuring me.

"That's for you to figure out, isn't it?" I didn't mean to be so sarcastic. "It's not on any map, you won't find a title . . . it's not supposed to exist. Donny said—" I stop from saying anything else.

"There's a drawing in the file, of a map, it's the only way you'll find it." I tear my gaze from hers and close my eyes. I see the cabin in my mind and for one soft moment, joy floods me. But it's only for a moment and then it disappears and I'm hurting all over again.

I play with the ring on my finger, feeling the empty spot. "Anything else I should know?" Kaarns asks.

"Start there," Spikes says.

I look up and catch him studying me. I fidget in my seat but manage to wait until his partner has left the room.

There's a quietness between us. Not an easy quietness. More like a stirring volcano, full of questions, declarations and unspoken answers. It's heavy, uncomfortable, suffocating.

"What?" I finally ask.

"I'm trying to decide if I want to go back to the conversation about your mom or find out why you don't like that cabin." He says it so matter of fact that it catches me off guard.

Well, that's easy enough for me to answer.

"Mom and I talk a lot." I lead the way, more ready to discuss Mom than bring up memories of the cabin. "Every morning and night, in fact."

He chuckles and leans forward so his forearms rest on the table. He plays with my file, his finger in between the two edges, as if he's about to open it.

"Mom it is," he says. His voice carries that laughter, and I can't help but wonder if he's mocking me or not.

I don't say anything.

He opens my file, rifles through the papers until he pulls out two sheets.

I see a lot of highlighted colors with a map of those colors at the top. I read that map and something curdles inside my stomach.

Pink is for Mom.

Yellow for Donny.

Blue means Alexius.

Green equals unknown.

Shit. Having them go through my life, it's unnerving.

I always expected it when I had done something wrong. But not now. For the past year, I had lived without the fear of the future and what could be used against me. I didn't think about my life being placed under a microscope again.

It was freeing, living without that fear.

It took me a while to get used to that weightlessness.

There's a sharp pinch inside my heart, like in the very middle, where it really matters, and the fear of losing that freedom rushes over me like a jacked soda pop.

He pulls out another sheet, this one that has a printed image of Mom clipped to the corner. It's an older photo, one I recognize from an article years ago. Mom had done an interview about raising a convict, or rather, what it was like raising a convict. She'd hoped it would raise awareness, but I think it did more personal damage than anything.

I remember her mentioning she'd lost some friends and even one of her side jobs of making meals for a wealthy family. Losing that income had hurt her, forced her to move into a shadier neighborhood where I had to buy her protection.

I made sure that family became aware of the price we all ended up paying. I don't think they ever found who broke into their home and robbed them blind. I know I never told.

"Caryn McCoy." Spikes says Mom's name with a hint of emotion, as if he knows her or recognizes her.

I nod.

"You were placed with her when you were, what?" His index finger traces lines on the page until he finds the information he sought. "Fourteen? You were her fifth foster child and her last, is that correct?"

I nod. His voice hasn't wavered; it still carries the same familiarity and I'm not sure how to take that. Does he know her? How? From when?

"You were placed in her home after your first stint in juvie," he continues to paraphrase what he's reading, "and she requested you to return after your second time as well. Then, if I'm reading this correctly, you went to live with her following your first adult conviction and then after your second . . . which ends up being your fourth time in jail, correct?" He looks at me then in surprise. "She didn't give up on you then?"

His question really doesn't require a response, which is good, because I'm not sure I can give him one. It hurt to listen to him, to hear the surprise in his voice, to feel my own condemnation and embarrassment as he recounts my past.

"You went back to her each time. Each time, she opened her doors, her arms, her heart and accepted you," he says, his voice trailing off as he continues to skim the page.

I don't want to hear anymore. I'm not sure I can handle more of the pain his voice inflicts on me. "What's your point?"

"She must be one hell of a woman, is what I'm thinking." Spikes drops the paper onto the table.

"She is. Leave her alone. She doesn't belong in this." I know Mom is probably going crazy wondering where I am and what's happening to me, but there's no way in hell I want Spikes or his partner contacting her for information.

"I'm kind of thinking she does."

I drop my hand that's on the table to my lap and fist it. "Leave her alone. Please."

He cocks his head but his lips don't move. They don't move to tell me he'll do as I've asked, demanded. They don't move and there's a bubble inside me, full of anger, rage and fear . . . an anxiety that never bodes well . . . and I clamp my own lips tight to stop from saying anything damaging to myself.

I breathe deep. One. Two. Three. Four. The bubble starts to recede, shrinking to a manageable form and I twist my lips into something I hope resembles a smile.

"True, we talk every day," I say, "but I don't think she knows anything about Alexius. She's really only met her the once, when I first started. When we talk, it's mainly about the two of us and our lives. She has this need to make sure I'm safe."

"Safe?"

I nod. "Out of trouble, making good decisions . . . she holds me accountable and it's been good. I promised her this time would be different and I meant it. I don't want to end up back in prison. I'm a different person now."

His lips tighten, but for a moment, I swear I catch a glimmer of approval on his face.

"Yeah, she said the same thing."

He drops that bomb without warning and my back straightens, fists tighten and I'm about to unleash an explosion of words that shouldn't be said when he raises his hand and stops me.

"Before you go all crazy, she has been calling me. Us—" he jerks his head back toward the window behind him — "almost every fifteen minutes wanting an update on how you are."

"She doesn't know anything." The words shoot off my tongue like a rocket.

One brow on Spikes' face rises.

Oh shit.

"Really?" he says. "Because that's not what she says." Double shit.

15: IS THIS PUZZLE MISSING PIECES?

2:05 a.m.
DETECTIVE KAARNS

"Gotcha." I pound my fist into the palm of my hand with delight. She's dirty.

Follow the clue, that's what Spikes told me to do. Well, the clues led me to Caryn, Starla's foster mom. All I had to do was leave a message for her to call me, not answer a few times and presto . . . she wants to talk. She'll do anything to save her daughter.

Her words. Not mine.

"How long till Mom arrives?" I glance behind me.

"Thirty minutes." Danvers doesn't even look up; his fingers are dancing along his keyboard in search of information on the so-called *secretive* cabin Starla mentioned.

"Mom will be here in half an hour. Interested in a drive up to the cabin with me after?" I ask Spikes. "Make her sit there and sweat a little?"

He leans back in his chair, tilts his head to the side, then gives me a thumbs-up.

I turn to the team behind me. "Okay guys, I want more information on Starla's history with her mom, anything you can pull up online and such. I also want every speck of dirt we can find on this cabin. Aerial views, layout, deed, inspections . . . everything. I want to know what to expect when I pull up."

"Other than what's in the file, there's no official record of the cabin," Trina, another member of my team, says.

That's not possible. Even if Dixon had this built himself with no inspections, he had to have bought the land the cabin sat on.

"Found something." Trina lifts her head, her eyes scrunched tight. She reaches for the eye drops beside her before she continues. "It's like, seriously dry in here." She leans her head back and adds three drops to each eye. "I found a really old title from back in the last century. It's hard to read, but the surname Dixon is on there."

I move to stand behind her and stare at the screen. The name is really hard to read, even with her having blown it up, but she's right.

"So it's land that's been handed down. Grandfathered in, probably, which would explain why we can't find anything on it."

I push my tongue to the ridge of my mouth and press hard. Damn it. I hate when I don't have enough information.

It's one of my downfalls, I know. Spikes is always telling me to lighten up, that the harder I try, the more frustrated I get.

"Anyone up for more coffee? I'll see if there's a fresh pot brewed," Trina pushes her chair back, stands and lifts up her arms in a stretch. "It's been a while since I've had to pull a double shift like this."

Danvers pulls away from his screen and pulls his arms back in a stretch as well. "Come on, our first serial killer case? Fun times ahead." His grin is wide, excitement shining in his eyes, and as much as I want to remind him how many victims we have, I understand the feeling.

My body hums with the same adrenaline that's filled this room.

In a single moment of silence comes a ping on all our phones. Shit. Pings can only mean one thing.

Sure enough, a text is there with words I've read too often within the past twelve hours.

More remains discovered in an additional garden bed on the property.

They're still at the Kincaid location.

I can't remember how many garden beds were there. I remember there were a lot. I remember the groans from one of the crew members when they arrived. I remember the dazed looks as we all stood there, staring at the red fabric and bone that stuck out of the soil like a flag, announcing its presence.

"How long was the contract with the Kincaids?"

It didn't take a genius to do the math. The longer the contract, the more bodies we'd probably find.

"Seven months in total. From the file, it was a complete overhaul of the property with multiple garden beds. Grass was pulled up, multiple patio areas and walkways . . . I attended a wedding there last summer and everything has been changed." Danvers hands me a file from one of the piles on the table.

"What about other locations?" I look at the whiteboard to see if we've mapped out a pattern.

He jumps up from his chair and grabs a marker.

Ahh . . . good kid. He's on the same wavelength.

He adds another column to the board, one for the length of the contract.

"Let's be sure to place which ones Bishop worked on too. There should be something in there, a time log or something. She's just as dirty as the other two, we just need to prove it."

"What are you hoping to see?" Trina asks. She's tapping her pen against her cheek in thought. "The longer they remained on a project, the more victims we'll find?"

I nod. That's exactly what I'm dreading we'll discover.

I have so many unanswered questions, and I get that we're in the early hours of the investigation and this will take months for everything to be processed, every 'i' dotted and 't' crossed, but . . . how could multiple murders happen in my backyard without us knowing about it?

These people had to have been operating for years to have killed so many people without getting caught. But how? Why?

Something is there, niggling at the back of my mind, but I can't grab hold of it. Not yet. But it's there . . . and eventually I'll figure it out.

"Spikes, another body has been found. Same location, different garden." I keep my voice low, not wanting to startle him. I know he heard me from the way he dropped his right arm to his side and squeezed his fingers. It doesn't take long before he interrupts Bishop from explaining why we need to leave her foster mother alone, pushes his chair back with enough force to make me smile and stomps out of the room.

Bishop looks surprised. Stumped. Frustrated.

My smile is even wider now.

The moment Spikes enters the room, everyone stills. "Update."

One word. He utters one word and somehow manages to convey every single frustration we're all feeling.

Trina starts to rattle off everything we've found, where we're at and the direction we're headed.

Spikes turns to me. "Where are you on Burnard?"

I groan. "Nowhere. The chief was in the room when I went back to him. He walked Burnard out and told me to smarten up."

Spikes eyes narrowed for a split second. "Smarten up? His exact words?"

I nod.

"Where's Jordan?"

Jordan Pittman was the undercover we had placed in Soil and Springs Landscaping. He was the brains and brawn behind the investigation. He'd posed as a foreman for Alexius and proved to be her downfall.

"With Dixon now." He hasn't come out of the room for two hours. The team in there has been feeding us information he provides, but so far it hasn't been much.

Dixon's lawyer won't let him talk.

"The husband or ex-wife?"

"Donald. But he's clammed up tight with his lawyer. Alexius is the same. So far Bishop here is the only one talking."

He grounds out a groan, a sound from deep in his throat that resembles a muffled roar and cuss at the same time.

"Not enough. What has her foster mother had to say?"

"Not here yet. You wanting to wait to interview her before we head to the cabin?"

There's a look on his face that dropkicks my heart to the curb.

I'm not going to like what he has to say next.

"About that, I think we bring Bishop with us. There's something there, something she's running from . . ." He shakes his head and looks at Bishop through the mirror.

"Are you kidding me?" No way. No effing way is that woman coming with us. What is he thinking?

"She wants to cooperate," he says as he reads me with the ease of a children's book.

"She's as dirty as the rest of them." How can he not see it? What is blinding him to her? Sure as hell isn't her looks or charm. Actually, I'm a bit surprised she's even engaged to Donald Dixon, the man to whom appearance is everything.

"Please tell me you're not giving her a deal."

"She hasn't asked for one."

"Yet."

He shrugs.

"When's the mom get here?"

I look to Trina who glances at her watch. "Anytime," she says.

"Let's give them time alone," Spikes suggests. "See if anything is said from either one."

I lean against the wall and study my partner. He's tired, I can see it in his eyes. "Why aren't you pushing her harder?"

"She doesn't need it. We'll get what we need from her, I'm not worried. Trust me, okay?"

I trust him. It's her I don't trust.

It's not very often that I challenge Spikes or make him explain his reasoning, but this case . . . it's not the time to drop the ball or go soft.

"I don't get it," I say. "I need you to explain what you're doing and why, because it doesn't make sense to me."

"She's been used. She's involved, sure, but not by choice. I think Dixon pulled the ultimate con job on a con and when she finds that out, she'll go atomic."

A Cheshire cat type smile spreads across both our faces as understanding hits me. "She'll stop protecting Dixon then." Our heads bob in unison. "I like it."

"Have I steered you wrong yet?"

No, and he knows it. But I don't do blind faith and he knows that too.

"How are you going to break the news then?"

Spikes nudges his head toward the group behind us. "What have you found on the ring? Ten bucks it's not the real deal."

Trina inhales with a sharpness that could cut butter. "He wouldn't do that, would he?"

Spikes barks a laugh, the sound similar to the sea lions lying around Fisherman's Wharf in Seattle.

"Does Bishop seem Dixon's type? Dixon likes a fresh, styled, expensive woman dressed to the nines who shines on his arm when they're out. Bishop is more scarred, comfortable, and budget-friendly. She's a 'relax on the couch with a beer and popcorn' kind of woman. Not a champagne and caviar at a five-star resort."

"She's the opposite of Alexius," I say. "Maybe he was in the mood for something different?"

Spikes' brows lift half a mile up his forehead.

"Midlife crisis?" I suggest.

"You on his side now? Giving him the benefit of the doubt?"

I reel back as if clocked in the jaw. "Hell no. But, if she's for real, if she's really in love with Dixon . . ." — I can't believe I'm saying this — "no woman deserves to be treated like that."

Spikes rubs his chin, the creases around his eyes deepening as he watches Starla play with the ring on her finger.

"It takes a sick man to twist a woman's heart like that, for sure," he mumbles.

"About the ring . . ." Trina speaks up. She waves a piece of paper in the air. "I think I found something. It's an Amazon receipt for a cubic zirconia princess cut ring. Any guesses on the price?"

"Is it the same one as on her finger?"

Trina's fingers fly across her keyboard, her eyes squinting as her nose basically hits the screen of her laptop. We all wait, eternal seconds turning into minutes before she leans back with a smile on her face.

"Sure is," she says as she twists her laptop around so we can all see the blown-up image of the ring Bishop's currently playing with.

"Bet he told her it was a family heirloom or something." My mouth twists into a grimace as I push away any remorse I feel for Bishop right now. This is going to kill her, but at least she'll be alive.

Unlike the victims buried in gardens throughout town.

16: WHEN MOTHER CALLS . . . YOU ANSWER

Tuesday 2:30 a.m.

I hate police stations. Hate interrogation rooms even more.

I roll my neck and yawn, unable to hide my exhaustion any longer.

The image of my nice, comfortable bed with my new pillows plays with my mind, teasing me, taunting me.

I'm about to use the desk as a bed as best I can, my head cushioned in my arms, when I hear a familiar voice outside the door.

Damn it, she came. Why?

The door opens and Mom rushes in. She drops her large shoulder bag onto the table and I stand, expecting her to give me a hug, but she plants her hands on her hips instead.

Her face is blank, no hint of anything she's thinking or feeling, and that crushes me.

My eyes smart and I look away from the emptiness in hers. Spikes stands behind her, half in the door, half out. It's like he's unsure if he wants to come in. He decides not to because he steps out and closes the door behind him with a soft thud.

"Mom? You shouldn't have come." I muster the courage to be the first to speak. My voice croaks, but I'd prefer to pretend it's from tiredness and not fear.

Fear or disappointment. Which one is worse?

"Not come?" The exterior of her face changes then, the facade of emptiness draining into one of heartbreak. A single tear hangs on the edge of her lashes and that one drop nearly breaks me.

I sink back down in my chair, wrapping my arms around myself and let everything I don't want to feel rush to the forefront of my mind.

I've failed. Again. I've broken my promise without even meaning to — without knowing how — and the crushing weight of what is happening buries me in a hole far deeper and darker than I've ever experienced.

"Oh no you don't," Mom snaps. "You are not allowed to wallow in self-pity or anything else right now. Pull yourself together, Starla Bishop." She places her finger beneath my chin and raises my face.

I swallow, nod and straighten my spine. "I'm sorry," I whisper, hoping she can read all the words I want to say but can't.

"Don't apologize. Change."

My jaw clenches at the words she's raised me on.

"I'm trying, Mom." She knows I've done nothing but try for the past year.

That's when she comes over and gives me a hug. A hug only a mom can give. One that's full of love and acceptance and smells of vanilla and coffee.

We stand there, neither one wanting to let go, to break the bond. I'm the first to accept that I'm in a situation a hug can't save me from.

She sits in Spikes' chair, pulling it close to the table.

"Tell me what's going on," she says, reaching for her purse and pulling out a notebook and pen. "I've been writing down everything the news is reporting and what Officer Kaarns has told me."

She opens to a page full of scribbles. It took me years to learn to decipher her chicken scratch, but this is even worse.

"Give me the Coles notes, please," I ask.

"They've arrested Donny and his ex-wife for murder. There's a lot of bodies, Starla, all over Bervie Springs. They're finding them in various gardens, backyards . . . basically every project they've worked on and there's no clue how long this has been going on for."

Mom's voice is calm, which surprises me. If it weren't for the slight shake of her hand as she holds her pen, it would be like she's reading me an article of something happening elsewhere.

Not here. Not with me involved.

Again.

"Have they arrested you yet?" she asks.

I shake my head.

Surprise fills her eyes before she masks the emotion.

"I'm waiting for it to happen, though. It doesn't look good, does it?"

She sighs, her shoulders dropping; the slight smile she's attempting disappears.

"You're Alexius' right hand, aren't you? They have to assume you're involved. Right? What about Jordan, the other guy that works so close with you and Alexius? Have they brought him in too?"

Good question. "I have no idea. Probably."

"We need to find out." Mom frowns. "We need to know what's going on. All the information we can get the better." Mom scribbles more on the page.

"Where's your lawyer?"

"I haven't asked for one yet."

"Why not?" She doesn't agree with me, it's in her voice, even though she hasn't heard why.

"I'm being cooperative. Once I call a lawyer, all that will change. Besides, a lawyer has never done me well and we can't afford a good one."

"Well, Donald sure as hell can. He should be providing one for you. Have you talked to him?"

"Mom." I shouldn't have to say this. "You know they won't. I've been asking for updates, I'm trying to tell the detective how he's not the one they should be focusing on, but no one seems to be listening."

"You're kidding me, right?" She glances over her shoulder, then leans forward. "Concentrate on yourself, Starla, not him. God, I wish I'd never told you to take the job." She reaches for my hand, covering it with hers. The warmth from her skin seeps through mine.

"You look exhausted." She searches my face, noticing every telltale sign of how tired I am. She reaches into her purse again and holds up a pack of gum before withdrawing one to give to me. "Have this gum," she says, loud enough for everyone in the building to hear.

"You don't have to yell. They can hear you just fine."

"Well—" she glances over her shoulder again — "you never know. Remember that time someone barged in and snatched the granola bar from my hand?"

That was the last time I'd been charged for possession. The stash wasn't mine, but it was found on me nonetheless. You'd think I'd have learned my lesson, but no, rather than let a friend get caught, I thought I could handle it.

"Spikes doesn't seem that . . . uptight." No doubt he's in the other room, listening to every word, hoping I'll spill something.

I won't.

Nothing incriminating anyways.

"I thought you were clean? Safe?" Mom is still leaned half across the table, but her voice is lowered, thankfully.

"I am. I have been."

She frowns, the wrinkles on her forehead growing deeper. "So you're just here to give them information? What have they asked so far?"

"Locations on projects, how well I know the Dixons, that kind of stuff."

"It's horrible, Starla. Can you imagine? Burying people like that? Killing them? I never would have thought . . ."

"Donny didn't do this."

The look on her face is full of sympathy and I hate it.

"I know him. He didn't kill anyone."

She snorts. "Starla, honey, I told you there was something off about him. If he didn't murder those people, he sure as hell helped cover it up for that she-devil." She leans back in her chair, arms crossed. "There's no way in hell I'm letting you go back to prison for a crime you didn't commit. And don't you dare try to take the blame to protect that man."

I want to argue that I wasn't going to, but she's got that Mama Bear 'don't mess with me' look.

"I told you to be careful, to not get in the middle of that relationship and what do you do? Not only get in the middle, but—" she leans forward — "become part of their crazy cycle." She's dropped her voice so only I can hear. Thank God.

"Engaged after six months," she continues, her voice whisper soft still, "I . . ." Her lips thin into a straight line and she shakes her head as she says the words she's been wanting to say for a long time.

"You what? Say it. Get it out of your system." It can't be any worse than what she said in the beginning when I told her he'd proposed.

"There's something about him, love. Something about his relationship with Alexius too. It's . . . unnatural." Her hushed whisper is like an exhaled breath.

As much as I'd love to get into all this, and I really don't, now is not the time.

"You've slept with a murderer, Starla. I just . . ." She shudders and I wonder if this time is too much for her. "Sorry. Sorry. This isn't what you need." She pushes back wisps of escaped hair from her braid and scribbles on her notebook again.

"We need a plan. While you insist on waiting for Donald to hire you a lawyer, we need to figure out how much you reveal before he does."

An innocent woman wouldn't worry about how much to hold back.

She obviously believes I'm guilty. Maybe not of murder but of something.

Knowing that hurts. Hurts more than it should. I can't blame her . . . why should she believe in the good when all I've done is broken my word and her heart?

I scrub my face and yawn.

"Anything that will clear you, you need to tell." Mom says this as if it were old news. As if I didn't already know this.

"I am."

"Honey, I know you're tired, but you can't give in. What could they possibly have on you that would make them think you're involved? What have you done?"

"Why do you believe I've done anything?"

"Because they have you in here."

I yawn again. But this time it's from pent-up emotions. "Maybe." I have to tone my voice down. Mom isn't the one I should be attacking. "Maybe," I say, softer this time. "I'm just here to help provide information on contracts, timing and stuff. I am Alexius' right hand, like you said."

She nods. "It's possible." She looks around the room, her thoughts going a mile a minute, if the way she air-taps her pen is any indication. "So you haven't done anything? No contact with old suppliers or anything?"

I almost want to laugh.

I've talked to this woman at least twice a day for the past year. She's probably kept a journal of all our conversations. She grills me all the time about who I've met, who I've spoken with, which means she should know the answer to this.

Well, she'd know the answer I've given her. Some things I kept to myself.

"What about all those favors Donald asked of you?"

I shoot daggers with my eyes toward her. She said that way too loud.

Those favors were between Donny and myself. Just little things I could do to help him out.

"Whatever you're hiding, stop. He's not worth it."

"He's worth it and more," I argue. "You, of all people, know how much he has helped me. Helping him now, it's the least I can do. I love him."

Her sigh is more than loud enough. "Love can make a person do stupid things, Starla. You of all people know that. Why are you letting this happen to you again?"

I'm not letting anything happen to me.

"This isn't the same, and you know it."

"Looks like it to me. Just exchange con jobs to murder and you're back sleeping in the same bed."

That hurts. I drop my gaze to my lap and play with my engagement ring.

It's not the same. Then, I was young and foolish and let myself be used as a trap.

"If you don't want to take the fall, then don't keep secrets."

On that, we agree.

"I'll tell all I know about Alexius," I say, looking directly into the mirror. "About her secret trips to the woods, the late-night experiments, the blood she collects . . ."

17: FIRST INKLING OF PREMONITION

Eleven Months Ago

Mom and I were curled on my couch, reminiscent of my teenage years when we'd watch movies with a bowl of popcorn between us. She'd come to visit for the weekend with some excuse about wanting to attend the local weekend market.

We both knew it to be an excuse. I'd been out of jail for a few months now and I had a lot to make up for.

"Things honestly going okay?" Mom asked during a commercial break.

She wasn't asking how I was doing or how work was going. She was asking about my promise, that this time would be different.

"It's harder than I thought it would be," I said, going for honesty.

She sighed, curled her knees tighter to her chest and gave me a look that I knew all too well.

She was worried but didn't admit it. "Who have you talked to?"

I jumped up from the couch at her question and headed to the kitchen for another bottle of wine. Mom had brought three different kinds and we'd already finished the Chardonnay.

"Rosé or Moscato?" I called out.

"You pick," she said, her voice laced with impatience.

I uncorked the rosé and brought it back to the couch, pouring each of us a full glass.

"Are you going to answer the question?" Mom sipped her wine and looked at me over the brim of the wine glass.

"I haven't spoken to anyone," I replied. It wasn't a lie. I haven't spoken to anyone from my past. Not in person, at least.

"Who's contacted you?"

I pulled my hair out of its ponytail, not answering right away.

"Starla?"

"A few people," I finally admitted. "But I didn't take their calls. I returned one or two messages, but that was to only tell them I wasn't interested in their offer."

She scowled, her lips tightening as whatever she had to say rested on the tip of her tongue.

"Why would you call them back?" she finally said.

"I told you—"

"You shouldn't have," she said, cutting me off. "It shows you are interested, that you need a better offer. So, did they?"

I leaned my head back on the couch and closed my eyes. I didn't need to ask her to clarify what she wanted to know.

Had they called back? Absolutely they did. Did they give me a better offer for the job? It'd been hard to turn down, if I were being honest.

It had been on the tip of my tongue to say yes, that I was interested, that they could count me in as a team player. But I'd made a promise I wasn't ready to break.

"I told them I wasn't interested. No matter the offer. No matter the incentives. No matter the team they put together." I lifted my head and looked at her, straight in the eyes. I wanted . . . no, I needed her to hear me, to listen and to believe.

"I said no," I repeated.

It took her too long to accept my truth. I couldn't blame her, though. In the past, I'd have been bored of whatever I was doing and anxious to get involved in another con job. Anything to add excitement, to make me feel . . . period. That need remained a constant thread in my life, probably something left over from being raised in the system.

"This time," she said.

That hurt.

"I think I can be happy here." I took a sip of my wine, tearing my gaze from hers so she can't see the pain her words caused.

"For how long? That's what I'm worried about."

I let out a long sigh. At least she was being honest. I couldn't fault her for that.

"I don't have all the answers, Mom. I've only been here a month. So far I like it." I lifted my hands and pointed around the room. "Free apartment that is fully furnished, a vehicle . . . what's not to like?"

It took her a bit, but she finally nodded, as if accepting my answer.

"What's the Frost Queen like?" she asked.

I didn't stifle my smile. Mom kept coming up with nicknames for Alexius and all of them were quite accurate despite only having met her that one time.

"She's happy when her hands are covered in dirt or when she heads to the city to teach."

"And the other times?"

"Let's just say I doubt we'll become best friends any time soon," I said.

I can't seem to get a read on Alexius. Her spirit animal was probably a chameleon. An old crusty one, too.

"But you like working with her?" The confusion was clear in Mom's voice.

"Not with her. The job. The people. I like what I do. I don't see her often, so when I do, I grin and bear it, I guess you could say."

Mom harrumphed. She didn't like to hear that.

"What about Donald Dixon? Is he still around?"

I snorted. Around? The man was like an unwanted trail of toilet paper on the bottom of a shoe. I couldn't get rid of him.

He was there in the morning when I picked up coffee. There when I sat out in the gardens having lunch. He checked in on me if I was out helping with projects. He was just . . . there. Always there.

"There's something about him I don't trust." Mom angled herself toward me more, her wine glass in hand.

"He's a used car sales manager, Mom. I doubt trust has ever been a word associated with him."

"It's more than that," she said, her finger tap-dancing against her lips.

"Well, whatever it is, how about we agree to not discuss the Dixons for the rest of the weekend? They're both out of town anyways."

I rather enjoyed the days when they both left town. Alexius drove into the city twice a week to teach with Donald going with her at least once a week. He normally took off most weekends and hunted.

Whenever they left town, my life calmed. The workload remained the same during the week, but the stress of dealing with clients' projects ended up diminishing when Alexius was not around.

And Donald, well, he took on the role of being my fairy godfather with enthusiasm. He might as well be a guard, the way he was always there, watching me.

"Did they go away together?" Mom's voice was piqued with interest.

I shook my head. "He's stocking up on his leather supply and she's at some lecture this weekend."

Her brows wrinkled together. "I think you told me he makes his own key tags, right? When does he find the time? You'd think it'd be cheaper to buy them in bulk."

I shrugged. "Not my problem," I said. I also intended to keep it that way too. I didn't really need another project added to my already overwhelming list of things to do.

Mom took another sip of her wine, reached for the TV remote and scrolled through the options until she selected the next movie on my list. I have a lot to catch up on after spending so much time behind bars.

My phone dinged with a text message. It was Officer Burnard. I frowned, then groaned in disbelief.

"What's the problem?" Mom asked.

I held out the phone to her so she could read the message.

"He wants to do a random drug test now? It's Friday night," Mom, who grabbed the phone from my hand, said as her fingers flew over the keyboard.

"What are you doing?" I asked, trying to snatch the phone away.

"Telling him to suck it. This is just a power trip."

I managed to force the phone from her grip and deleted the text she'd almost sent.

"You want to get me in trouble? They're called random for a reason."

While I agreed with her on her assessment, the last thing I wanted was to get myself in trouble only a month in.

I texted back asking for him to come here, rather than me into the police station. My attempt at politeness obviously worked because he promised to be by in less than ten minutes.

While we waited, my mother glowered in disgust and made unintelligible mutterings as she tidied up my already cleaned apartment.

From the moment he entered, handed me a brown bag with a bottle inside for me to pee in, to when he left, my mother barraged him with comments about abuse of power, respect and belief in the process of change.

It took her a good twenty minutes to cool down after he'd left.

"I've never had Burnard apologize so much for a random drug test," I said with a teasing note in my voice. "Sure you don't want to move here? I could use you as my personal attack dog."

I'd brought up the subject a few times, her moving to Bervie Springs and starting over with me.

"Let's give it more time." It was the same response she'd given each time I brought up the idea.

It wasn't that she didn't want to. It was the fact she needed to make sure I'd be around, that I wouldn't end back in prison, that she wouldn't be uprooting her life for nothing.

I got it. I needed to rebuild her trust. I could do that.

My phone dinged again with another text.

"So help me," Mom ground out between a clenched jaw, "if he is bugging you again . . ." She grabbed my phone and held it up. "Starla." One word. Two syllables. But my heart rate sped up, my chest tightened and any breath in my lungs disappeared at her tone.

"I thought you said no," she said as she turned the phone around in her hand so I could see the text.

The message was a simple one.

Saturday. Noon. Fifty percent cut as agreed. Address to be provided day of.

Well, shit. I could explain this away but she wouldn't believe me, no matter how hard I tried or how much truth I told.

"I don't handle lies, you know that." Mom's voice was razor-edge sharp.

"I didn't lie."

The perfected look of a 'mother who knows better' came on her face.

"He won't take no for an answer. He tried this last week too. I didn't show up then, I'm not showing up now."

I could tell she didn't believe me.

"We have plans tomorrow, right? The market, remember? Why would I invite you here for the weekend if I planned to be on a job?"

The moment the truth in my voice hit her, I let out a long breath. I sank back against my couch and pulled my legs up beneath me.

Nothing was said for minutes, minutes that felt like a decade.

"I believe you," she finally said. "But if you dare to ditch me tomorrow with some paltry excuse, I'll be on the phone the minute you leave my side, serving your sorry ass to the police. Is that understood?"

The truth is, I had asked Mom to come this weekend for that very reason. Accountability. So that I wouldn't be tempted to take the job, steal the goods, and land back into my old life without a second thought.

We both knew it too.

18: WHAT HAPPENS IN THE SHED STAYS IN THE SHED

Ten Months Ago

The office was quiet. Blissfully quiet. No phones rang. No equipment disrupted the noise from outside. No one spoke to me.

I never realized how much I craved silence until I moved here.

I dropped my head into my hands and massaged my temples with my fingers. I had a whopper of a headache that just would not go away no matter how much Tylenol I took or water I drank.

I'd spent close to thirty minutes so far working on an invoice for a project without a file. It wasn't the first time I'd come across this. No file equaled off-the-books, which was fine if that's how they wanted to do things. But at least give me a heads up or something.

My phone buzzed with a text.

Come see me.

I groaned. I hated being summoned like that by Alexius. It was like being told to play nice with the new girl at school, something I had to do whether I wanted to or not.

I grabbed my notebook and headed toward the nursery area. It took fifteen minutes of walking through the rows and different plant areas until I realized she had to be in the Shed.

I've yet to step foot inside the Shed. That was Alexius' secret domain, her private place where she worked her mad scientist skills.

I hit the doorbell attached to a camera and waited.

"Starla, come on in," Alexius called out.

A buzzer sounded and the door clicked, opening slightly. I pushed it wider and stepped into the until-now forbidden room.

It was a laboratory full of light, pouring in from the ceiling and overhead fixtures. Greenery filled almost every available surface and soft music played over speakers hanging from overhead.

"Alexius?" I called out, not seeing her at first glance.

"Down here."

I headed to the second aisle and saw a leg sticking out from beneath one of the wooden tables.

My eyes widened as I took in her Shed. I was walking in a jungle; the humidity soaked the shirt to my back right away. Why was it I never saw Alexius all sweaty?

"Anything I can help with?" I asked as I walked closer.

She inched her way from beneath the table and stood, wiping the dirt from her hands on her cargo pants and black shirt.

"Actually, yes. Come here, will you?" She walked to her desk, pulled out a metal stool and indicated for me to join her. "I would have come to you, but I have a time-sensitive experiment happening today so I'd prefer not to leave."

I looked around, expecting to find lab equipment and instead found a container with pods holding individual plants and tags with times listed.

"What's the experiment?" I was clueless when it came to the work she did.

"I'm testing out some new blood," she said, a twinkle in her eye.

I reeled back. Did she just say blood?

She pointed to a room in the back that was sectioned off by what looked like two vinyl curtains. "Go see what's back there," she said, the challenge in her voice very real.

I slowly stood from my stool, unsure if I really wanted to see whatever was behind there and yet, I parted the curtain and stepped into a completely different reality.

Cooling containers full of bottles with red liquid lined the wall opposite of where I stood. On either side of me were two metal tables. Beakers and other equipment filled open shelves.

My first instinct was to look over my shoulder, but I was still alone.

Part of me wanted to walk toward the fridges and look at what I assumed had to be blood. The other part of me wanted to run as fast as I could away from these crazy people.

Who the hell kept blood like that?

Alexius worked with soil, not people.

"Still alive in there?" Alexius's voice was muffled from behind the curtains.

I stepped back, slowly, until I was out of the room. I breathed in deep, inhaled the moisture from the room and took my time before I looked Alexius in the face.

When I did, her lips were turned up into a wide smile.

"I figured you wouldn't believe me until you saw it in person. Most people don't." She hitched a shoulder as if it were no big thing.

"What was in those bottles?" I asked.

"Blood."

"I'm sorry?"

She let out a slight sigh. "Blood, Starla. Did you look at the bottles? They're all from different animals, dated from when the blood was collected. I have everything from possum to deer, rabbit and even wolf. I'm using a new type of blood today, which is why I prefer not to leave the area."

I swallowed hard. "Is that even . . ." I couldn't think of the wording to use.

"Legal? Ethical? Of course it is. Nurseries use bloodmeal all the time in their soil. I just prefer to use it straight from the source rather than mix it with other ingredients."

Was she playing me? I haven't yet figured out how to read her and that doesn't happen very often.

"Why would you use blood?" The question slipped off my tongue. I had to admit, the concept was horrifyingly interesting.

A switch came over Alexius as she turned toward me.

"Blood contains three primary plant macronutrients," she explained. I could clearly see the teacher persona take over. A jolt of excitement flashed across her face as her voice changed from patronizing to patient.

"Which are?" I had no idea what macronutrients were or why they were important, but it seemed like a good idea to play student.

"Nitrogen, phosphorus and potassium," she said. "It's what plants need in order to not only survive but grow."

The reason for blood wasn't clear and that must have shown on my face.

"Blood is rich in nitrogen. It's one of the best things I've used for growth and luster. It's amazing the difference it makes."

My stomach rolled and swayed as I looked at the plant containers in front of me. It didn't take much of an imagination to see pools of blood soak the soil and work its way through the green stems.

"Did you know in some communities, women will collect their menstrual blood, mix it with three parts water and use it for their vegetable gardens?"

The idea of eating a blood salad had me bent over and gagging.

Alexius patted my back as I struggled to breathe through the retching.

"It's really quite interesting, if you think about it," she said.

It really wasn't. I thought back to some of the salads Alexius would eat during lunch, the different times I'd join her. Please tell me I hadn't eaten any of her experiments.

I didn't want to ask.

"It's what I'm doing my doctoral thesis on, thus the experiments. I want to see if there's a difference between the types of blood and how plants react."

I breathed in deep through my nose, forced the image of a red-soaked lettuce leaf from my head and opened my notebook, the need to get out of her Shed strong.

"I'm trying to invoice for the Kincaid project, but I can't find any paperwork for it, just a few notes from Donald," I told her.

She shook her head and stretched her shoulders. "He had it in his head that he didn't like what we did and decided to replant things."

I frowned. "Does he do that often?"

She shrugged. "Often enough. Makes a mess of things too." When she didn't say more, I tapped my pen against the notebook. "So . . ."

"Do up an invoice and bill it to internal. We can't charge them for something Donny decided on his own without their approval." That made sense, but there had to be a way for the company to not take a hit.

"What if we were to get approval before he did this, in the future? Maybe offer them a discount while providing a new plan? If it's an upgrade, they might be more inclined to pay."

"Instead of having it come out of our pockets," Alexius said with approval. "I like how you think. Now, if we can only get that man of ours to follow procedure, then we'll be fine."

"He's not mine," I said, my voice firm.

Alexius lifted her shoulder in a 'don't really care' kind of shrug. "As long as you are here and managing him, consider Donny your responsibility."

I turned from her, not liking the implication in her voice.

"If Donald is a problem, he's yours. I just work here." I needed this to be clear. I wasn't going to get involved in any of their bullshit business. I've worked hard to stay out of things and I preferred to keep it that way too.

"Starla." Alexius stood, arms crossed and looked me straight in the eyes. "You wouldn't be where you are today if not for us. If Donny needs something from you, I expect you to do everything you can to make sure he's taken care of." Her eyes narrowed, her gaze intensified. "I don't care what it is he asks of you, am I clear?"

I stood as well, met her toe to toe and refused to back down. I was about to tell her where to go when Mom's voice popped in my head.

"Gentle, daughter. The choice is yours — do you want to succeed or end up back in prison?"

I swallowed the gaggle of harsh remarks back down.

"If my job description is about to change, then I'd like it in writing."

Alexius rolled her smoky, grey-lined, mascara-coated eyes.

"Of course," she said. "But trust me, we wouldn't put you in jeopardy, everything we ask of you is fair . . ."

In other words, do as I'm told because without them, I'd be reliving my past all over again. Yeah, yeah, I got it. Except, I was getting tired of the messaging.

A ding sounded, breaking the tension and Alexius turned to focus on her plants. It was then that I noticed a jar of what I now knew to be filled with blood and a dropper.

I didn't care if she had more to tell me, I wasn't going to stay and watch her drop blood onto her plants.

No way. No how.

19: THE BEGINNING OF THE END

My shift was over, lights turned off and I was about to lock the door behind me when Donald turned the corner of the walkway and waved.

"Damn it," I mumbled beneath a smile.

"I raced all the way here, hoping I'd catch you in time," Donald said as he sauntered my way.

My brow rose in a silent question.

"What would I do without you, Starla Bishop?" Donald said, his megawatt-billionaire-smile in full force.

"Same thing you did a few months ago when I wasn't here." I couldn't count the number of times we'd had this exact exchange. It was getting tiresome.

"I was running my wheels, always on the go but never getting anything done," Donald said. "With you here, why, everyone says it's a miracle the change they've noticed in me."

I pushed the door open to hide my gagging reaction.

"What can I do for you?" I didn't head back toward my desk, instead I stayed close to the door, the message that I didn't want to be here, clear.

At least I thought it had been.

"A few days ago, Alexius mentioned you were interested in helping me more often," he said. "I'll be honest, I was a little surprised, but pleased. I can use all the help I can get." His smile remained just as blinding as before.

My hand rose to my face, my fingers squeezed the bridge of my nose. What the hell was he talking about?

A few days ago, I'd walked into the Shed for the first time since arriving and prayed I never had to return. My sleep had been full of blood jars and animal cries and I was never going to forgive her for it.

"I did?" I didn't recall a conversation where I'd offered to help Donald. In fact, it had been the exact opposite.

"You will help me, right?" His smile drooped.

The sigh I released was very long and very telling. Did I want to help him? No. I didn't need to add more to my plate.

"I'm sorry," he said, his hands clasped together. "Maybe I got things mixed up. Maybe she said she'd talk to you or . . ." His voice trailed off as he struggled to find an adequate excuse.

I bit my lip while a small war raged on inside of me. I didn't want to help him. I didn't. And yet, Alexius had made it very clear if he asked for help, I was to be there, ready and willing.

"Of course, I will." The words slipped out before I could swallow them back.

Instant relief flooded Donald's face. He reached over for my hands, holding them between his own, and held tight. "Thank you, thank you, thank you," he said. "Honestly, I screwed up big time right now and without your help, I don't know what I'll do."

He led me over to the waiting chairs that were meant for customers. When we sat, he leaned forward, his elbows resting on his knees while I sat on the edge of my chair, my back straight.

"You're pretty good with graphics, right?" This came out more as a statement and less as a question.

"I'm okay," I said. Alexius had introduced me to some online design sites and after playing around, I felt pretty proficient.

"I'd say you're better than okay. Considering the flyers you created, I was surprised to find out you had no design skill set until now."

My face flushed from the praise. I lowered my head, in hopes he didn't notice.

"Don't be so humble," he said. "Think you could work your magic and make up a flyer for me? I dropped the ball on a huge sale I'm having for the dealership. I totally forgot until today, when a truck of used merchandise I'd bought at an auction showed up."

How could a person forget about vehicles he'd purchased? He must have spent thousands on those vehicles. Something about his sob story didn't add up.

"When is the sale?" If he said tomorrow, I was going to leave and tell him to contact Staples or some other big box company who could do rush jobs.

"This weekend," he said with a chagrined smile. "I figure if you could put something together within three days, that leaves me time to get a rush printing job on it and . . ."

The look on my face must have told him exactly how I felt about the short time frame.

"I just want a flyer, that's it. Nothing fancy. Something that looks decent with sale prices. I'll provide everything for you, don't worry."

Who said I was worried?

"So how does this work exactly? Billable hours to you or Soils and Springs?"

He looked a little taken back at my question. What, did he think I was going to do this for free?

"Yeah, okay, that makes sense. Can you keep track of hours where you do work for me? And whether it's council or sales?"

Now it was my turn to be taken back.

"Council? I seem to remember a fancy admin office right beside yours when I first visited your office a few months ago. Don't you have someone to do that stuff for you?"

His nose wrinkled. "I share her with everyone. I'd rather have someone whom I can trust. Someone like you."

Trust? Oh honey, he should know better than to give someone like me his trust so easily.

"I could be screwing you over, for all you know," I said, my face void of all emotion. He thought I was easy to read, that he could play me, but he couldn't.

All this crap about needing me, trusting me, believing in me, it made me nauseous.

"You're not." He carried a smug tone in his voice, and his lips lifted into a smirk. "If you were conning me, I'd know."

I wanted to laugh. None of my marks ever knew. That's why I was so good. I only got caught because each time I had gone behind someone's back to line my own pockets even more. Greed is my nemesis. That and pride.

Mom always warned that pride was one of the seven deadly sins. She liked to remind me each time I landed in prison too.

"Besides," he continued, his voice less certain, "what would you have to gain? I've given you everything you could possibly need."

Was that a question? I hope he didn't expect me to answer that.

"I trust you, Starla Bishop," Donald said, his voice softer, with a hint of sincerity mixed in. "If you're playing me, then you're playing me. I hope it's worth it."

I leaned my head back, part exhaustion and part exasperation in my motion.

"It's obvious I have more faith in you than you have in yourself, and that's okay. Like I said the day we met, I'm here to give you a new life. I can only offer it. What you do with it is up to you."

Was he trying to parent me? I couldn't decide.

"Send me the stuff you want on the flyer and I'll start tonight. If this is going to be a regular thing" — because apparently, I didn't have a choice — "I'll send you an invoice at the end of each week. Does that work?"

Donald popped to his feet, huge-ass grin on his face and reached his hand out, supposedly to help me stand.

I ignored the gesture.

"This is just the beginning, trust me," he said. "I'll send everything over after dinner."

It wasn't until I walked into my apartment later on that I realized I'd smiled at him as I walked away.

My smile hadn't been one that said goodbye, goodnight or even you're welcome.

My smile had been full of promise, positivity and even of thanks.

I thanked him with my upturned lips because of the faith he'd placed in me.

It wasn't until I was alone at home that it hit me how much I appreciated that feeling. Mom always believed in me, even when I didn't deserve it. But, to have someone else . . . the chinks of chain mail wrapped around my heart didn't seem as tight as before and that was a feeling I wasn't familiar with.

20: LOVE IS A DANGEROUS WEAPON

Tuesday 4:00 a.m.
DETECTIVE KAARNS

I'm rereading Bishop's file, trying to get a sense of the woman and get some questions answered.

But all I'm getting are more questions.

I've looked into a few of her sentences. She's got quite the reputation. A friend of mine works for the NYPD and recognized Bishop's name right away.

"She's a smart one," my old roommate told me. "Pulled off quite the heists too. Rumor is she pissed off the wrong person on her last job; it's why she ended up back behind bars."

I don't get it. How could someone so smart fall for a douche like Dixon? She's not only drinking his Kool-Aid but eating his drugged brownies. Why?

She's a con outsmarted by another con.

From everything I'm reading, she's the one who normally outsmarts others.

She landed in prison the first time for petty theft. The second had been for stealing personal information and working with a group who pretended to work for a collections agency. The last one had been for a pigeon drop and it was amazing she'd gotten away with it for so long. The fact Bishop had worked with someone associated to the mob was probably the reason.

It was also the reason she'd gotten caught.

But Dixon . . . it didn't make sense.

A pigeon drop isn't an easy con, but done right, very profitable. Seeing that three quarters of a million had been confiscated from Bishop's apartment tells me she knew her shit. Convincing someone to entrust her with their money, or better yet, get them to take her money only to make a switch . . . she's got skills.

So why fall for Dixon?

Does she really love him? The guy is a slime ball. Everyone knows that. Sure, he's got connections and can get anything and everything done, but five minutes in his presence and you'd feel like you'd just been licked by a slimy snail.

"What are you mulling over?" Spikes pulls out a chair next to me and steals the file I've been staring at.

"Trying to figure Bishop out, that's all. Something's not adding up."

He just nods as he looks over the sheets then pulls my notebook close.

"You called Darlington?"

Elaine Darlington, my old roommate.

I nod. "Why not? Use all resources, right?"

He doesn't say anything, just gives me an unreadable look. "What? Did I do something wrong?"

He shakes his head, pushing away both Bishop's file and my notebook. He stares at the wall behind me, pulling his lips in and out, an odd habit he has when he's working through a problem.

"What's going through that old head of yours?" I hate when he's quiet, not sharing his thoughts, making me work for them.

He takes his time replying but when he does, I lean back in my chair, arms folded and listen hard.

"I once worked a case, five years into the force maybe. Jilted lover who kills the new girlfriend," he says. "When we brought the boyfriend in, he told us this wild story of being the woman's first lover. She thought they were soul mates and couldn't handle him being with someone else. He'd put a restraining order on her but it was like something snapped within the perp."

There were times I love when he gives me long explanations, but today is not that day.

"What's that got to do with this case?"

A minute passes.

"Spikes? Where are you going with this?" I rephrase my question.

He still says nothing. Another thing he tends to do. Which means he wants me to figure shit out.

"Do you think love really changes a person?" he says as he pushes his seat back and stands.

I do a double take at his question.

"You're asking me? You're the one who's been married since the Ice Age. You tell me."

"If someone wants to change bad enough, anything can happen."

That hangs between us. Anything can happen yes, but because of love? Or would it be from desperation or low self-confidence? How much does that play into everything? Did Dixon step in at the right time and use it to his advantage?

"Even help them hide bodies?" I ask.

He gives me a shrug. "People do strange things for love," he says. "Or, better yet, because of it."

21: WILL YOU DO ME A FAVOR?

Nine Months Ago

It was after seven in the evening, I'd just finished helping Alexius replant shrubs for the Starr property and wanted nothing more than to climb into the shower to wash away all the dirt and grime that caked my body.

What I didn't want was someone to knock on the door just as I was about to pull back the curtain.

Shower or answer the door? The answer was obvious. The only people who knocked on my door were telemarketers or school kids tempting me with popcorn tins and chocolate mint cookies.

Considering payday wasn't till the end of the week and I was broke, I closed the bathroom door and blocked out the rest of the world in the shower.

Showering alone was a luxury I still wasn't used to, even now, almost three months out of prison.

Twenty minutes later, hair wrapped in a towel, I was about to open the bathroom door when there was a knock on it.

"Starla, I don't want to scare you, but I'm out here."

My heart pounded from the unexpected knock. I recognized the voice but couldn't connect it to the idea he was in my apartment.

How? The door had been locked.

My hand went to my chest and clutched the towel tight. "Donald?" I called out, my cheek pressed to the wall as I spoke.

"Just me," he said.

"Um, why are you here? How did you get in? Everything okay?" My casual attempt to keep my voice steady backfired on me as the last word came out in a squeak.

"I knocked, but there was no answer. I got worried and wanted to make sure you were okay."

I turned and stared at myself in the mirror. My brows knotted as I processed his words.

"But you heard me in the shower, right?"

His chuckle grated. "I should have left, I know."

I waited. He should have, yes. So why hadn't he?

"Listen, I'll just wait in the kitchen, okay? So you don't have to worry about me seeing anything . . . indecent."

I counted to ten, hoping that was long enough for him to be completely out of view before I opened the door and stuck my head out.

I couldn't see him. I did, however, hear my kitchen cupboard doors slamming shut.

I scooted into my bedroom and closed the door behind me. I also twisted the doorknob so it locked.

I threw on a pair of yoga pants and a sweater, pulled my hair into a wet bun and surveyed myself in the mirror.

Why was Dixon here? It bothered me he could just walk in. He shouldn't be able to. Sure, he had a key, since he technically owned this building, but that didn't excuse him.

Making sure I was okay? I didn't buy it.

I pushed my shoulders back, chin raised and headed to the kitchen.

"Donald, I have to say . . ." I was ready to stand up to him, to tell him how I felt about my privacy being intruded when I saw the table set, a vase of flowers set in the middle and lit candles which cast a glow along the walls.

"Sorry." He held up his hands in mock surrender. "I shouldn't have come in, I know. Honestly, I was worried. I knew Alexius had you working hard and she mentioned you looked pale. I had thought of asking you out for dinner until she mentioned how worried she was about you. So I brought dinner to you, but when you didn't answer . . ."

He looked like a schoolboy ready to be scolded for accidentally throwing a basketball at a girl's head.

"Alexius was worried?" She hadn't said a word to me. In fact, she'd left me alone at the Starr property, telling me she had to be back at the Shed for a client meeting.

"She shouldn't have left you alone to finish planting those bushes."

No, she shouldn't have. In fact, I'd been surprised when she'd left. That had been the first time she'd trusted me enough to leave me alone on a project.

"So is the dinner from her or you?"

"Me. And the flowers too." He grinned, that boyish charm tempting me to smile back.

I knew better than to give in to temptation.

"You could have called. Or better yet, left, once you realized I was in the shower." I crossed my arms and I refused to smile.

He looked over the table, then back at me.

"You're right. I should have. Listen, I'll . . . you've had a long day. Enjoy the dinner and I'll see you tomorrow, okay?" He headed toward my front door, his steps slow, as if he hoped I'd tell him it was okay.

I wasn't going to.

Give an inch and you've given it all. I learned that the hard way in prison.

He'd crossed a line. Without boundaries, he'd cross more of them too.

Be smart. Mom's voice rang in my head.

"Why dinner?" My voice stopped him.

He turned, looked at the table, then back to me.

"Why not? We both need to eat and there's something I wanted to discuss with you."

I tried to read him. Was he being honest? Or did he have other intentions? Did he think I'm an easy mark, someone who's lonely and will do anything for a night of company?

Was I lonely? Not really. Since arriving in Bervie Springs, I'd done everything Donald had asked me to do. I'd volunteered, gotten involved in the community, made a friend or two.

Truth be told, I enjoyed my life right now. I had my own place that came fully furnished, could pick and choose if I wanted to be alone or have a coffee with one of my new friends, no schedule other than having to work . . . it was nice.

I'd spent years being surrounded by others, never having a moment to myself, being held accountable, or rather being told how to spend every waking minute.

I liked being alone.

"I had Lou make your favorite." Donald left his place by the door. Perhaps he sensed my hesitation, and he began to unpack the food containers from the brown paper bags.

Fresh bread, salad, pasta swimming in a cream sauce followed by a dessert I knew I couldn't resist. Crème brûlée.

"What's the catch?"

I didn't wait for him to speak, just sat, tore off a piece of bread and groaned as the butter and garlic touched my tongue.

Bliss. Pure garlic bliss.

"Can I sit?"

I nodded. "But don't talk. Not till I'm done."

He laughed but didn't say a word. Not while I ate. Not while I poured us each a glass of wine. Not until I'd set our cleared dishes in the sink and settled on the couch.

"Thank you for dinner," I said. My stomach was full, my skin was clean, and my spirit was happy.

"You're a hard one to figure out, you know that, right?" Donald stared at me, his eyes half-hooded, his lips half-twisted in a smile.

"Your point being?"

He set his wine glass down on the old oak coffee table. "You've been here almost three months and I hardly know anything about you. In fact, I discovered more about you being in your apartment for ten minutes than I have in all the times we've talked."

I looked around to see what he'd discovered. Thanks to online shopping, I'd covered the walls with framed maps of cities around the world. London, Paris, Rome, Vancouver, Moscow and an island in Hawaii. All places I've wanted to visit but never will.

I have plants everywhere in a variety of colored pots, plants Alexius told me to take home. A soft green blanket Mom knitted for me one Christmas. A few throw cushions covered in encouraging words.

What about me was in the room?

What had I revealed by my decorating choices?

"I see a woman with dreams, passion, desires and heart." Dreams? Passion? Desires? Heart? From what?

"I see a woman finding herself, and it's nice to know I had a hand in that."

Ahh. There it was. His pride, ego, larger-than-life attitude. It was all about him and what he's done, accomplished, made possible.

"Yes, you've done well." My tone was borderline sarcasm edged with cynicism. I sipped more of my wine, curled my legs beneath me and suddenly wished Donald would leave.

"Sorry, that came out wrong," he said, with the decency to blush a little. "What I meant was—"

"Stop." I held up my hand. "It doesn't matter what you meant. It's the truth. You hand-picked me, gave me—" I waved my hand holding the wine glass around — "all of this . . . of course you should be proud."

He lifted his shoulder in a shrug. "You were the best candidate for the program. Still are. In fact, I just sent in a report singing your praises."

I breathed in deep, sure my hand trembled but thankful it didn't. "Report?" My voice shook but only slightly.

He pretended to ignore it.

"Yeah, just a little thing, really. Don't worry about it. Honestly."

I uncurled my leg, planted both feet on the ground and wished I could ask him to leave.

"It's just a bunch of paperwork. If this program is a success, then other towns will use it too. It's a good thing." His eyes lit up with excitement and I saw the politician in him. Everything, the program, me, it was all political for him, another notch on his belt, one step closer to becoming mayor.

"So, what did you say on the report? That I've become a model citizen, staying out of trouble, following all your rules?"

"Something like that."

The way he said it, he thought it was funny. But it wasn't. This was my life on the line; these reports determined my fate.

If anything, these past three months proved I needed this job. I needed something substantial in my life, that kicked my ass, provided hard work that wasn't demeaning or demoralizing.

"You've become a strong member of our team, Starla. Both Alexius and I have noticed the changes you've helped to implement within the office, the crew and not to mention how you've managed to help me with my dealership."

I didn't say anything. When it came to Donald, the less you spoke the more he talked. And talking was something he excelled at.

"It's taken a lot of pressure off Alexius," he said, "leaving her free to focus on her own studies and experiments. We're happy you're here."

A warm glow grew within me. His words meant a lot.

"With that in mind," he continued, "I wanted to run something by you, get your thoughts."

Mom's voice tingled in the back of my head. *Be careful. Stay safe. Don't get involved.*

"With the dealership?" I asked.

He shook his head.

"What are you doing?" I couldn't help it; I was always intrigued by ideas.

It was how I tended to get in trouble and yet, I never learned my lesson.

"This is a little side project of mine. You know I own several apartments here in town, including this one. I've put a bid in to own more, including some houses."

I felt my brows rise and questions of why he needed me swam through my mind.

"I'd like to do some extensive . . . renovations on a few projects."

When he didn't say more, I shifted in my seat.

"I'm not into construction," I said.

He laughed. "No, no, that's not what I'm hinting at." He swallowed and finished the wine in his glass before leaning over to place it on the coffee table. "What I'm hoping is . . . perhaps you know people skilled in certain . . . areas . . . who could use jobs and not mind being paid under the table."

"People from my past, you mean?"

It didn't make sense. He looked uncomfortable asking me something that was completely logical.

Why not ask an ex-con if they have connections?

A dozen, if not more, names filtered through my mind.

"I know people, sure."

Relief mixed with excitement filled him. He leaned forward, clasped my hand and the smile on his face became infectious. I smiled too.

"See, I'm not that bad, am I?" His boyish charm poured out of him like water through a sieve.

With my cup raised to my mouth, the intent to cover my smile, I winked. "Never said you were."

"Oh, come on now," he said. "You've held me at arm's length since the day we met and all I've tried to do is get to know you."

It was true.

"Why?"

He looked like he couldn't understand my question.

"Why try to get to know me?" I repeated. "I'm your employee. A charity case. You've been nothing but kind, gave me this furnished apartment, a vehicle, a job . . . why?"

He looked away, not able to meet my gaze.

"Why, Donald? Why am I so special? Because I know you didn't have to do any of this. So why me?"

"You intrigue me," he said quietly with a shrug. "I've never quite met someone like you before. You're honest, free, you say what you mean, you mean what you say and you don't hide behind anything or anyone."

The rawness of his words, the way he praised me, built me up . . . it was unnerving. I didn't know how to respond. I've never had someone compliment me like that.

I didn't sense any subterfuge, a hidden agenda or even slight sarcasm.

He spoke the truth.

I didn't know how to reply.

He stood and ran his hands down his pants to straighten them. "Alexius would kill me if she knew I'd overstayed. We . . . I . . . appreciate all your help, everything you've done since you arrived. I meant it when I said I couldn't imagine what life would be like without you in it."

He headed toward the door. I stayed in my seat, almost frozen. What the hell was I supposed to say to that?

This whole conversation had a weird vibe to it and I struggled with how to respond. Lines were being crossed and I should be doing something about that.

Except I wasn't sure I wanted to.

I was at war with myself. If any of my old cellmates could see me now, they'd get a kick out of it all.

"I'll get you a list." I cleared my throat. "Of some people I think would be able to help you with those renovations," I said. My paltry words seemed inadequate and disjointed.

He was hoping for something more. His shoulders drooped but his smile remained.

"I appreciate that. Some of the places will need to be gutted completely."

I stood then, crossed my arms around my chest.

"You'll almost own all of Bervie Springs, you realize that, right?"

His laugh was genuine. "That's the goal, Starla. That's the goal."

I could still hear his laughter as he left my apartment.

22: YOU WERE WARNED

I liked to sit on my back porch early in the morning with a cup of coffee. There was something about the stillness as the sun rose, the quiet chirp of the birds, the teasing caress of the wind as I sat there; in those moments, everything felt perfect.

Right then, nothing from my past or my future mattered.

As soon as I drained the last drop of caffeine from my cup, I stood, went into the house for a refill and did the one thing I did every morning like clockwork.

I called Mom.

It was our routine. Every day. There were days it felt too much, but then I would remind myself what it felt like to be away from her, to not be able to call her when I wanted . . .

"Good morning. Wasn't that a beautiful sunrise?" Mom's bright voice was exactly what I needed this morning.

I hadn't slept well last night.

"It was gorgeous."

There was a slight pause, a quick inhale.

"What's wrong?" Mom asked. She read me like a book, whether I wanted her to or not.

"Just didn't sleep well, that's all."

Did she believe me? Probably not.

"Starla, what's wrong?" Her words, sharp, to the point, instinctive, brought tears to my eyes.

What the hell was wrong with me?

"Nothing happened. I just . . . I couldn't shut my mind off last night, that's all."

"Why?"

"Donald Dixon dropped by last evening. I came out of the shower with him in my kitchen."

"Excuse me? Who does he think he is?"

"He said he was worried about me."

"Why would he be worried? What happened? It had to be something for him to be in your apartment." She stopped, gasped. "You're not sleeping with him, are you? You're not in some crazy threesome with him and the Ice Queen, right? Oh God, Starla, so help me . . ."

A chuckle, one from deep inside, burst out at her words. The image of a threesome with Alexius . . . like that would ever happen.

"You're kidding me, right? A threesome? What shows are you watching, Mom?"

I wished I were there, in the same room with her. I imagined her face beginning to glow with embarrassment.

"There's this show about a S.W.A.T team in L.A. and one of the characters is in a threesome with a couple . . ." She cleared her throat, her voice trailing off as I continued giggling.

"No, I'm not in a threesome. I'm not in a relationship, sleeping with a*nyone or anythin*g else, thank you very much." And yet, even as I said that, a whisper of my dream, the reason I'd been up most of the night, unable to sleep, brought my own face to a flush.

Me. Donald. In bed together, doing things I haven't done in a very long time . . .

"Good. I mean . . . gah. I hope he left. You kicked him out, right?"

"No. He brought dinner. Alexius kept me late last night helping her replant shrubs in a garden bed she'd torn apart."

That still wasn't that good of a reason for Donald to invade my privacy, though.

"He . . . um . . ." I pushed the door open and sat back outside on my deck, enjoying the soft blue in the sky. "He wanted to ask me a favor."

Mom didn't say anything. But she didn't need to. She had her own opinion of Donald and it didn't lean toward the favorable.

"It's not bad. He wanted to know if I had any connections—"

"No." Mom interrupted me; her voice strong, decisive, serious. "No connections. You promised, Starla Bishop. Do not do this. One small favor leads to another and another and before you know it, you'll be hauled off again, back to jail, and God help me, I couldn't handle that."

"It's not like that, I promise. He's buying real estate and wants to hire people like me to do the demolition and renovation."

I paused. I said a phrase Mom hated to hear. *People like me*. Yet, it was the truth.

People like me didn't get regular jobs.

People like me weren't trusted.

People like me were expected to fail.

"Then why not contact the prison himself? He's got the resources. Why does he need to go through you?"

Good question.

The only answer I came up with was that he wanted or needed an excuse to talk to me last night.

I wasn't going to admit that, though.

"You be careful, Starla. I'm not sure what it is, but I'm starting to think trusting him isn't the right decision. Remember, I warned you when you first started not to get in the middle of those two. It doesn't make sense for him to like you. There has to be a reason, and the last thing I'd want is for you to get hurt."

What hurt, and this surprised me, was her surprise that someone like Donald would be interested in someone like me.

"I should probably get ready for work," I said after a pause. "I thought maybe I'd try to beat Alexius into the office this morning and catch up on some paperwork."

"You don't need to prove anything to her," Mom reminded me, for the umpteenth time.

Mom was wrong though. I had everything to prove. That's what life was like now for me.

I had everything to prove and I'd do most anything to prove it.

* * *

I was elbow deep in paperwork, catching up on unpaid invoices and tracking shipments when Alexius strolled in, her high heels clicking on the tile.

Normally Alexius came into the office with clothing more suited for working in her gardens, but today she was dressed to impress in a soft cream-colored suit.

"Well, this is a surprise." The slight lift of her lips didn't hide the lie in her voice.

I pasted a smile on my face, tried to add some warmth, but failed miserably.

A few days ago, I'd discovered a camera in the office. I'd expected one when I started, waited for it to arrive in that first month. I'd relaxed a little when it didn't show up.

Until now.

I could have handled having the camera when I'd started, but why now? What had I done to force Alexius to add the camera months after I'd started?

Did Donald know? Had it been his idea?

"I thought I'd get started tracking some of the late shipments," I said as she leaned over my desk.

"What are we missing?" She reached for the file where I kept a weekly report of what we were expecting, her finger tracking each line as she read.

"The juniper already arrived. It's what we planted last night." She handed the file back.

"Not the order for the Moes project. That's been on back-order for a few weeks now. Remember, you left me a note to upgrade the sizes since you didn't want as much ground cover to be visible?"

She straightened, an odd look on her face.

"Hmmm. Keep me updated, will you?"

I nodded. I sent her a daily email on each project, so of course she'd be updated.

I checked the company calendar to see where Alexius was headed this morning. The whole day was blocked off, with no explanation.

"I'm headed to see a new client. Donald wants to invest in some property and start a tree farm, of all things." She brushed her hair over her shoulder.

"Oh?" This is the first I'd heard of this, but it wasn't like I was in the know when it came to their business. I only did what I was told to do.

The less I knew the better.

"He didn't tell you? I thought he would have, considering how close you two have been lately."

My head raised with a jerk.

"Oh, come on," she said. "Like I haven't noticed."

"No, no." I shook my head, my gathered ponytail brushing the back of my neck. "It's not like that."

"I'm not upset, if that's what you're worried about. As long as Donald is happy, then I'm happy," she continued as if I hadn't spoken.

"But I . . ." I didn't know how to reply. She'd caught me off guard.

Donald and I close? What did she know that I didn't? Because apparently, there was a lot I didn't know.

"It's okay," she repeated. "I imagine the idea of finding comfort after being in prison must be . . . nice."

Speechless. My brain couldn't get past the idea of seeking comfort from her ex-husband. I just . . .

"Oh," she inhaled with a sharp gasp. "I misspoke." The smile on her face held no apology despite her words. "Well, let's keep it our little secret, shall we?"

A heat wave surged up my neck, blazing across my cheeks. She giggled.

"Don't be embarrassed, Starla," she said, misreading the flare on my face.

I wasn't embarrassed. I was furious. The mean girl in front of me mistook me for someone to be bullied. If it weren't for the fact I needed this job . . .

I turned from her, dropped my head and fiddled with the papers on my desk, needing to distract myself, to breathe through my anger and speak like the adult I needed to be.

"Is there anything you need from me before your appointment?"

The moment her eyes twinkled, my hands fisted beneath the desk.

"Actually, now that you mention it." She pushed files I had sitting on the corner toward the middle of the desk and half rested her hip against it. "I appreciated some of your questions last night as we replanted the shrubs. How do you feel about working on a design for me? Nothing too extravagant, a dozen or so shrubs and perennials for a corner of a park some dogs destroyed?"

I immediately went through my mental files of all our ongoing projects and didn't remember that one.

"I noticed it this morning on my run," Alexius said, reading my thoughts. "Since Donald arranged that we have all the town landscaping . . ." She played with the files she'd moved, picking one up, leafing through the papers.

Her request surprised me. Last night, she'd rebuffed any suggestion I'd made, not once making me think she'd ever consider me helping her.

Designs were her baby, or so I'd been told in the very beginning.

"Sure, I mean, if you think I'm up to it, I'd love to try," I said.

She reached for a notepad, wrote down the address and file number. "Look up what we had before and do up some designs for me. If you feel adventurous, use that program on the computer too. I want extra dirt and feel free to suggest something different than what we've had in the past."

She stood, brushed her skirt to get rid of nonexistent wrinkles and gave me a pat smile.

"If I like it, you can work with Jordan on it."

Jordan was a new employee that had just started last week. Alexius seemed to take a liking to him.

I nodded, not giving her any words. I couldn't. Anything I said, in the tone I'd give, would let her know she had the upper hand.

"Oh, and Starla, I'm serious about Donald. I have just one request. Be gentle with him, okay? He hasn't fallen for anyone, seriously, since . . . well, since me."

The look on her face, raw, honest, vulnerable, had me nodding in agreement.

A soft smile graced her face before she turned away, her heels clicking on the tile.

I sat there, unsure of how I felt.

Donald, interested, in me? Sure, he'd said things last night that left me wondering, that didn't help when it came to my dreams, but for it to be real . . . I didn't know what to think, how to react.

My hands trembled slightly as images from my dreams played out, the tangle of sheets around our legs, the way my body responded . . .

The phone rang, interrupting my train of thought, thankfully.

"Thank you for calling Soils and Springs Landscaping," I greeted, my voice level, with none of the emotional turbulence I felt coming through. "Starla speaking, how can I help you?"

23: HIDDEN MOTIVES

It was love at first sight. His beautiful, melted chocolate eyes held mine moments before he kissed me with his tiny tongue. He was only ten weeks old but I'd already fallen under his spell.

"What would you name him?" Monique, the pet shop owner, stood at my side, cuddling a puppy of her own.

"Charlie," I said as I stifled a sneeze. "I always wanted a dog but never could have one." I leaned in and rubbed my nose with the cute little Pomeranian puppy in my arms.

One whiff was all it took for the sneeze I tried to ignore to happen, over and over and over again. I set Charlie down on the ground and reached for a tissue from my bag.

"I thought you were going to take some allergy meds before coming in?" Monique set down the pup she held and led me away.

I gave Charlie one last longing look before heading to the sink Monique led me to.

"I did," I said as I lathered up, hoping to wash away all the hair I might have picked up. "Obviously not enough, though."

Monique leaned against her counter, her hands braced against the wood, and chuckled. "For someone so allergic to dogs, you sure do come in often."

How could I not when she placed a placard outside her shop door with the words *PUPPIES* written in bright pink?

An alarm sounded on my phone, alerting me that I was almost late for my appointment with Donald. He had asked me to join him at his lot before heading into work today.

Between the random check-ins with Officer Burnard and then Donald always wanting to see me for one reason or another, I rarely had any down time.

I grabbed a coffee from the shop down the street, in a complete rush, and almost sideswiped a woman on the sidewalk.

One minute I had a cup of coffee in my hand and then next minute, that cup was on the ground, the coffee covering both our feet and, unfortunately, the front of her jacket.

"Oh my gosh, I'm so sorry." I dug into my purse for a spare napkin or two, as if that would help.

"Well . . . that wasn't how I planned to start my day, but . . ." The woman looked down at her stained jacket, her coffee-covered shoes and shrugged.

Absolutely embarrassed, all I could do was apologize profusely and repeatedly while staring at the stain on her jacket.

"Honestly, not a problem." The woman shrugged out of her jacket. "This has seen more stains than you could imagine." She held out a hand, a smile plastered on her face, taking me by surprise. "How about you buy me a cup of coffee while grabbing another for yourself and we'll call it a wash?" Her eyes twinkled at the play on words and I found myself back in the coffee shop, ordering two coffees.

"There's a dry cleaner just down the street," I mentioned. "If you take your jacket there, I'll cover the cost of cleaning it."

She laughed. "Oh honey, this jacket will just get thrown in the wash, like it has every other time I've spilled something on it. Don't you even worry about it. Besides, I'm just passing through."

"Oh? Headed to the city?" Making small talk was not one of my specialties.

We headed to the side counter, where we waited for our drinks.

"Where I could get lost in a crowd? No thanks," she said. "I prefer small towns, the ones that give off that family vibe, you know? Guess you could say I'm on a scouting mission, looking for the perfect place to settle down with my family." Her smile was bright, beautiful and full of promise.

"Bervie Springs might fit that bill," I suggested. "I'm new, so I'm still getting settled, but if you're looking for a place where no one locks their doors, everyone says hi and they hold welcoming parties for all the newcomers, then this is it." I wasn't sure if she heard my hint of sarcasm or not.

"If I were a serial killer, you might have just sold me on moving here." That twinkle was back in her eyes.

"Are you?" I knew enough con artists and criminals to know one often speaks their truth, even when it sounds like a joke.

"A serial killer? No." She waved her hand in the air. "Unless you were an ant. Then yes, that's a label I'd wear with pride. I hate those things." She shivered a little and I found myself actually believing her.

"Ants? They're harmless." What an odd conversation to hold in a coffee shop.

"I'm Starla, Starla Bishop," I said, deciding it was time I introduced myself. We were interrupted by the barista, who handed us our to-go cups.

"Thanks for the coffee, Starla," she said as we headed back outside. "I'll have to take a walk around downtown, get a feel for the place. Who knows, maybe you're right, maybe this is just the kind of town I'm looking for."

I smiled. "Then hopefully we'll meet up again . . ." I hesitated, feeling slightly off balance because she knew my name and yet, I don't remember hearing hers.

"Ava. Silly me, I never did introduce myself. I'm Ava and who knows, maybe we'll bump into one another again."

She went one way and I went another, my steps rushed as I headed toward the Dixon Deals car lot. He had about fourteen vehicles out today, all covered in banners and balloons. His lot looked like any other small-town used car lot — lots of cars, flags, flashy banners and empty of customers.

Before I could even approach the wood stairs that led up to the open door of his trailer, Donald stepped out, wearing a bright blue suit with a canary yellow tie. If his goal was to be seen by drivers that passed by, mission accomplished.

"Oh, you have coffee," Donald said as I approached. "I was going to suggest we walk and talk."

"We still can," I said.

"But I wanted to buy you the coffee." He pulled at his tie but it did nothing to hide the whine in his voice.

I lifted my shoulder in a shrug. "Technically you did," I said to appease him. The smile on my face seemed to satisfy him considering the way he jumped down the stairs.

"Let's head toward the town hall, if you don't mind. There's someone I'd like to introduce you to." Donald glued himself to my side as we headed toward the street.

"Who's manning the lot while you're away?"

"I just hired a new lot attendant," Donald said. "I should have introduced you, sorry about that."

I wasn't sure why he apologized, so I ignored the comment. He kept up a steady stream of updates about the town, events he was in the middle of planning for the town, and sharing gossip about some of the older families when I stopped at the crosswalk and refused to take a step more.

"What's wrong?" It took him a minute to notice I wasn't at his side.

"What did you want to talk about? Who are we going to meet?" I didn't like being ambushed and from his cageyness, that's the vibe I got from him.

I sipped my coffee, staring directly into his eyes, daring him to continue the charade.

He didn't.

"Remember our deal? How you'd do everything I told you to do?"

My eyes narrowed, pinning him down like a boy with a stick about to pop all the balloons. "What are you asking me to do now?" So far his requests hadn't been difficult; they'd kept my evenings busy and at times, I'd even called them fun. But it didn't give him the right to expect me to follow through one hundred percent.

"I want you to talk to a therapist."

A therapist? What the . . .

"Hear me out," he said, hands up, palms out. "Her name is Leigh Kits and she is an old friend. I trust her. She's discreet and—"

"Discreet?" I cut him off. "Of course, they're discreet." I ran my fingers through my hair, messing up my ponytail as I did. "Don't make this mandatory, Donald."

"I only want what's best for you."

Why did he have to say that? It was like he knew I was about to argue and those words stopped me. Every. Single. Time.

"What kind of therapist is she?" I asked. "What does she specialize in?" I clarified at his confused look.

"She's a therapist," he said, like that should explain everything. It didn't. In fact, it told me squat.

"I'm all talked out."

"Now, Starla, don't be like that. It would make me very happy if you went and talked to her, even just once." He glanced around and waved at a few people who walked on the other side of the street before focusing his brilliant white smile at me. "Please?"

What made this, me talking to a therapist, so important to him? I felt forced and being forced into therapy was never good. I've spoken to enough shrinks throughout the years to know that.

"Why is it my responsibility to make you happy? You're overstepping, Donald, and I'm really not comfortable with this." I refused to go any further until I received clarity on this.

"It's not." For a moment, Donald looked affronted.

"Sounded that way to me." I took one step, then two steps back from him.

"Just come and say hi, that's it. Please?"

"Why?" It didn't take a genius to know he was hiding something from me.

It took a little bit of time for him to answer. Thoughts crossed his face like trains on a track during rush hour. I knew he thought about lying to me, that he considered twisting his truth, but then realized that would be a mistake.

It's always a mistake lying to me.

"It would look good on the program, okay? I have a therapist willing to step up and volunteer their time. You'd be the first, but by showing how successful this program is, it's going to open a lot of doors."

"For you."

"For this town. For inmates like yourself."

"And for you." I was goading him, I knew it, he knew it, and I'd continue until he finally admitted the truth behind his request. Sure, this would be good for his program and the town, and absolutely, having programs like this across the state would be amazing, but bottom line, this reflected on him and him alone. "And for me," he mumbled.

I almost didn't hear his admission. It was a good thing I watched him say the words. But the minute I did, I walked in the direction of the town hall and this therapist who waited for me.

I wasn't sure why I did it. Spending time with a shrink wasn't at the top of my list of priorities and yet, I found myself shaking hands with Leigh Kits and following her into her office. We talked for thirty minutes, discussed my life outside of prison, and before I knew it, I agreed to see her monthly.

Donald waited for me as I left Leigh's office. The smug smile he gave me earned him a scowl. Fine, I went, and I'd go back, but he didn't need to be so damn proud of being right.

24: THE CABIN

Seven Months Ago

The early morning sky, silk with shades of pink blending into a soft yellow, greeted me as we drove along the highway.

I stretched out my hand and wove my fingers through Donny's as we drove.

With my head turned, my gaze traced the silhouette of Donny's face, starting from his forehead to the elegant lines of his nose, lips and chin. I couldn't believe this was my life.

The past month had been a whirlwind of emotional highs, from Alexius giving her blessing to Donny sweeping me off my feet despite the walls I'd built to protect my heart.

It had been sudden, relentless, and I'd eventually fallen in love despite all my mother's warnings.

It'd surprised me, and yet, I couldn't be happier.

"Not much longer," Donny said. "I'd hoped to get there before the sun rose . . ."

He'd woken me up three hours ago, told me to pack a weekend bag, made some coffee, and then whisked me away to someplace where we could be alone.

"I need to be with you, and just you, this weekend," he said. My heart raced even thinking about his words.

He wouldn't tell me where he was taking me, just that it was his little slice of heaven.

His little slice of heaven was in the middle of nowhere.

He'd made so many turns, driven down so many back roads, I felt turned around.

"Tell me about where we're headed," I said, my voice sleepy, my eyes fighting to stay open.

He caught my yawn and smiled. "You're going to love it, I know it. It has the softest bed you've ever slept in, a claw foot tub in front of a large bay window so you can watch the sun set while soaking in a bath and the perfect hammock to relax in during the afternoon. We're surrounded by nothing but trees."

It sounded perfect.

The vehicle slowed; we turned down a barely-there dirt road which went on forever.

I couldn't stop my gasp as a beautiful, old, wood cabin came into view.

"It's been in my family for years," Donny said. "I've never brought anyone here." His voice caught and when I was able to tear my gaze from the cabin to his face, a light sheen of tears in his eyes melted my heart.

"Other than Alexius," I said, expecting him to agree with me as we drove closer.

I'd come to accept I'd have to share him with her.

It surprised me when I'd realized I didn't mind.

Alexius stayed away from us, from our secret relationship that we hadn't made public. Sometimes I caught her looking at me, a question on her face, but other than that one time when she gave her blessing, she'd never brought it up again.

Our relationship was personal and other than Mom knowing about it, I liked keeping it a secret.

"Not even her," Donny said, parking the car in front of the cabin.

"This has been my hideaway, handed down to the men in my family for years. No women have walked through those doors. I've done some renovations to make it more comfortable, added a modern kitchen, and updated the bathroom, but most of what you'll see is original."

There was an honesty in his voice that left me with no doubt he told the truth. I completely ignored that little wiggle of doubt in the back of my head whispering questions of how could Alexius not know about this place, as someone he'd been married to for years?

As far as I could tell, he had yet to lie to me.

"Why?"

He shrugged. "Something about male bonding, rituals and other nonsense the men in my family have been raised with. It was all fine, until now. Until you." He squeezed my hand.

"Why me?" Our relationship surprised me on a continual basis. That someone like Donny could fall in love with someone like me; my stomach was all tied up in knots thinking about it.

"You're the only one I've ever wanted to share this part of my life with." He raised my hand to his lips and kissed it.

The knots increased. I was getting used to the feeling.

I'd never been in love before.

Not until now.

I'd been thinking about how to tell him, how to share this part of me with the man I didn't deserve and everything came up lackluster.

When he'd told me he loved me, it was in the middle of the night, a gentle whisper as he held me tight. He didn't mean to say it, the surprise in his voice, the way it caught on the word 'love' told me he was as shocked as I was.

I hadn't said it back. He hadn't pressured me too either.

"Ready?" He stepped out of the vehicle, walked around the car and opened my door. "This will be our own little hidden paradise," he said as he helped me out.

The cabin was everything he'd said it was and more. I would have sworn the cabin had been professionally decorated if I didn't know Donny as well as I did. It could have graced a magazine spread.

"Do you like it?" He showed me around; his steps carried every ounce of pride as I fell in love with our hideaway.

He drew me a bath, and while he puttered around the place, I relaxed, not believing life could get any better.

An hour later, I wandered through the rooms, looking over photographs and little knick-knacks, being surprised over and over again at the little things he'd kept around the rooms.

The majority of it were handmade pottery items, from bowls to water jugs to vases. All held a reddish tinge to them, from earthy to an almost pink eggshell color. Some looked to be painted where others had the red right in the clay. They were all wrapped with leather in one fashion or another, some just around the handles or top of the jug, some completely wrapped around a bowl or cup and a few of the plates I found looked like the leather was literally inside the clay.

I'd never seen anything like them.

Years ago, I'd taken part in a pottery activity in prison, something to keep our hands busy or some other nonsense. The act itself was calming, and I really enjoyed the experience until a fight occurred between two members of opposite gangs and the pottery wheel's disassembled parts became weapons.

I turned a few of the items over and noticed a name carved on the bottom portion. It was probably the collection name it had come from and the date created.

The oldest went back almost one hundred years. I replaced that bowl immediately, worried I'd drop it.

I had discovered more about the man than I thought possible.

I stepped outside, walked around the wrap-around balcony and took in the view from behind the cabin.

Three hundred feet beyond a clearing lay a valley, with hills and trees and a view not many have seen. My breath caught as I took it all in. I'd been dropped in the middle of a historical novel where you'd expect to see deer wandering through the untouched land.

I couldn't see Donny, but I wasn't too worried. Behind the house stood a couple of sheds, one with a door partially propped open.

I made my way toward the shed and called out to him.

Before I made it even halfway across the grass, he popped out of the shed, closed the door behind him and gave me the widest smile I'd ever seen.

He looked relaxed, at ease, happy.

More than happy. Peaceful.

"Hey, beautiful." He gathered me in a hug, lifting me off my feet and twirled me around. "I thought I'd have to come wake you up," he said, setting me down on the grass but keeping his arms tight around me.

"How could I sleep? I've never been to a place like this before," I gushed as I looked around. I was in a fairy tale and all that was missing was tiny creatures who could sing to me.

"I'm glad you like it. I'll have to give you a tour, but first, you must be starving."

He led me back to the cabin and into the kitchen.

"I didn't think you could get delivery out here," I teased.

Never, since arriving in Bervie Springs, had I ever seen him cook a meal. I wasn't even sure he knew how.

"I'll have you know I can make a decent omelet," he said as he pulled out ingredients from a fully stocked fridge.

I hadn't had an omelet since prison. In fact, I tried to stay away from anything related to breakfast eggs since I've been out. Toast, yes. Eggs, no.

He glanced at me when I didn't reply. "You do like eggs, right?"

There was a huge part of me that wanted to lie, to be brave enough to try something that made me gag, but I couldn't do it.

Donny had asked me to always be truthful with him, no matter what.

"I could make pancakes? There's a blueberry patch in the back we could pick and use?" He placed the carton of eggs back in the fridge.

"You don't mind? There's just some things I haven't eaten since prison, and eggs is one of them."

A mixture of sympathy and pity followed by understanding crossed his face.

"Don't think anything of it." He grabbed a bowl off a shelf and handed it to me. "How about you grab some berries? They're right off to the side of the deck."

I took the bowl, noted its off-pink tinge, a reminder of the sunrise this morning and turned it over. "I love all the pottery you have in the house. I had no idea you were a collector."

His eyes twinkled as he looked at the bowl in my hands.

"Another thing that runs in the family," he said. "I think my granddad made that one, if I'm correct. Beth, right?"

I looked twice. He was right. Beth, 1943.

"What are the names for?" I'd assumed they were part of a collection, but if they were handmade, then that didn't make sense.

"For the important women in our lives," he said, his face glowing with an excitement that was almost infectious.

"Well, if that's the case, do I get to put in a request?"

He ducked his head, but I was sure I'd noticed a slight dimming to that glow.

"How about we wait a bit on that one," he said. He must have noticed the disappointment on my face because he leaned down to give me a kiss.

"Smile, beautiful. I'm not saying no. It's just that they're meant as a memory item. It's another tradition in my family. We only make them after a death occurs."

* * *

It was the perfect weekend. Every moment, every experience was beyond anything I'd ever lived through.

It held a lot of first moments for me. First time I'd been to a cabin, first real woods experience complete with outdoor campfires, first time sleeping in the hammock beneath the stars until I couldn't stop shivering.

I was living on borrowed time. I had to be. It was the only explanation for the turnabout in my life. A tiny bubble of pressure occupied a small space of my heart, a warning that it wouldn't last. It couldn't. I didn't live a fairy tale life.

"Stop it," Donny said, giving me a squeeze with his arms tight around me as we sat in front of the fire, our last night here.

"Stop what?"

"Thinking. You're so tense. Relax, listen to the song Nature's serenading you with."

Months ago, I would have rolled my eyes at his words. Nature serenading me? Who talked that way? Donny, that's who.

His hands ran down my arms, and together we listened to the wind, to the crickets and owls, to the creatures awake in the moonlight.

"Everything until now doesn't matter, you realize that, right? It was all a lesson, but your life is different now. You are different. The girl you were when we first met has disappeared. That was the Old Starla. The hard-crusted, sarcastic, locked-up Starla." His voice was low, methodic, and full of pride.

"And New Starla?" I looked up at him, wide-eyed.

I shouldn't have needed his approval, but I did. When he smiled, praised me, built me up, I was renewed, reborn.

I'd never felt like that before.

"Ahh, New Starla, completely unrecognizable from Old Starla. You glow with a vibrancy that's blinding, there's a peace in you that feels soul deep and something about you calls to me in a way I've never experienced before." Donny leaned down and kissed me, sparking lightning through my body with his touch.

When we finally pulled away from one another, his eyes twinkled.

I looked down and he held a small box in his hand.

My heart stopped. My breath disappeared. My mind stilled. The universe collided into one moment, a moment where everything I'd known, everything I'd believed got swallowed up into a black hole of nothingness and my future spread out before me, with infinite possibilities that were mine for the taking.

When my heart beat again, when my lungs filled with air, I realized Donny was speaking, saying words I couldn't understand. Words of love and forever and eternity wrapped around me in a warm embrace. Tears trailed down my cheeks and my hands shook as he opened the box to reveal a square-cut diamond ring, the size of Manhattan Island.

His words didn't make sense. He loved me? He wanted to marry me? Spend the rest of his life with . . . me?

"Starla, love? Please answer, please say yes." The edge of Donny's lips tilted and there was a hiccup of doubt in his voice.

I half turned in my seat so that I could look at him directly. "Are you sure, Donny?"

He placed his finger against my lips, to stop me from saying more. "I've never been more sure of anything in my life."

I searched his eyes and all I saw was love.

Who was I to deserve such a man?

This wouldn't last. It couldn't. All I'd ever wanted was to be loved like this and now that I was . . . I'd become a different person. Someone I didn't even recognize. All my hard edges disappeared when I was with Donny. I was so unrecognizable that Mom told me she was worried.

That should bother me, and yet, it didn't.

25: LIES PILE UP

Tuesday 4:00 a.m.

I'm alone again.

In the interrogation room.

I hate it. Hate its drab walls, the fan blowing on my neck, the mirror and stupid camera. Hate the table, the chair I'm sitting on, even the blanket that offers no comfort.

The only thing, or reason, stopping me from storming out is that Donny is a few doors down.

Mom is at my place, hopefully resting. I hate that she came, saw me like this, that she feels helpless.

I'm full of hate right now.

I'm tired. Exhausted. Grumpy. Afraid?

I need sleep or coffee. Preferably sleep, but unless Spikes comes back and tells me to leave, I won't be getting that for a long time.

No one has come in for almost an hour. Maybe longer. Maybe shorter.

I rest my head in my crossed arms and close my eyes, hoping for a few minutes where I can maybe feel a slight relief.

There's a knock on the door.

For the love of . . . I lift my head and hope whomever walks in feels castrated.

"Sorry, was it nap time?"

Kaarns closes the door behind her and sits in Spikes' seat. She's got a smug look on her face. One that says she doesn't care despite saying sorry.

"Daddy let the young one come play? Is that how this is going to work?" Snide, sarcastic, completely insensitive but at this point, I don't care.

Her perfectly filled brows rise as she looks at me. No words. No mud-slinging comment back, taking the high road while silently sneering on the inside.

Bitch.

"I can't help but notice your ring," she says, her back straight, her voice almost sympathetic.

I immediately take notice.

"What about it?" The bright florescent lights in the room have the diamonds sparkling, the only reason why a smile tugs at my lips. I can't help but look at the empty space where I'd lost one of the smaller diamonds. Hopefully Donny insured it.

"Have you ever had it appraised?" Her voice is direct, like her gaze, which makes me a little uncomfortable.

"Why would I?"

She shrugs. "If I got a ring that size, I'd be interested in the value." She says this in a matter of fact way, like two friends chatting over wine.

Friends, we are not.

"That doesn't matter," I say. In the life I used to live, there were diamonds aplenty. This ring . . . it wasn't fake, Donny wouldn't do that to me.

"I've been trying to figure you out," Kaarns says.

"Why don't you just ask me what you want to know?"

Her head dips in a nod.

"You don't seem the gullible type," she begins. "Going through your file, reading your background, I don't understand how you could fall for a guy like Dixon." She holds up her hand before I can comment. "What do you see in him we don't? You know his reputation, right? Sleazy, will do anything for a buck, untrustworthy—"

"And yet," I interrupt, "he's the first person everyone in this town goes to when they need help."

She nods again, but I'm not sure if she's agreeing or just placating me.

"You're judging him based on what, exactly?" I ask. "Innocent until proven guilty, remember?" They're so adamant he's guilty, it feels like an uphill battle to prove otherwise.

"We have a lot of evidence telling us he's guilty, Starla. Him and Alexius. If I were you, I'd be more worried about your own state of affairs than his." The warning in her voice is thunderous despite her kitten-soft tone.

"I haven't killed anyone." I'm proud of how sure I sound. "I've never buried a body, nor have I ever seen a dead body buried in any of the gardens," I remind her.

"So you say." The doubt in her voice is clear. "Listen, I'm here to do you a favor. I thought you should know the truth about your ring."

Why is she so fixated on my ring? I glance down at the sparkling gem. What truth could she tell me?

The knot that has my insides all messed tightens and I'm sure I don't want to hear whatever Kaarns is going to say next.

"The one good thing about Dixon is he keeps all his receipts," Kaarns says.

The tightening inside me releases a little. She's going to tell me what it's worth or not worth, which is something I don't care about. If he bought it on sale, good for him. Hell, he could have bought it from a pawn shop and I wouldn't care.

"Doesn't it seem weird that his ex-wife still wears her ring? Or that no one, and I mean no one, knows about your engagement?"

I lean forward then, a genuine smile on my face. She's trying to make me doubt what I have with Donny, but it's not going to work.

"Just because she wears the ring doesn't mean anything. Call it a self-defense mechanism." I shrug. The way Donny made it sound to me when I'd asked, Alexius preferred men to believe she was married. It made her life easier.

"Right, but you've seen her ring. It could cover half this town's annual salaries for a solid five years."

I chuckle. "A bit of an exaggeration, don't you think? Besides, the ring doesn't belong to Donny. It's from Alexius' side of the family. An heirloom passed down from bride to bride, and yes, it's worth a fortune."

This news catches Kaarns' attention. From the surprise on her face, she didn't know that detail.

"Isn't that a little . . . odd?"

I nod. I'd thought the same thing but once you get to know Alexius, all the oddities are taken in stride.

"You do realize all the money is from her side?" I ask. They have to realize that. Did they honestly believe a used car lot owner could afford the house, the ring and the lifestyle? Little Miss Princess held all the power.

"And about my engagement, I was the one who asked we keep it under wraps. I know what it looks like, someone in Donny's position to be engaged to someone like me and so quickly. I didn't want to do that to him, for him to have to go through that kind of rumor mill."

"You?" Kaarns leans back in her chair, the surprise still present on her face.

I nod. "He wanted to tell everyone, throw a big party and all that. I was the one to kibosh the idea, squashed his excitement. There's no rush to get married and it would be better for the residents of Bervie Springs to become more comfortable with me before he tells anyone."

"Gotta say, Bishop, you caught me off guard," Kaarns says, her voice dripping with appreciation. I dip my head and look down at my ring, my smile growing.

"I thought for sure," Kaarns continues, "that you were going to tell me Dixon was the one who wanted to keep your relationship a secret. It made more sense to me, considering your ring is a fake and all."

My head pops up and I stare at her, repeating her words in my head.

"I'm sorry," she says. She means it too.

I don't want to believe her. I can't believe her. She has to be lying, hoping to trip me up, for words to spill from my tongue to condemn my fiancé, to give them something, anything, to help their case.

I refuse to believe her, except, when I see her face, read the message in her gaze, there's no satisfaction, no pride for ripping my heart to shreds.

"Fake?" One single word. One single syllable. One single explosion.

My ring, a fake. A fake. My gaze drops back to my lap, to the ring that still sparkles with a brilliance that takes my breath away.

Except, that brilliance is now tarnished.

There's a hole in my heart now, and it's expanding and widening, all my dreams, my happiness, my future draining through.

"You thought what you had was real, didn't you?" The disbelief that carries in her words wraps around me like a noose.

I can't say anything. There are no words, no expression that can convey how splintered I am. I'm just . . . broken.

"I want to go home, please," I say. "Just to sleep. To dream this nightmare away."

26: LOVE IS FLEETING

Tuesday 4:45 a.m.
DETECTIVE KAARNS

Bishop didn't know.

It's hard to sit here and watch her heart break. It's not the first time I've been caught in the middle of a relationship, where I've witnessed realizations and understandings become crystal clear.

But this one feels different.

She really didn't know. Not just that, but she honestly, really and truly loves Dixon.

I had the best of intentions when I came in here. From one woman to another. If my boyfriend was screwing around on me, you can bet your ass I'd want to know. I thought she'd be the same.

I hadn't thought she truly loved him. Sleaze-bag Dixon. What does she see in him? How could he have made this life-tough woman fall in love with him?

It's mind boggling.

I hand her a tissue as large teardrops trickle down her face.

Got to hand it to her, though, she's holding it together. She may be crying, but she's not sobbing, slamming the table, throwing her fake ring across the room.

"It's been a long night, I know," I say in response to her plea to go home to sleep. I'd prefer her to be behind bars, so being stuck in this room is as good as she'll get.

Her eyelids droop and exhaustion is written all over her face.

"I put on a fresh pot of coffee before I came in. Why don't I grab us both a cup," I offer before I stop myself. Now I'm sounding like Spikes.

She first shakes her head, but then nods. "Cream and sugar please, if you don't mind."

I stand without saying a word and leave the room.

Spikes is waiting outside the door.

"Good job in there," he says.

I let the left side of my lips raise into something that resembles a smile.

"Dropping the bomb like you did, quite impressive. Caught her off guard, which is what we needed."

"Thanks." The praise is nice. "I want to up the ante though. Share the audio recording Jordan got from Dixon. Make her mad, not just heartbroken."

Spikes doesn't say anything, just stares at the worn carpet beneath our feet.

"That'll work," he finally says. "I want her at the cabin."

What? Why? That didn't make sense. We finally figured out where the cabin was located and how to get there, so why bring her?

"We should just book her," I say instead.

"She knows more than she's letting on. Once she stops protecting him, we'll get more."

Spikes still isn't looking at me. He's not studying the carpet, he's thinking. I know how he works by now.

"Did you manage to get the extra cadaver dog?" The belief is that bodies are buried at the cabin. We have a team from the city and an officer with his cadaver dog combing through Bervie Springs.

He nods. "We head there first, though. They'll follow." He glances up at me then. "More bodies were found."

I almost don't hear the words, his voice is so low, but I do and it's like being sucker-punched over and over and over again.

More bodies. The count grows almost every hour. They're spread out all throughout town.

"We have to nail them," he says. "Nail them with as much evidence as we can find." He pulls out his keys from his pocket and plays with them, the jingle of the metal clinking together as he works free the leather keychain from Dixon's dealership.

"All these bodies . . . spanning decades . . . why?" He flicks the keychain with each word. "How do they pick their victims? What do they do with them and where do they keep them? There's so much we're missing, so much to piece together. Alexius isn't saying a word, Dixon's saying too much . . . what's their game?"

Same questions we've all asked ourselves the past few months, ever since we linked the disappearances back to the landscaping company.

"Jordan has some theories," I remind him.

The copious amounts of blood Alexius goes through for her experiments, to black market deals; the information Jordan got from Alexius was ridiculous.

I never asked how he gathered it, though. I've never had to go undercover, not like that.

Spikes nods. "I've heard. They bear some weight." He glances down to the room where Jordan, who worked undercover for the Dixons, is interrogating Dixon now. "We'll see how it all plays out."

He straightens, wipes his hand over his face and rolls his neck, letting out loud cracks. "You go play the recording while I speak to the chief. I need more information on these Dixon Deals."

He walks away, his shoulders sloped, hands shoved into his pant pockets.

The man looks tired. He didn't return to Bervie Springs to lead an active murder investigation; he came here to retire.

I pull my phone out and prepare the recording as I step back into the room and sit across from Bishop again.

Her hands are clenched in front of her and a vein in her neck is pulsing, but other than that, she appears calm.

For now.

"What's in your hand?" she asks, her voice barely steady. She's coping pretty well; I'll give her that.

"I know I've hit you with a lot, but I have more," I warn.

Her body almost folds in on itself. Until now, she's been strong, decisive, steadfast in her faith in Dixon, but now she looks broken.

Do I feel guilty? A little. There's a part of me that wants to cringe, knowing I'm the cause. A small part that acknowledges this woman loved a man. But let's be honest. She was in love with a murderer. I'm not so sure she was as caught up in the mess as I first believed.

So, there is that.

"You want me to turn on Donny, but I'm not going to. The ring is fake," she says with false bravado. "It doesn't matter. Maybe things are tight and he plans on replacing it later. Maybe . . ." Her words trail off as she realizes how weak her excuses sound.

"Maybe it's all been a con," I suggest. "Why? We're trying to figure that out. Aren't you the least bit curious?"

In her shoes, I'd want to know what the eff was going on. But I'm not and I hope never to be. I know better than to fall in love. I did it once. That was enough for me.

I place my phone on the table between us.

"What now?" There's a look of resignation in her eyes.

"There's something I think you need to hear," I say.

I want to warn her, but I also want to gauge her reaction, see her response. That's more important right now. The victims have to come first.

I hit the play button and sit back. Bishop copies me.

"I'm curious about the program you set up with the prison." Jordan's voice is clear on the recording. I've listened in a few times while he sat in the interrogation room with Dixon and can't help but be amazed at how calm he's been.

I would have knocked a few teeth from Dixon's mouth if I'd had to deal with him. He treats Jordan like a kid, like he doesn't know how all this works, but thankfully, Jordan's using that to his advantage.

"What about it? Pretty genius, don't you think?" Dixon's voice is just as clear as Jordan's.

The moment Starla hears Dixon's voice, she jumps. Not much, but enough that I notice. Her shoulders lean forward a bit too, as if she wants to get closer to his voice.

"What? Get a con to do a con?" Jordan asks. "Yeah, pretty smart. I'm surprised you got away with it, in all honesty."

"Hey now," Dixon draws out. "It's a legit program, all the 'i's dotted and 't's crossed. You won't find anything illegal about it."

I'm watching Bishop as Dixon's voice fills the room. So far nothing. But we haven't gotten to the good part yet . . .

"Other than you have Starla doing most of your dirty work for you," Jordan says.

Starla's face scrunches together. She's trying to figure out what's going on, I can see it.

"Don't know what you're talking about," Dixon says. I hear disinterest in his voice. Could Bishop?

"Not many people do, from what I can tell. How many dummy companies have you set up?" The sound of Jordan flipping through papers can be heard.

I can answer that one for him. So far we have about twenty companies we've been able to uncover. How this man has gotten away with all of his crap is beyond me.

"Again, I don't know what you're talking about."

I hit pause on the recording. "Do you? Know what Jordan is talking about?" I ask Bishop.

She shakes her head.

My finger hovers over the play button. "He's about to explain it. I want you to listen to how he explains it all. He's proud of it, Starla, proud of what he's gotten away with. You can hear it."

I hit the button as she leans forward even more, her elbows resting on the table.

"Whatever it is you're charging her with, you won't be able to link me to any of it," Dixon boasts. "Her fingerprints are on everything. From hiring people, to ordering supplies to signing contracts."

There's more shuffling on the recording.

"So you're saying," Jordan clears his throat, "that Starla should be the one sitting here, answering my questions and not you."

"That's what I'm saying."

There's a pause. Bishop looks at me. I look at her. She's got a shocked expression on her face, but she's a smart one, she'll figure this out.

"I couldn't help but notice the ring on her finger," Jordan says, his voice mildly curious. "It's the talk of the station. Pretty nice ring too. I was surprised, considering I'd never seen her wear it around the office."

There's laughter that starts first as a snicker, then into a full-blown belly laugh. It's not infectious though, it's demeaning and disheartening and as Bishop recoils, my heart goes out to her.

"Gotta say, Dixon," Jordan continues as if the laughter doesn't affect him. "I'm a little surprised that someone of your . . . reputation would get involved with someone like Starla."

"Looks good, doesn't it?" Dixon says. "Put something shiny on a woman's finger and they never look beyond it."

There's a small gasp from Bishop.

"So," Jordan says, "you reel them in, profess your undying love, put a ring on their finger and . . . ?" His unanswered question lingers, the silence growing as Bishop waits for his answer.

He doesn't give one.

He hasn't called for a lawyer yet either, which is surprising. Alexius has. But not him. He's cocky, thinks he can worm his way out of this, no doubt.

"Was the engagement real?"

What we don't see is Dixon's shrug.

"How do you think Starla would react if she found out you'd only used her?" Jordan finally breaks the uncomfortable silence.

"Starla is . . . was . . ." He stumbles over his words. "She almost makes me wish things were different." There's a wistfulness to Dixon's voice.

Starla's hand falls from her mouth, along with a trickle of tears.

I want to hit the pause button, I want to remind her he only used her, but something stops me.

"Her time is coming, though. Alexius is ready to move on."

"So, what Alexius wants, Alexius gets? What about you? Sounds like you could have fallen for Starla."

There's a snort. Probably from Dixon.

"There's only one woman in my life. My wife. My true wife. Everyone else is a plaything, for her. Except she didn't want Starla. She let me have her."

"What do you mean?"

"Figure it out, lover boy. You know Alexius, don't you? Don't think I didn't catch the two of you . . ."

Bishop waves her hands and I press the button to stop the recording.

"I've heard enough," she says, her voice resembling a broken pottery vase. "I was used, I get it." She leans her head back and stares up at the ceiling.

I know I could be pushing, pressing, prodding her, but I let her process all the feelings, all the words, all the plans.

I see her playing with the ring, twisting it on her finger until it slides off and she lays it on the table.

"I'm sorry," I say, meaning it.

She nods. "So am I. I fell for the oldest con in the book. I knew it, Mom even warned me, but I thought . . . things were different this time." She breathes in deep and I see a transformation come over her face. "I'm not going back to prison for him," she says.

I let myself smile at her words. This is where I wanted her, needed her. Right here, in this moment, with this feeling, this determination.

Here is a woman awakening from being scorned.

Here is a woman who wouldn't be used.

Here is a woman who will help us put away serial killers.

27: MORE AND MORE ANSWERS

Six Months Ago

For the next week, it was all hands on deck. In trying to fix problems Donny had created, Alexius was in a frenzy to get projects completed.

I found myself on a crew with Jordan, the new favorite. Most of the regular hands liked him; he held an air of authority about him they were used to working under.

Me, I wasn't sure.

He watched me. A lot. To the point it became intrusive and uncomfortable.

We were working side by side on a corner lot property. My job was to pull the weeds. His was to tell me where those weeds were, or so it seemed.

Alexius had just left. She'd come by to check on us and hand deliver lunch to her new boy toy. Of course, just as she pulled up, he had to take his sweaty T-shirt off.

It wasn't the first time I'd tried to ignore that impeccable six-pack of his.

"Want a break?" he asked as he looked through the bag of food. "There's a couple wraps in here. I'm more than happy to share."

I straightened, my hands going to the curve of my back as I stretched the kinks out. "I'm good, thanks."

He'd set the bag down and pulled out a clean shirt from his gym bag. Thank God.

"You're going to tell me you'd rather pass up a chicken caesar wrap?" He chuckled a little beneath his breath. "Don't even bother. I know they're your favorite." He pulled the wrap out and held it out to me.

"And just how do you know that?" I stood but kept my hands close to my sides.

"I overheard Don tell Alexius the other day in their kitchen."

I wasn't sure how to respond to that. Was it the fact Donny and Alexius talked about me or the fact Jordan had been in their personal space? Even though it was my decision to steer clear, it still stung a little.

"Alexius brought that for you, so no thanks."

He turned the sandwich over so it faced me. "Actually, I'm pretty sure this was meant for you." My name had been written in black ink on the plastic cover.

To say I was surprised Alexius had thought to bring me lunch was an understatement. I could count on two hands the number of times she'd provided lunch for me while I was on a job.

We ate our lunch in relative silence. Before I could suggest we get back to work, Jordan leaned toward me and flashed me his 'I used to be a teen-heartthrob' smile.

My guard was instantly up. I knew better than to trust those smiles. Those smiles always carried a price once accepted.

"How long has this thing with you and Don been going on?" He leaned back, his arms behind him holding his weight.

I steeled my face to not show a single emotion, even though I felt a combination of shock, awkwardness and a little mixture of fear.

That last one caught me off guard.

"Don't bother denying it," Jordan said. "Pillow talk is a huge thing with Alexius."

I pushed a shoulder back until I heard a slight pop. "Do you hear me asking for the nitty gritty between you and our boss?"

"Whoa." Jordan's smile grew even wider. "Okay, so it's off limits, I get that."

If he was trying to appease me, it wasn't going to work. "How about everything other than work be off limits?" There was something about him I didn't like.

His smile faded and for a moment there was a look of unexpected openness. "I'm not your enemy."

Where had I heard that before? Oh yeah, from basically everyone.

"I don't care if you're my enemy or wanting to be my friend," I told him. I was ready to get back to work. "We work together and that's enough, okay?"

"So you're just here doing an honest day's work and nothing else?" The doubt in his voice crawled up my skin like a colony of fire ants.

I snorted in reply. "What, don't believe someone like me could be honest?" I turned my back, tired of this whole conversation. I was ready to get back to work.

He seemed to get the hint. There were thirty minutes of blissful silence before his voice had me pulling out my headphones.

"What?" I added the extra emphasis of exasperation when I turned toward the direction of his voice.

"I have to do a run into the city for workers," he said in a way that made it sound like he was repeating himself.

"And so?"

"And so, I was wondering if you'd done any of these pick-ups? It's my first and I'm not sure what to expect." He stuck his shovel in the ground and leaned on it.

"Not a clue," I went to put the earbud back in place. "Donny takes care of that."

"So, you don't know where they go after, or how long they're promised work? Is there a list or anything to keep track of them?"

"Again, I have no idea." Was there a problem with his hearing? "I've never done a run. You'll have to ask Donny about his process." I heaved a sigh that lifted my shoulders to my ears, held it for a moment, letting every muscle in my shoulder and back tighten. There was a sense of relief when my shoulders dropped.

I looked around the area I'd been planting shrubs, thought about what was left and what needed to be planted.

"Want me to dig some holes?"

I backed away. "By all means," I said to him. If he wanted to do the heavy work, I didn't mind.

While he dug, I sat on the tailgate, a fair enough distance away, and drank a bottle of water. My shirt clung to my skin and I couldn't wait to head home for a cold shower. It was days like this I wish I had a pool.

A half hour had passed and I still sat here. Not that I minded, but he was digging way too many holes for what I needed.

"The holes don't need to be too deep," I called out, as if he didn't know.

"I know," he said, finally dropping the shovel to the grass and joining me on the tailgate.

I jumped off as he jumped up.

"I'm getting the feeling you don't like me," Jordan said to me.

I shrugged.

"You gonna fill those holes too? I didn't need them that deep or that many." I surveyed the mess he'd made on the grass with his piles of dirt. A dog could have done a cleaner job.

"I'll take care of it, don't worry. If you want, you can do the mulch on the section we completed earlier today."

I eyed him with suspicion. "What are you hiding?"

No one dug a hole that deep unless it was to bury something of value. I would know. I'd buried enough suitcases full of money and jewels to know the difference between a hole meant for a shrub or something else.

Jordan's brow creased. "Why would I hide anything? I wanted to be sure we weren't planting something on top of water lines."

I pointed to a folder beside him on the truck. "The plans are in there. There's no lines and if you'd looked at that in the first place, you'd have known that."

Rather than wait for a reply that would be layered in lies and half-truths, I grabbed a shovel and faced the pile of mulch in the distance. Donny had warned me he didn't trust the guy. I thought it had to do with the fact Alexius seemed to be into him, but now I wasn't so sure.

28: A MOTHER ALWAYS KNOWS

Tuesday 5:15 a.m.
DETECTIVE KAARNS

Caryn McCoy.

I'm tasked with speaking to her, drawing out more secrets Bishop won't tell us.

Bishop believes her mom is headed to her apartment. We've got a team there, going through every nook and cranny. Keeping Caryn McCoy here is the goal for the next hour.

I don't think it'll be hard. Seems to me, Mommy dearest has a lot of things she needs to get off her chest.

"Ms. McCoy?" I stop her in the hall with a warm smile on my face.

"Yes?" She looks at my name badge first, then to my face. "Officer Kaarns? We spoke on the phone once or twice, right? Please, tell me what I can do to help." Despite the weariness in her voice, I hear strength, determination and wariness too.

My smile remains while I open a door to a room where there is a couch and chair. "Would you mind giving me a few minutes of your time? I have some questions I hope you're able to clear up for me," I say. "There's a coffee shop in town that opened a few minutes ago and I sent someone to grab some real coffee and muffins, hope you don't mind?"

On the coffee table were two take-out mugs and a box of freshly made muffins, open with the intent to tempt her into the room.

"Different room, same tactics," she says as she passes me and enters. She sits on the couch and takes the cup of coffee. I have no idea what was bought, but I sure hope it's strong.

"At least the couch is more comfortable. Why don't you bring Starla in here, rather than force her to sit on that horrid chair for hours?"

I sink to my seat, place my notebook beside me on the armrest and reach for my cup, not responding. I'm going to need coffee to keep up with Mama Bear apparently.

"Ms. Bishop is here for questioning," I try to explain, keeping my voice light but no-nonsense.

"But not charged?"

I shake my head. Not yet.

Her shoulders visibly lower, as if believing her daughter to be safer than originally believed.

I sip my coffee, thankful for the strong brew before I reach for my notebook, open it to the page I need and look Caryn McCoy in the eye.

"Ms. McCoy," I start.

"Caryn, please. I have a feeling we'll be here a while," she said.

I nod. "Caryn, I know this might be asking a lot, but would you mind walking me through the beginning when your daughter first came to Bervie Springs?"

With coffee in hand, Caryn leans back on the couch, and looks off into the distance.

"When she first told me of the program, I thought it was too good to believe, you know? I've tried to always support Starla, to have jobs lined up for her when she got out of prison, but this time, there was nothing, and that scared me. When she told me of this job and everything that came with it . . ." She looks at me from a side glance before staring down at the coffee in her hands.

"You were aware Starla was secretly engaged to Donald Dixon?"

Caryn nods. "Why keep it a secret? That's what doesn't make sense. If he loves her, he shouldn't be worried about her reputation, right?"

"That seemed odd, I'll agree there." I didn't want to lead her, but rather, push the issues she presented to see if she would tell me more.

"Right? If they're so in love, then why not tell everyone? I warned Starla to be careful. Three is always a crowd and I don't care what he says, he's still tied to his wife in ways that leaves no room for anyone else."

I drop my gaze and scribble things down on my pad, hoping she'll continue to talk.

"The foolish girl fell in love and look where she is now, back here, in a mess like we both knew she would be," Caryn says, lifting her coffee to her lips, then lowering it without taking a sip. "I warned her but she wouldn't listen."

"Sometimes it's hard, looking in from the outside," I murmur.

"Starla's whole life has been hard to watch. She's bright with a good heart that gets taken advantage of. She's loyal," Caryn says, looking me directly in the eyes, as if trying to give me a warning.

I nod. I've seen that loyalty first-hand. It's too bad it's wasted on someone like Dixon.

"That girl is blinded," Caryn continues, "blinded to all the good things happening to her. Every gift has a price. All the jewelry, first the free apartment, then moving her into that furnished condo, giving her a vehicle, then handing her a lucrative business . . . it's like he's grooming her for something."

I look up just in time to see her body shudder as she says the word 'grooming'.

That hadn't been a thought, not until now. But Spikes had probably already figured it out. I wrote it down, with a note to talk to my partner.

"Starla isn't involved in the murders or hiding the bodies. My girl wouldn't do that. She's broken the law before, yes, but never for something like this."

"We have her tied to several of the victims," I say softly, knowing this will be difficult to hear.

Caryn's breath breaks as she inhales. "No, she wouldn't."

I set my pad of paper down on my lap and lean forward. "Caryn, she's living in the house one of the victims lived in. That bed she's sleeping in, the furniture she uses . . . it all belonged to someone we found buried."

Caryn's eyes grow wide; her hand slowly rises to cover her mouth and she shakes her head in slow motion. I read the horrific realization of what I'm saying register.

"No, no, she wouldn't . . . Alexius was the one who made that happen. She—"

"Alexius?" I scribble her name down. I hadn't been expecting that little tidbit of news.

Caryn nods enthusiastically. "She saw the apartment Starla was in and didn't like it. Told Starla she'd talk to Donald about moving her to another place. Next thing you know, Donald showed up with a trailer and some guys, packed everything up and moved her into a fancy new condo before her shift at the landscaping company was done."

"Alexius instigated the move but Donald chose the new dwelling?" More insight into how the two worked is beneficial.

"It was all too good to be true, wasn't it?" A neediness to Caryn's voice seeps in and I wish I could tell her it's all going to be fine, that Starla isn't involved, but I can't.

No hope is better than false hope.

I wait for tears, but none appear. Caryn takes a deep breath, steels herself then looks me straight on.

"My daughter got mixed up with the wrong crowd. Again. But this time . . . it wasn't knowingly. Let me help you see this, please."

I look over my notes and re-read my scribbles. Condo. Car. Jewelry. Business.

Dixon handed Bishop the world on a silver platter, giving her everything. But why?

Did Bishop never question his gifts? Did she never wonder why the places she lived were fully furnished?

Maybe it's my nature to question everything. Maybe this is why I'm not in a relationship, why Spikes says I make a great detective. But not everyone is perfect. Not everyone has good motives. Not everyone is willing to turn the other cheek.

"Tell me more about this business Starla was handed," I say.

29: THE HISTORY STONE

Five Months Ago

I couldn't get enough of the cabin. We came up every weekend now, to escape and focus on our relationship.

Donny had promised to show me his pottery shed this weekend and I couldn't wait. I had visions of creating bowls, plates, vases, items to fill my little apartment.

We'd created a bit of a routine on our weekends away. Donny hid himself in his 'man shed' where he worked on his leather keychains he handed out to customers while I puttered around his cabin, doing a little cleaning and a lot of reading.

I was always shocked that for a cabin no one else knew about, it came completely stocked with groceries and supplies every time we arrived. Donny teased me, claiming he had cabin fairies. He thought it was a game, keeping secrets like this, but it bothered me.

Who stocked it? Who else knew about this place?

At lunch time, after putting together a grilled chicken salad, I rang the bell Donny had brought with us. Rather than me coming down to his shed, all I had to do was ring the bell, something similar to a cowbell, and he'd come up. I teased that he was hiding something from me, but he promised there was nothing to hide.

I set the table while Donny washed his hands.

"I still don't understand why you don't just find a local supplier who can produce the keychains for you. It'd be a lot less work," I said, a repeat of an issue I'd brought up earlier in the car.

"I like working with the leather. Sure, it takes longer, but it's soothing for me. Peaceful. Almost like working with the pottery wheel. If it ever becomes arduous, then I'll farm it out. But until then . . . I like doing it all by hand."

I gave him the bowl with the salad and waited for him to fill his plate.

"Where do you get the leather? I don't think I've ever run across an invoice," I asked.

He shrugged. "You probably won't either, not for a while. I have . . . quite the supply, enough for a year or so I'd think." He didn't say anything more as we enjoyed our lunch.

"Can I help you mark them?" I asked while washing the dishes. I wouldn't let this go. I wanted to be a part of this, I didn't like that he spent so much time in that shed working on something we could do together.

He patted my arms. "I'm not sure you have the strength to push the press," he said, teasing me.

"You'd be surprised what these skinny arms can do," I said as I reached around his chest and squeezed. The smile on my face grew, the happiness in my heart filled every crevice inside of me and again, I couldn't get over how amazing my life was.

"Could we go for a hike? You keep promising to take me, but we always seem to get sidetracked." I gave him a wink and a hip jab.

"You've never seemed to mind," Donny said, nibbling on my ear.

I wriggled out of his hold and snapped a wet towel toward him. "Enough of that," I said, my voice showing the smile I'd wiped from my face. "I demand exercise and not the kind we get in bed."

Donny caught my hand, twirled me in a circle, then dipped me low, giving me a long, lazy kiss.

"If you want a hike, then a hike you shall get. Fill up some water bottles, will you, while I take care of something." Without explaining what that meant, Donny left me and headed into a small room off the side of the kitchen and closed the door behind him.

He had a small study that he normally kept locked. It was the one room in the cabin he'd asked me to not enter. Why, I'm not sure, but it was such a small request, I didn't let it bother me much.

Not only did I have the water bottles filled, but I'd put together some small snacks, pieces of cheese with sliced meat and crackers.

"I hope that wasn't work-related," I said as he stepped out and closed the door behind him.

He gave me a sad puppy dog look. "Sorry, I know I'd promised, but something came up that I had to deal with. All done, though." He held up his hand in a promise. "No more work this weekend."

"What came up? Something council related or lot related?"

"A little of both," he said as he hefted the small backpack with our water and snacks over his shoulder. "A council member is buying a car for his daughter and the guy covering the weekend shifts forgot to give him a Dixon Deal."

"And you couldn't have taken care of that on Monday?" I knew I pouted, I knew I whined, but I was possessive of our weekends. I never said anything during the week, when he'd get calls late at night or during meals.

"Come on, pouty face," Donny teased me by sticking out his own lower lip. "It's too beautiful a day to be fighting."

I waited till we were past his sheds and onto a path I never would have known was there until I brought the subject back up.

"What kind of Dixon Deal did you give?" Donny was famous for his deals, but they always changed depending on the customer. He led the way on a beaten path through a copse of trees, holding low branches for me as we walked.

"Oh, you know," he said, giving me a look over his shoulder that I couldn't read. "Just one favor for another. It's handy to know people in high places."

My foot caught on a root and I reached my hand out, grabbing hold of the backpack.

Donny turned and grabbed onto me, his grip tight on my arm. "Careful," he said as he moved more to the left so I could walk beside him. "I forgot you have shorter legs," he said, giving me a wink.

"What kind of favor do you need?" My curiosity grew the more evasive he became.

"Why so curious?" His gaze remained straight ahead but it was his voice that caused me to halt in my steps.

"Is it an issue? Me asking?"

He still wouldn't look at me. "It's just dealership stuff, nothing you need to worry about."

I didn't appreciate his tone of voice.

"Who said I was worried?" I remained where I stood. "I'm just curious. You have me helping with other things, not just for the landscaping, but your real estate and such, so maybe I could be of some help there too?"

He had the decency to appear to think about it, but we both knew he wasn't.

"You do enough," he finally said. "Come on, there's a clearing up ahead I want you to see."

Together we walked about a hundred feet until the trees thinned and ahead of us was a field full of wild grass and flowers. The grass came up to mid-calf and the area had a rugged beauty to it. A large misshapen rock rested in the middle of the field.

"This is my favorite place to come and sit, to watch the sun set in the evenings," Donny said, pulling me toward the rock. "I used to come out here as a child, sit here with a book and read for hours." He pointed to an indent, one of many on the stone.

The surface was full of scratches. Some were straight lines, some looked like odd s's. But the rock was full of them.

"My father used to tell me a story about this rock. We call it the history stone." He placed his hand on the stone, almost with a sense of reverence. "One of my ancestors knelt here and begged God to give him this land. He wanted a family, a place to call home, a land that would be full of familial history. Some say he was running from the law and hid here." He looked at me over his shoulder and smiled. "Imagine that, me coming from a family of criminals."

"We have something in common then," I said back, my voice hushed but full of teasing.

"I knew it the minute I met you, that there's a thread linking us," Donny murmured.

Donny knelt on the ground. "My ancestor fell asleep in this very spot. When he woke up, he realized he'd slept on a protruding rock. It took two days, but eventually it emerged from the ground like this."

He pulled out a knife and started to etch a line onto the rock.

"What are you doing?" I asked as I ran my hand over the surface, feeling all the indents and marks.

"Marking history." He continued to etch the stone.

I wanted to ask why, to figure out the reasoning, but something in his voice told me not to. Maybe the history he marked was us. Having me out here, telling me the story.

I memorized where the marking was, a solid line amid hundreds of others, but that line was mine, at least in my head and my heart.

When he was done, we continued on, out of the clearing and back into the woods. We walked for a few hours, stopping to rest, to watch a deer in the distance, for me to fawn over all the variety of wild flowers and bushes.

I was ready for a nap in the hammock by the time we made it back.

Donald had remained quiet throughout the walk, even after grabbing us both a beer. It was hard to give him space.

"What's going on?" I finally asked. "Ever since we came to that rock, you've been stuck in your brain."

He twisted off the beer cap and flicked it into a small pail, taking a long drink before he took a seat in a wicker chair.

"That rock is important to me. It's hard to explain it."

I sat beside him, held my bottle in my hands.

"I'm willing to listen if you want to try," I offered. I really did want to know. I wanted to know more about the man I was engaged to be married to.

"This land, this house . . . it's my history." He took another swig. "That rock, my father brought me here to mark it, his father brought him, his father brought him and so on. We measure all our successes on there and have for generations. That's why it's so marked up."

He took out his keychain and rubbed it between his fingers, something I'd noticed he did when lost in thought. We sat there for a few minutes until he replaced the keychain in his pant pocket, finished the last of his beer and stood.

"I'm going to do some more work, that all right with you?" He didn't look at me, but stared at the locked shed.

I swallowed hard, unsure of what had happened or where his head was at. Was he okay? I'd never seen him like that, so lost in thought, so distant from me.

"Sure, I'll nap a little on the hammock and then get started on dinner." I wasn't sure he even heard me. By the time I'd finished speaking, he was on his way to the shed.

I laid in the hammock but my mind wouldn't slow down enough for me to nap. I'd never been in a relationship with a man like Donny before.

I wanted to change. For him, for myself, for the life that I could have. It wasn't easy, but having Donny there, encouraging me, guiding me . . . change came easier than it had in the past.

I was different. Even Mom noticed.

White fluffy clouds floated above me, shading me from the sun. I couldn't imagine a better life. An easier life. A more perfect life.

30: BIG BAG FULL OF . . .

Four Months Ago

Life had a way of going full kilter and gifting you a bag of diamonds when you expected lemons.

It was six thirty in the evening and I was on my way to the Ladies Auxiliary group where I helped out in the kitchen for their weekly evening tea parties.

Donny was the one who had encouraged me to get involved. These ladies were the cornerstone of the community, he'd told me, and if I'd wanted to be accepted, it would be by lending a hand and showing I was ready to work.

The evening tea was put on by the founding families of Bervie Springs. My role was to help make the sandwiches, serve the tea, turn a blind eye to the alcohol and just make myself available.

Basically, smile pretty, show them I was useful and eventually they would remember my name.

I used to scoff at women like them. Entitled old grouches who looked down at the world with their gold-tinted glasses.

Donny had begged me to give them a chance. He said they needed to know someone like me, that it would change their lives in ways they'd never imagined.

I didn't believe him then and I didn't believe him now, but it had been months and I still attended the meetings and volunteered.

Tonight, it was their bi-monthly Welcome to Bervie Springs night, where all the new families came to be fawned over, told about how awesome their new town was and encouraged to get involved.

It was also my first one that I was asked to attend as a guest and not part of the serving party.

My plan was to walk to the clubhouse, a mere four blocks away, with my pumps in a bag, when a car honked behind me as I started on my walk. Alexius pulled up in her brand-new Veloster that Donny had picked up for a steal of a deal.

"Starla, you can't go to the welcome night wearing that," she said as she pulled up to the sidewalk and turned off her car.

I looked down at myself. Crisp clean jeans and a button-up blouse, I thought I was presentable. "I have heels," I said, in hopes that would make a difference.

"Honey," Alexius said, her voice saccharine sweet. "That's not going to cut it tonight." She stepped out of the vehicle with a garment bag in hand. "Come on, let's get back inside."

She gave my small apartment a quick glance before shaking her head. "Why does he keep you in something so small when he has nicer places available?"

"It's bigger than what I'm used to," I said with a slight shrug. Having a place to myself that was bigger than the prison cell which I shared with three other women.

I viewed my living space through Alexius' eyes. To her it would be puny, dirty, beneath her. To me it was a palace.

"You deserve better. I'll talk to him," she said as she unzipped the bag and pulled out a dress suit. "The blouse you're wearing will go nice with this," she said, surveying me. "Show me your heels, though."

I viewed myself as a confident woman. No, I didn't have the best clothes in the most up-to-date styles, but I didn't look like a bag lady either. But when next to Alexius, I always felt underdressed, like the ugly stepsister.

Thankfully she gave a little nod when I pulled out my plain black heels. "Understated, but nice. You don't want to look flashy," she said as she handed me the outfit and pushed me into my bedroom.

By the time I'd finished dressing and reapplied my lipstick, I felt taller, more sophisticated and too much unlike myself. Imposter, the mirror screamed at me.

Imposter meet New Starla.

Alexius smiled when I came out of my room. "That's much better. They almost won't recognize you. In fact, I can guarantee half of them won't." She handed me a small handbag. "Look inside."

I did as I was told. Inside was a beautiful gold necklace with a heart charm that nestled a diamond in the middle. It was elegant, expensive and not me at all.

I'd never worn a diamond until I'd met Donny. His ring was tucked away in my bedroom, in its box on my dresser.

"Are you sure?" I asked her as I held it up, the gem twinkling.

"There's earrings too," she said.

Diamond studs. If my cellmates saw me now, the things they'd say . . .

Actually, I wished Mom was here. To see this. To see her Cinderella turned into a princess.

"You look lovely," she said as she gathered the garment bag and her own handbag and headed to my door.

"When I first came to town, Donny called himself my fairy godfather. But I'm starting to think you deserve the role too."

She gave me this 'you finally get it' type smile. "Let's go, we're late as it is," she said.

I followed Alexius down my sidewalk and sank into the plush leather seat of her car, AKA my coach.

Walking into the clubhouse, where all the ladies cackled and the men laughed, I once again couldn't believe my life.

Donny was there, standing by the unlit fireplace, talking with one of the queen bees who presided over the night. She held a glass of wine. He probably had scotch.

I stood in the doorway as he looked me over, his gaze trailing over my body before he gave me an appreciative look. He liked what he saw and even though he wouldn't express it in public, just knowing was all that mattered to me.

I walked through the room, introduced myself to those I hadn't yet met, mentioned I worked for Soil and Springs Landscaping and pretended to be someone I would one day become.

Everything held a surreal feel to it. From the wine in my hand to the way people spoke to me, I waited for the bell to ring, for my evening to end, for the handcuffs to replace the jewelry I wore.

"Starla, you look beautiful," Donny said as he joined me by one of the windows where I stood staring out into a garden I knew Alexius had designed. "This look suits you."

My face warmed beneath his compliment.

"I have someone I want you to meet." He placed his hand on my arm and my body tingled from the contact I'd been craving all night. He led me to a man who stood in the back of the room, alone. I didn't recognize him from when I had perused the room earlier, so he must have arrived after me.

"James Delany, meet Starla Bishop. She's the one I'd mentioned will handle your contract and such," he said as we shook hands.

I tried to hide my surprise. I knew nothing about this, but pretended I knew everything.

"Mr. Delany, nice to meet you." I shook his hand with a confidence not felt.

"James, please. Mr. Delany is my father and he's a crotchety old man."

We laughed, as if his comment were the wittiest thing we'd heard all day.

"From all Dixon has told me, this is going to be a great relationship," James said.

Donny laughed again while I just smiled. What had Donny said? What contracts? I hated being left in the dark.

"Feel free to snag a plate of food before you head out." Donny gestured toward the food table. "Starla will be in touch." He shook James' hand, handed him one of his keychains and then led me away, his hand on the small of my back.

"Anything I need to know?" I said quietly as we walked.

"Sorry about that," he said, his head bent low toward mine. "Can I come over tonight to explain? It's a new venture for me, and will be great cash-wise for you."

As if that mattered, and he knew it. I had already scheduled house cleaners, carpenters and deliveries for him without worrying about income. He always promised to give me a cut and I always told him it wasn't necessary.

I'd been able to build a nice little bit of savings since I arrived in Bervie Springs and even sent money Mom's way. I was doing fine and had no concerns, no bills either.

"This time I'm not taking no for an answer," Donny said. "I made the contact, so I'll take a twenty percent cut, but you'll be doing all the leg work, so the rest is yours. Besides, I set it all up under your name." His eyes twinkled as he dropped that tidbit of news.

"Under me? Whatever for?" I was both confused and thrilled at the same time.

"New Starla deserves all the good things I can give her. Why not a new business?" He looked around as he said this.

I'd truly been dropped into my very own fairy tale.

"How did you get it under my name?"

He shrugged. "Don't you worry about that," he said. "Just consider it a Dixon Deal marker cashed in."

One of the queen bees called out Donny's name. He presented her with a wide white smile before he leaned close to my ear. "Diamonds look good on you," he said, leaving my side.

If anyone were looking at me, they would have caught the bright red flush that grew from my neck to my forehead.

Yes, diamonds did indeed look good on me.

31: ONE QUESTION WITH TWO POSSIBLE ANSWERS

Tuesday 6:00 a.m.

Defeat isn't a word I generally accept.

Even when the cuffs are slapped on my wrists, I'm dressed in new prison garb and thrown into the den with new cellmates.

But right now, with Spikes standing over me, I'm close to accepting defeat.

"Will you?" His rough voice is full of exhaustion.

He wants me to direct them to the cabin. To the place where Donny proposed and then proceeded to break my heart.

I knew this was a possibility when I told them about the cabin. "Do I have a choice?"

Someone knocks on the door and hands Spikes a tray of coffee and a fast food bag. The smell has my stomach rumbling loud enough that he drops the bag on the table without a word.

"For me?"

He nods. He sets the coffee tray down as well, takes his cup, leaving two more in the holder. Which either means he bought me two cups of coffee or one is for his partner.

Inside the bag are wrapped breakfast sandwiches and at this point, I don't care that there's egg trapped between cheese and meat.

"It's a long drive. These aren't going to cut it." I pick up the bag and tray.

* * *

Once on the highway, I rest my head against the seat, my eyes closed, not wanting to see the scenery and remember.

And yet, remember is all I do.

Every early morning drive. Every sunset as we drove home. Every time our fingers entwined, our bodies relaxed, our future only moments ahead.

Spikes is at the wheel, Kaarns beside him. Their voices are low as they discuss details of the case they don't want me to hear, except they must think I'm deaf.

Someone's phone buzzes and Kaarns swears.

"Another one?" Spikes' voice is gruffer than before.

My stomach somersaults and the egg threatens to come back up. I want to cry, scream, roll into a ball and pretend none of this could be true, but I can't get those images out of my mind. Of the hand rising out of the ground, the red fabric . . .

"When's the turn?" Kaarns' voice has a note of urgency to it.

"Have we passed the cross with the teddy bears yet?" I keep my eyes closed.

Seconds pass before the car begins to slow and the turn signal comes on. I open my eyes to see a weathered cross surrounded by stuffed bears pass by.

I wait till we turn before I straighten.

"Second right, first left, then search for a tree that's been hit by lightning and split down the middle. You've got another fifteen minutes before that turn though."

"Where the hell is this place?" Kaarns says, frustration radiating off her in waves.

"Calm down," Spikes says. "Us being there isn't going to make a difference."

A look passes between the two that I can't read. A silent look that could fill caverns with debris discarded by history.

"Why are the two of you taking time away to come out here?" I'm not sure why I need to know. When we get to the cabin, there's no way in hell I'm stepping foot outside this vehicle. I'd almost rather be back in the interrogation room.

"You told us to look for the cabin, except we can't find anything on it, so now I'm curious," Spikes says, eyeing me in the rear-view mirror.

"Curious about what?"

"What he's hiding."

I shudder, a natural instinct I wish I could control.

Spikes' brow raises at my reaction. I can see the dare in his gaze, wanting me to reply. Instead, I turn my face toward the window.

I'd love to take him up on his challenge. I'd love to tell him everything Donny is hiding . . . but I won't. It's not time.

There's a squashed fury churning inside me. I'm containing it — so far.

We pass the tree and I have to remind myself to breathe. We're so close, it's like I can feel the cabin beneath my skin.

"Slow down." The words escape past my tight jaw. Everything I'm doing, coming here, directing them, it's betraying Donny, betraying us and the future I've been holding on to.

"Where the hell are we? There's nothing on the map," Kaarns mutters. She holds the map up to the windshield, hoping to see something that isn't there.

"See the gap in the trees on your right? Turn there."

I see Spikes hesitate; it doesn't look like we're turning onto anything, but that's the intention. Branches above the vehicle crack and break as the mammoth SUV passes through and I cringe, knowing that this turn won't be hidden anymore.

The time for secrets has come and gone.

I close my eyes just in time. I don't want to see the cabin as we pull up. I don't want the memories to surface, the feelings to overwhelm me.

I don't want to feel at all. I need to place what could have been into a box, slam the lid down and wrap every inch with packing tape, then throw it away.

"Holy shit." Kaarns breathes the words I'd first felt when Donny brought me here.

"Dixon's good at keeping secrets," Spikes mutters, looking at me again through the mirror.

I wipe every thought off my face as we pull up and park. They both step out and wait, but if they're waiting for me, they'd better pull up chairs.

Spikes knocks on my window. I shake my head. He goes to open the door but I click the lock button. He hits a button on his keys and opens the door before I can lock it again.

"We need you," he says.

No one needs me. Those are just words spoken as a lie with the intent to guilt me.

"No, you don't," I say. "Please . . . don't make me go back in there."

I see the way Kaarns softens, how her shoulders drop and the fierceness on her face relaxes a smidgen.

"Good memories here?" she asks.

I lift my shoulder in a shrug. Anything I say, anything I admit won't matter.

I know what's going to happen.

We all know.

They're going to walk through the cabin, open closets, see the skeletons and call their crew to come and dig up every single inch of this property and more.

"Starla, you know this place better than us. Walk us through it, show us his spaces . . ." Spikes' voice drops as he looks around the front yard. "The wheelbarrows, why so many?"

Kaarns pulls out her phone and starts taking photos. "I'll send everything back to the team," she tells Spikes, who is pulling nitrile gloves over his hands.

The wheelbarrows were new. A total of six were set around the area, all filled with dirt and a few planted perennials. I recognize them from the hothouses at Soil and Springs.

It's been months since I last came out to the cabin. Life has been hectic, busy for both Donny and I and timing never worked out. He'd mentioned making changes, and perhaps this was one of them.

Spikes looks at me for an answer but I've got nothing for him.

He walks over to the first potted plant, sticks his covered hand in the dirt and then motions Kaarns to him, who then takes photos. They do this with all the wheelbarrows in the yard, the time at each lengthening.

Kaarns' mouth is set in a straight line as she walks across the lawn to me. I want to curl into a ball and hide.

"When was the last time you came out here?"

I search her eyes for an answer I don't want to know but she's stone cold.

Shit.

"Months," I say, my voice wavering.

Her brows raise in skepticism.

"If I dust those—" she points to the place where Spikes is standing — "will your fingerprints be on them?"

I shake my head. "No."

"No? I find that hard to believe." Her hands shake as she holds her phone.

I don't want to know the reason.

"You didn't order them and bring them out here?" she asks. "You didn't plant," her voice catches on the word, "them and intend for them to be used as lawn ornaments?"

I shake my head.

"I need you to answer verbally and be very clear with your wording."

The fierceness of her voice, the intensity of her words has me shaking. Ribbons of fear wind themselves around my body, each thread full of barbed wires and even though I want to answer her, I can't.

I. Can't.

Spikes' steps are slow, heavy and methodical. He's looking straight at me and I want to cower. Instead, I raise my chin and challenge him to accuse me of something I didn't do.

I'm expecting it, prepared for the words but instead he tears off one glove and opens the back of the SUV, pulling out a bag, stuffing both gloves into it.

"Bag every glove you use," he says to Kaarns, who nods. She pulls out a pair from her pocket and pulls them on.

"Inside or outside?"

I don't realize he's talking to me until he repeats himself. I know there's no choice, I've got no option but to lead the way. Everything in his voice tells me that fighting is pointless, so up the steps I go to reveal an electronic lock pad.

"Do I get gloves too?" I turn and ask. Sure, it's been months since I've been here, but Donny is methodical about cleaning.

Kaarns passes me a pair.

"Code?" Spikes says. His fingers hover over the keyboard.

My mind scrambles for the answer. "Donny changes it all the time," I say, as if that explains my hesitation. "Try zero two seven zero," I suggest. I think that's the number he gave me last.

I hold my breath as he punches in the number.

"What's the significance?" Kaarns asks. She's standing behind me, within my personal space. I step to the side. She moves closer.

"Not sure there is one." I don't look at her as I say this.

"Birthday? Anniversary?" She directs this question toward Spikes.

He opens the door once we hear a click. "What was the original code? The first one he'd told you?"

I try to think back. There have been so many numbers that I'm hard-pressed to give a definitive answer.

"I think zero one eight zero." We all hear the uncertainty in my voice.

"Body count," Kaarns and Spikes both say together.

My body freezes, blood crystallizing at their words. Nine bodies? There are nine dead bodies hidden in the gardens?

I swallow bile that rises like a shaken pop can in my throat. My throat is on fire and I rush to the bathroom just off to the side, where I lean over the toilet and dry heave. What the hell?

I hear murmurs as I wash out my mouth. I'm in a nightmare. None of this can be real. It can't be.

"They'll send another team from the city. I sent them directions. Should be here by tomorrow," Kaarns is telling Spikes as I leave the bathroom.

Both turn toward me. Both have a look of disgust on their faces. I hope it's not directed at me, but I have a feeling it is.

"I haven't been out here in months," I tell them, hands held out, palms front, as if that were all it took to tell the truth.

"Why?"

I look to Kaarns, her arms crossed as she waits for me to answer her, then to Spikes.

"Life has gotten . . . complicated lately," I say. "There's not enough hours in the day for me to get my work done, so I've been using the weekends to get caught up." Even to me, that sounds like a weak excuse.

"Get a car to come out here," Spikes tells his partner. "We're not leaving till one arrives." He's looking around the room — at the furniture, the pottery, the prints along the wall — at everything but me.

I don't mind.

"Photograph it all," he continues. His back is rigid, his voice harsh, the mask on his face deadly. "Record us walking through the rooms. No one is ever alone." He throws me a glance as he says this. "Ever."

This is a different man from the one I'd seen since being brought into the police station. This was a man filled with fury, a police officer bound to see justice served. This is a man no one should cross, ever.

I swallow hard.

One hour later, we make our way to the back porch.

We'd gone through every inch of the house, opening closets, boxes, rifling through drawers; I was asked about almost every single item in the house and both my voice and my patience were close to nonexistent.

"I wouldn't expect Dixon to collect pottery," Kaarns says, her shoulders a little more bowed than when we'd first arrived.

"He makes them." The words came out before I could stop them. Maybe this was their goal, to exhaust me to the point where I have no filter, where my words are more honest than intended, where I have no leverage left.

If it is, he wins.

I point to the shed ahead of us on the right. "That's where he keeps his kiln and supplies. The other shed—" I point to the left shed — "is where he works on the leather."

Spikes' hand goes toward his pocket and he pulls out keys.

"Yes," I say, nodding to the leather in his hand, "he makes those by hand."

He looks at the keychain for a moment, then at the shed, and then to Kaarns, who has a look of horror on her face.

"What do you mean by hand?" Spikes' voice is controlled, one level, without inflection, like he's trying really hard to remain in control.

I cock my head to the side, trying to read the two, to figure out what's not being said.

"He's a hunter," I say. "He uses the skin to make his own keychains."

When I look at Kaarns, she's gone green.

Spikes turns to me and holds out the leather keychain.

"What?" I ask, bile riding up my throat like a surfer.

"You say he's a hunter, and we just found out skin has been removed from most of the victims, as far as we can tell. So, the question is—" he looks at what he's holding — "is this human or animal skin?"

32: THINGS GET UGLY WHEN PARENTS FIGHT

Three Months Ago

The mosquitoes buzzing around me played connect-the-dots with my skin. My tank top stuck to the sweat on my back and not for the umpteenth time had I cursed Alexius for banning all kinds of bug repellants in her hothouses.

I was at the point where my skin and sanity were more important than ensuring her plants remained toxin free.

I'd been out here for the past two hours. Between the humidity and Alexius' piss-poor mood, I was ready to call it a day and head to the local pub for a beer.

"What have you done?"

Donny's furious voice tore through the greenhouse.

I looked up, my heart stopping mid-beat as he barreled down the outer pathway toward where Alexius worked on a new bed of geraniums.

"What needed to be done," Alexius' cold shrill rang out. "Now leave me alone."

I hunkered down, not wanting to be noticed, and let out a very long breath. Perhaps now would be a good time to take a break.

"You should have consulted with me," Donny said. "You have no idea how this has affected me." The low timber to his voice, the way it rumbled through his cavernous chest, it said more than his words had.

Whatever Alexius had done; she'd better undo it. I knew voices like that. I knew the consequences that came with pushing too far, too fast.

"What I've done?" The words whipped out of her mouth like a slap. "You're the one who has screwed things up so royally. I'm the one having to clean your first-class mess, thank you very much."

"How about talking to me first before you make decisions like that." Donny's anger climbed and I tried to make myself invisible.

"Consult with you?" Her laughter was full of sharp knives coated in sarcasm. "Trust me, Donny, that day will never come."

The thing about this particular greenhouse and the way it'd been constructed, everything carried. Every whisper, every labored breath and especially heated exchanges. It didn't matter where you were, what you were doing or how far away you tried to get, you heard everything.

Every. Damn. Thing.

A few days ago, I'd walked in on Alexius enjoying a little afternoon . . . siesta with a new work hand. For holding the title of Ice Queen, she sure melted in the right arms.

"You have no idea what you've done." Donny now stood beside Alexius. From where I sat on the ground, I had the perfect view of the showdown between the two.

Alexius was bent over, focused on her plants. Donny stood to the side, arms crossed, chin pointed out.

He was pissed and she was indifferent.

"I really don't care." Alexius straightened, placed her hands on the slope of her back and bent backwards stretching.

"Well you should. Do you have any idea how much money we just lost?"

Alexius pulled herself back up and turned then. The tilt of her face, her squared shoulders, the way she leaned toward the sign; Donny should have known better.

"Do you have any idea how much money you're costing me? This company?"

He snorted. "What about the money I've saved you? Have you thought about that?"

"What? By bringing your transients in to help do all the heavy labor? That's not saving us any money. I still have to pay for your driver, all the food, the cost of the rental properties and my own staff to redo half their work."

Donny threw his hands up in the air.

"You do that for you," Alexius continued. "For your name, your position, your image. It's why you brought that dimwit in too. Have you lured her to bed yet? No, wait, don't answer that. She'd be gone if you had. They all seem to disappear afterward, don't they?"

He stepped toward her. I shrank back, needing to disappear. I wanted to stop watching, listening, being part of their fight and yet, I was right there, in the middle whether I'd wanted to be or not.

What had she meant that they had all disappeared?

"Starla is different and she's a hell of a lot smarter than you give her credit for."

Alexius shrugged. "Best of the bunch, I'll give you that. But different? Not really." She stepped forward, closer, and the challenge in her body was clear.

Too clear.

I dropped my gaze to the ground, studied every minuscule drop of dirt, wishing I'd left the moment Donny had come in.

"You keep trying to find my replacement," Alexius said, her tone suddenly silky soft, "but you fail, time and time again. Don't think I don't know what you're doing," she said, her voice full of seductive tease that I knew would have one of two effects.

He'd either get lost in her voice or demand she get lost herself. I preferred option two.

"What am I doing?" Donny accepted her challenge and my heart sank.

I looked up and found the two nose to nose.

"What am I doing, Alexius?" Donny asked again.

"You'll never replace me," she said, her voice filled with indifference. "But you'll never have me. Not like that, not again." The minute his foot edged back, I wanted to shout for joy. Nothing was said. Like a piece of fine china, the air in the greenhouse had become fragile, frail and feeble. One jarred word, sound or even action would have destroyed any sense of tenuous peace between the two.

If I'd been smart, I'd have stood and announced my presence.

I should have listened to that tiny voice inside my head that screamed preservation.

I'd become a concrete statue, feet cemented to the dirt floor, any ability to move terminated by my own stupidity.

"You're not good enough for me, not anymore," he said to her. I felt the slap as much heard it.

Donny didn't move. Didn't raise his hand to his face. Didn't react at all to his ex-wife's violent reaction.

"I made you. I can break you," Alexius threatened. Her body vibrated with barely contained emotion and it hurt to watch her lose control.

"Good luck with that." The sneer in his voice shocked me.

He turned on her then and walked out the way he'd come in. Not once did he look my way and for that, I was thankful.

It took ten minutes for Alexius to remember my presence. "You can leave," she called out. "Word of advice, don't tell Donny you were here. He doesn't like being made to look the fool."

I slowly rose to my feet and brushed the dirt off my backside.

Alexius and I looked at each other from across the rows. Woman to woman.

No, I wouldn't tell Donny I'd been here. The less he knew, the better.

33: A LIE IS A LIE IS A LIE

It didn't take long for me to discover the cause of the fight between Alexius and Donny.

It was all he raved about over dinner.

He'd been backstabbed, belittled and betrayed and he wasn't sure he'd be able to get over it.

"What happened?" I asked, for the umpteenth time as I sat on the couch, legs tucked beneath me, wine glass in hand.

Before, when I'd asked, he'd mumbled something about it being a *non-issue*, something I didn't need to worry my *pretty little head* about, that he'd take care of it.

But despite all the text messages and phone calls he'd taken out on the back deck, nothing appeared to be solved.

"Let me help," I offered as I watched him burn a path on my carpet. "My head isn't that pretty that I can't help fix messes, you know that, right?" I hated to bring up my past and skills that went along with said past, but there was no reason Donny needed to shoulder this alone.

"She's selling a piece of land that I . . . well, I had plans for it," he said, his focus more on the phone in his hand than on me.

I wasn't surprised. He had plans for everything. Plans to become mayor, to own every piece of available property in Bervie Springs, plans to build an even bigger name for himself.

"What kind of plans?"

He didn't answer for a moment. "I was going to build an affordable housing complex," he said, his councilman voice in full mode. "You know I house transients from the city to here to work on projects and in Alexius' nurseries, right?"

I nodded. I knew a little about it, but not as much as I'd like.

Every so often, one of the laborers from Soil and Springs would take a company van into the city early in the morning and arrive before lunch with a vehicle full of homeless willing to work for little pay but free rent.

Donny owned an apartment building that he put his so-called workers in.

I'd walked through a few of the apartments once.

Prison life had been better, from what I'd witnessed.

"So why is Alexius selling it?"

He shrugged. "Some of my guys tore up the ground and pissed her off, I guess. I don't know. But she should have talked to me."

I heard my mother's voice in the back of my mind, 'Don't get involved, Starla.'

"Can't you just get one of your shell companies to offer a higher price?" I asked. So much for not getting involved.

He stopped his pacing and stared at me, like I'd either sprouted a unicorn horn or fangs.

"She'd know," he muttered with a shake of his head and a continuation of his pacing efforts.

"Not as long as it's not linked to you." That seemed like a no-brainer to me.

He stopped and turned, the dark cloud which hovered over his gaze lifting. He came to me and offered his hand, pulling me up off the couch before giving me a long, hard kiss.

"You're brilliant."

"I know," I said with a chuckle, thankful the tension had eased off his shoulders.

He let me go and was on his phone again, his fingers typing away furiously on the screen.

"Why don't you use the one you put under me?" I suggested.

He looked up with a grin. "That's what I'm doing," he said, "just talking with my accountant to make sure we have enough money in that account."

I grabbed my wine glass and headed to the kitchen. "Great," I called out to him. "Make sure there's enough extra so I can go shopping, will you?" I poured myself a fresh glass of wine and counted the seconds of silence.

He had to know I was teasing.

I sipped at the crisp rosé and offered him a 'I'm only teasing' kind of smile when he finally followed me into the kitchen.

"You wouldn't, would you?"

I batted my long lashes to go with my *pretty little head* and didn't answer.

"I mean . . . of course you can access that account, it's under your name after all, but . . ." His voice broke like a teen fresh in puberty. "You wouldn't, right?"

I pretended to act offended, but in reality, a part of me was. "You know me better than that, Donny," I said.

He nodded, shrugged, nodded again while his mouth flapped like a burst balloon caught in a cross wind.

"I mean . . . it's what you used to do, right? When you went to prison, so . . ." He swallowed hard but didn't complete whatever he'd been about to say.

His unspoken words hung heavy between us.

Yes, it was what I was good at.

Yes, it was what I was known for.

Yes, it was what sent me to prison. Multiple times.

"If you're afraid you've become a mark and I'm just playing you," I said, trying very hard to keep my voice gentle but hard at the same time, "then take it back. Give me something to sign and I'll walk away from it. From everything."

"What do you mean, from everything?"

I focused on my wine, on how it tasted as the crisp, tart juice sat on my tongue.

"What happened to your trust in me, Donny? If it's not there, then there's nothing here—" I pointed first at myself then at him — "between us. I'll leave Bervie Springs, go back to my mom, and figure shit out without you in my life."

He needed to know I was angry. Spit angry.

He covered the distance between us, placed his phone on the counter, screen down and took the glass I'd held from my hands.

"Baby, please forgive me," he said, his voice cajoling, "I'm an ass. You were right to call me on it too. The Old Starla would have taken advantage of this offer, but you, my New Starla, won't. I know that. I'm sorry for letting my insecurity come between us."

I wasn't sure what caused me to pause before I accepted his apology. Maybe it'd been the brief flash of shade in his gaze, the tilt of his chin as he lied bold-faced or how his voice became slightly higher pitched.

But whatever it'd been, I'd heard it.

Heard it and tucked it away to use for another day, another battle.

34: THE PRICE OF SECRETS

It was only one o'clock in the afternoon, but I craved a drink. Mom worried this job was making me an alcoholic, but she didn't understand.

My intention this morning had been to come in super early to finish up invoicing for some projects I was behind on. I'd assumed I could get them done and emailed before Alexius showed up, but once again I was wrong.

My empty, clutter-free desk had been covered with stacked invoices that appeared out of nowhere. I'd spent the morning sorting them into piles, mentally trying to figure out what needed my attention and what Alexius needed to be aware of.

Did I curse Alexius at the same time? Absolutely.

Some were for properties I'd never heard of, contracts that had start dates from three years ago or longer and some had obscene amounts of materials that I had to figure out how to bill for.

I wanted to pull my hair out.

My cell rang and Mom's number flashed across the screen.

I put her on speaker since I was alone.

"I haven't heard from you the past few mornings. I've been worried." No hi, how are you, just full-on parental guilt.

"Sorry, I've been up and out the door helping with some projects before coming in to the office," I said as I smothered a yawn. "Why worry, though?"

"Haven't you been watching the news?"

"Honestly, watching the news is not my favorite past time." I let the yawn stretch across my face that time.

"Don't get smart. There's been a murder in Bervie Springs," she said.

"Oh, that one." That was old news. A body had been discovered in a shallow grave outside city limits. "Last I heard they thought it was a hitchhiking gone wrong," I said.

The length and sound of Mom's sigh told me I wasn't playing the dutiful daughter like I should have.

"Honestly, I'm okay. Donny has stayed over most nights, and my doors are always locked." I hoped this would ease her anxiety.

"Why is he staying over?"

I dropped my head into the palm of my hands and groaned. "Why wouldn't he? We are engaged," I reminded her.

She snorted.

"An engagement you have to hide isn't real, you and I both know that. Stop kidding yourself, girl."

Another foray into a battle never to be won. For some reason, nothing Donny did won her over. He gave her a vehicle after accepting her piece of junk as a trade-in, he'd paid for a spa weekend at a swanky place in the city for both of us one weekend and had fresh flowers delivered to her home on a weekly basis.

"I'm okay with it, and that's what matters."

I pictured her, sitting at the kitchen table, coffee mug in one hand, phone in the other, a frown on her face that went along with the deep scowl lines on her forehead.

"You shouldn't be," she said. "If the man is truly in love with you, he'd be shouting it to the world, wanting everyone to see that rock on your hand."

I dropped an invoice back onto my desk and leaned my head back. Why did we have to argue about this?

"He is in love with me."

"He's playing you." Mom said. "You, of all people, should know that."

My arms were crossed on the desk, my left hand rested on my right forearm, my fingers pressing hard enough into the skin to leave white marks.

"It's because I know what a mark looks like," I take in a deep breath and release it, "that I believe him when he tells me he loves me."

"I don't get you, Starla Bishop. How can you fall for someone like him? He's playing you like a chess master and if you're not careful, you'll be back behind bars." Her voice was full of motherly concern, the type that confirmed she was only looking out for me and didn't realize just how much her words hurt.

In my mind's eye, I pictured a chessboard where our kings battled to the death, willing to sacrifice everything and anything in order to win.

If Mom's words were true, if Donny were truly playing me, then I'd be in on the game too. Didn't she realize that?

"I promise you, I will not go back to jail." It wasn't an easy promise to make. Opportunities to utilize my con-artist skills abounded aplenty but I ignored them all.

I used to think the risk had been worth it. That the likelihood of being caught had been slim, that I'd learned enough from my past mistakes.

I believed differently now.

"Come home for the weekend," she said after the stretch of silence became uncomfortable.

"Yeah, I'll see." The words slipped out.

"Starla." A warning tone invaded Mom's voice. She hated non-committal responses.

I riffled through the calendar on my phone. My weekend was empty, but Donny's wasn't. We shared a calendar together and he had the weekend blocked with *Trip to City* in block letters.

"You know what? A weekend away might just be the thing. Let me see if I can get through the crap-ton of paperwork on my desk and beg a day of vacation." I hadn't taken a day off since arriving, so it shouldn't be an issue.

Plus, if you added all the overtime I did with no complaints, it had better not be an issue.

"Oh, that would be lovely." Mom's voice gushed like a burst of fruit flavor from a jelly bean. "There's a new farmers' market which has downtown completely closed off to vehicles. It'll be a nice weekend for you to be home."

Out of the corner of my eye, I noticed Alexius heading up the pathway.

"Alexius is about to walk in. I'll text you when I leave, okay?" I ended the call before my boss entered the office and Mom had the chance to say something embarrassing.

Alexius stopped at the door, her hand on the knob, but didn't enter. Her lips moved, head twisted and a few seconds later, Donny appeared.

Their voices were raised, but I couldn't hear what was being said. Didn't take a genius to read their body language and know something was wrong. Between the frantic ways Alexius' hands gestured about and how rigid Donny's arms were at his sides, if things weren't already ugly between the two, it would soon be.

With a crack to my back and a straightness of my spine, I steeled myself to be placed in the middle of whatever argument the two were having.

By the time they entered the office and made their way back to me, neither one spoke to the other.

Alexius eyed my desk, came to stand beside me and riffled through the piles I'd made. Every so often she'd give a *harrumph* sound which made Donny's lips tighten even more than they already were.

I remained silent.

"Why did you hide these?" She finally spoke, not to me, but to Donny.

His gaze slid to mine for a millisecond.

"Pretty sure I'm the one who deserves an answer, not your precious Starla." Alexius' words were dark, drawn and filled with dangerous undertones.

"You always told me to stay away from these properties," Alexius continued as she picked up an invoice from one of the piles. "Why? So you could pick up a little side job here and there?"

He didn't say a word, which was unusual for Donny.

"We've lost hundreds of thousands of dollars, Donny. Do you realize that? It's all sitting here, money we could have invoiced, and you—" she vibrated beside me, her body shaking — "hid it."

I leaned back in the chair, physically trying to remove myself from between the two.

"Nothing was lost since you didn't know about it in the first place," he finally said, arms crossed, his chin jutting out. "You're overreacting, Alexius. Go play with your plants or something and I'll handle things with Starla."

Those words had me pushing my chair back, but Alexius' hand on the top of my seat stopped me.

"Excuse me?" Her tone was frosty. "This is my company, Donald." His name slithered out of her mouth. "If you're not careful, it'll be your blood fertilizing my plants."

Something akin to daggered goosebumps covered every inch of my skin at her words.

"Threatening me, love? You should know better than that."

Donny's gaze shuttered, like thick hurricane boards to protect windows. What was he protecting, though?

"I meant to be here earlier, Starla." Alexius focused on me, her words still clear, concise and full of calm anger.

I've witnessed such emotion only a few times in my life. The wife of a mob boss had looked at me with a similar gaze from across the street when I'd been hauled in last time by the police. She'd been the one to turn me in. She'd come to visit me once, while I'd been behind bars. She would have let me get away with everything, all the money, the diamonds, everything. Except I'd crossed some unknown line when she'd overheard me talking smack about her husband to another wife. That wouldn't do. She'd taken my comments out of context as I'd only been repeating what had been said to me, but . . . in the end, that didn't matter.

Lesson learned.

"You haven't sent any emails out yet, have you?" Alexius asked me as she pulled out another invoice.

I didn't have time to answer.

"What did you do, Donny? Come in late at night, create an invoice only to delete it or did you copy our template and do it from your computer?"

His reply was to sit down in one of the comfy customer chairs around the room, cross his legs and raise one brow. Classic 'figure it out yourself, bitch' look if I ever saw one.

I was seeing a side of Donny I'd never seen before and wasn't sure how I felt about it.

"You billed them and kept the money, didn't you?" Realization crept into her voice with each syllable. "Why?" She didn't sound wounded, furious or anything else. I got the impression she didn't understand his reasoning.

To be honest, I didn't either.

"Those gardens look like shit." Alexius turned the conversation from money to aesthetics. "What corners did you cut?"

"I used outside help." Donny's lashes lowered until they lingered against his skin.

One glance toward Alexius had me clearing my throat. "Listen, if you two don't need me—"

"I'm redoing them." Alexius spoke over me.

"Like hell you are." Donny jumped to his feet. "You'll leave those properties alone."

The two stalked closer to one another, hands fisted, shoulders pushed back.

"Afraid I'm going to find some skeletons you don't want dug up?" Alexius taunted her ex-husband, jabbing her finger into the middle of his chest.

"Do. Not. Touch. Them." The words tore out of Donny's chest, his voice unlike anything I'd heard from him before.

The two stared at one another, unspoken words and emotions filling the room until I felt like I was suffocating.

"I'm going to visit my mother this weekend." I managed to get the words out with minimal squeaks. I pushed my chair back, grabbed my purse and was prepared to run to the door when the two blocked my path.

"You can't leave," Donny said.

"This isn't a good weekend to take off," Alexius spoke over Donny.

My gaze darted from one to the other.

"I've worked enough extra hours that I deserve this." I focused my attention on Alexius. I didn't care if they were behind on a project, if all of their workers booked time off or anything else. I was not going to stay.

For once I'd heed Mom's words and take myself out of the situation I was being forced into.

With a grip that would surprise Wonder Woman, I hiked my purse over my shoulder, held onto the strap and pushed my way past the two. Donny tried to reach out, to grab hold of my arm, to stop me, but I wasn't having it.

"Starla, wait," Donny called out, running after me as I pushed the door open. "I'm sorry for . . . that." He indicated back toward Alexius.

I shrugged, like it didn't matter. It did, but he wouldn't hear that from me.

"I'm going to go spend the weekend with Mom." I pulled my arm from his grip. "I'll be back Sunday night sometime, okay?"

He shook his head. "I need you here this weekend, please."

"Why?" The word came out on an exhausted sigh. He didn't really need me here, he just wanted me here.

He glanced back toward his ex-wife, who stared at us through the window.

"A dog or something dug up one of the gardens and I need help to fix it."

"Tell Alexius. She'll send Jordan or something to do it." I wasn't his lackey. I was his fiancée. He should have recognized the difference.

"I . . . don't want her getting her hands dirty with this one." He couldn't tear his gaze from the woman he shared a house with.

"But I can?" Those three words conveyed everything he needed to hear.

I was disgusted, exhausted and done competing against a woman who stood so high above me that no matter how far I reached or how much I changed, it would never be enough.

"That's-that's not what I meant," Donny stammered. But it was too little too late. I pushed past him, ignored his pleas for me to stop and was thankful I'd made it to my vehicle before the gush of fury I'd wanted to say spewed out.

I knew I'd never be able to compete against Alexius, that she would always remain important to him. But I never thought he'd place her above me like that.

Not like that.

My stomach rolled as I contemplated the idea that just maybe Mom was right. Maybe I was getting played.

35: THE BEGINNING OF THE END

Sunday night, all I wanted to do was pour myself a glass of wine, watch a little bit of reality television and crawl into bed.

I turned down my street and groaned when I noticed Donny's truck parked in my driveway.

I'd ignored his calls, his texts and all the social media posts he'd uploaded with the goal of grabbing my attention. I'd ignored him because I knew I needed a plan.

I'd decided that if I was being played, I had to find a way to wrap myself in armor again. I'd spent the weekend contemplating what was important to me: being loved or my freedom.

I wasn't ready to face Donny. Not yet. Not when all the bricks around my heart hadn't been petrified with resolution.

I walked into a welcoming waft of alfredo sauce, combined with the warm scent of garlic bread. Donny stood there, with a glass of wine in one hand and a small gift bag in the other.

"I spoke to your mom," Donny said before I had a chance to say anything. "She mentioned you'd barely eaten all weekend."

"So you're here to do what . . . take care of me? Is this your way of apologizing?" I set my bag down and took the offered wine.

"And if it was?" he asked.

I placed a soft kiss on the side of his cheek as I passed him on my way into the kitchen. "Smells delicious," I said in reply. I expected to see take-out bags on the counter, but from the mess on the stove, it looked like Donny was in the middle of making me dinner from scratch.

"Please tell me you forgive me." Donny came up behind me and wrapped his arms around my waist. "I was an idiot and I treated you horribly."

I half turned in his arms and waited for more. More explanation, more apology, more promises we both knew he couldn't keep.

"I was upset and I took my anger out on you when I should have directed it toward Alexius. It won't happen again." He sounded earnest. He sounded desperate.

"We both know it will. Over and over and over again. Alexius will always come first."

He shook his head at my words.

"Donny." I sighed. "Try as hard as you like, but there's a chain wrapped between the two of you that will never be broken. There's no room for me and to be honest, I'm done trying to find some wiggle room." I had to close my eyes so I couldn't see how much my words crushed him.

His hold on me tightened. "Stand beside me," he said, his voice hoarse and full of desperation. "Stand beside me, as my partner. You—" he leaned his head against mine, his breath teasing my skin — "mean more to me than her, I promise."

I leaned my head back and offered a challenge I wasn't sure he could handle.

"Prove it," I said. I was done feeling insignificant. I was over being the weak link. I was tired of letting others control my destiny.

"I will. I can. I have a plan," Donny said as his arms loosened from around me. "Let's eat first and then I'll share it with you." A confident smile settled on his face and a hint of secretiveness twinkled in his gaze.

Intrigued, I sipped at my wine and waited.

"Aren't you going to open my gift?" He pointed toward the table where he'd set the gift bag down.

A quick lift of the bag revealed it to be feather light.

"Don't let that fool you. It's worth a king's ransom," Donny said, his lips lifting into a large grin that gave him a boyish look.

Buried beneath tissue paper was a beautiful robin blue scarf. The fabric was soft, delicate, and I knew it must have cost him a fortune.

"It's beautiful." I lifted it to my face, the soft fabric felt like a cloud on my skin.

"It matches your eyes."

"Stop spending money on me." I let go of the scarf and placed my lips against Donny's, giving him a kiss that told him just how much I loved his gift and all the money he spent on me.

"If you tell me to stop, I will, but I think you'll want to hear my idea first."

Talk about raising the stakes. Now I was really intrigued.

I kept my questions to myself until after dinner. I was starved and the smell of the alfredo sauce was too tantalizing to wait any longer.

It wasn't until we were washing dishes together that Donny brought up his idea.

"Remember your offer to buy the property Alexius was going to sell on me? What if we did more of that?" He handed me a rinsed plate that almost slipped through my wet fingers.

"Buy and sell property?"

"Buy." His tone was definite. "Alexius wants to get rid of a few we have and there's no way I will let someone else own them. Besides, it's time we built a legacy for us."

"For us?" If I closed my eyes, I heard the whispers of promise in his voice.

"For us."

I swallowed hard.

"What about that one property? Did you transfer the money? Get your lawyers to buy it?"

I wiped at the plate in my hand and set it to the side.

"We're in the process. Alexius has no idea. If it goes through, we'll place a bug in her ear that we are interested in others if she were to list them." If he were a villain in a cartoon, he'd be rubbing his hands in glee right about how.

Finished with the dishes, I wiped down the counter and put everything away before I asked the one thing sure to shake him.

"What happens when she finds out? Because she will. One way or another."

He shrugged, like it was no big deal. "We'll handle her when that happens. It won't, though. I've given her a project that will keep her head buried in her precious soil for the rest of her life."

"Project?" I wasn't sure I hid my surprise as well as I'd hoped.

He led me to the living room where I sat, curled up in the corner. He perched himself beside me, but on the edge, elbows resting on his knees while he cracked his knuckles.

Craaack. Craacccck. Craaaaaccckkk.

God, I hated that sound.

"You've seen her lab. You know I provide the blood for her soil. I've been changing things up the past little bit, giving her a new kind of blood, to see if she'd notice." His eyes twinkled; his knees bounced with excitement.

An emerging wave of goosebumps ran in tandem over my skin.

"That blood was gross." The words tumbled off my tongue.

He laughed. "Did she give her spiel about blood meal and nutrients?"

"Honestly . . ." I wrinkled my nose. "I found the whole thing disgusting. If I never stepped foot in her Shed again, I'd be happy."

"I didn't figure you to be squeamish," Donny teased, but I knew he found the information interesting.

"Not a blood person. If you get a cut, don't expect me to take care of you, not until you've cleaned everything up, at least."

He laughed, but not in a humiliating way.

"You surprise me more and more each day, Starla Bishop," he said, taking my hand in his. His finger lightly rubbed the area where his engagement ring should sit.

"Sorry, I didn't think to wear it this weekend."

"Does it bother you, not wearing it all the time?" His gaze didn't meet mine. I wasn't sure if he wanted the truth or if I should sugar-coat it.

All weekend Mom had been on me about our secret engagement, making me question the sincerity of Donny's proposal.

"At times. Mom wonders if you're ashamed of me still." It felt safer to place the focus on Mom than me.

It looked like Donny was going to say something before he stopped.

"Are you?" I asked, my voice timid, insecure, with a hint of distress.

Donny took my hands in his. His eyes welled like he was about to cry and I almost gave in, almost.

I could have said something to ease the pain of my words, but I didn't. If Donny wanted me, he was going to have to work for it. Prove to me he was worthy.

"Of course not," Donny said. "Do you have any idea how hard it has been not to tell the world that you will soon be my wife? I'm so proud of you, Starla Bishop. So proud and so very . . . hap . . . honored to have you with . . . stand . . . beside me in life."

He blinked, his lashes coated in unshed tears that meant nothing to me.

"But . . ."

I heard it, there, at the end, in the way he tripped over his words.

Donny often donned his masks. The ones he put on effortlessly while in the middle of a crowd, when he gave a speech or even just appearing in public where people recognized him.

A mask slithered onto his face, and I knew not to believe whatever he said next.

Knew but didn't care. What did that mean? Was I that desperate for his love and attention or did it no longer matter?

"Let me separate a little more from Alexius," he said.

I rubbed my face with the palms of my hands as I struggled to grasp exactly what he meant.

"Sure, we're divorced, but most people still believe we're together, that our relationship has just evolved. I don't want you to be the *other* woman, you understand?"

For an explanation, that wasn't a bad lie.

"By moving out? Selling her your shares of Soils and Springs? Making it clear you've *uncoupled*?"

Donny's fist covered his mouth for a moment as if he had something deep to explain to me. "I have a plan, Starla. Trust me, I have something in the works to make it very clear that the lives Alexius and I live are as far apart as two people can get."

Trust him? I wanted to. I really did.

36: BODIES IN THE GROUND

Tuesday 11:00 a.m.

I've been drifting in and out for the past three hours, the gentle swing of the hammock lulling me to sleep despite the craziness happening in front of me.

In no uncertain terms and with a look that demands I behave, Kaarns requests me to stay on the back deck where I'm in sight but out of the way. Considering more and more teams continue to arrive, I have no problem with this. The grounds are now full of police officers, their team members and a pair of dogs who either bark or lay down at different intervals.

I don't want to think about what having the dogs out here means. The image of the photograph Spikes showed me plays often in my head, too often for my comfort.

There's a hushed murmur over the yard and every time I pop my head up, I see more areas sectioned off with bold yellow tape.

It's probably better that I keep my head down, eyes closed and ignore everything that's happening around me. But it's hard.

Harder than I thought it would be, only because I keep hearing conversations I shouldn't be hearing.

There's a shattering sound from inside the house and I twist out of the hammock, my feet on the floor, heart racing as I try to imagine what was broken.

I walk into the house where Spikes is cursing out a young tech wearing a bright blue T-shirt.

"Crime scene, you understand what that means, correct?" The words come out of a clenched jaw. A vein throbs down the side of his face, starting beneath his hairline and ending under his chin.

Guess everyone has their breaking points. I didn't expect this to be Spikes', however.

"Ye . . . yes, sir." The kid swallows hard. "It slipped." He licks his lips and shows his gloved fingers.

"Everything is evidence," Spikes tells him. "Every. Fucking. Thing."

His eyes are closed as he turns around. "Will someone help the kid clean this up?" he calls out.

The moment he opens his eyes and sees me, he swears again.

"There's a lot of pottery," I find myself saying. "Give the kid a break. It's probably his first time out of the lab."

Spikes' lips thin into a straight white line before he takes in a deep breath, his chest filling up with air as he does.

He comes to me, places his hand on my arm and leads me into the almost empty kitchen. I square my shoulders, preparing myself for ugly news.

"You've heard of the trophy concept, right?" Spikes asks me.

I nod. Anyone who watches any crime drama series knows all about trophies.

"What would Dixon's be?"

I reel back, needing a ton of space between myself and that question.

"He doesn't have trophies," I say, trying hard not to imagine some of the things I'd seen on television. Things like teeth, fingernails, lacy underwear . . . I swallow the bile rising up and burning my throat.

"Oh, he has trophies." The way he says it, like 'trust me I know these things' kind of way, doesn't sit well with me.

In fact, it doesn't sit at all. I bend over the kitchen sink, emptying my stomach of all fluids. Spikes hands me a tissue to wipe my mouth, then fills a glass with water.

"Have you noticed a collection of things, whether at his place in Bervie Springs, in his dealership . . ." His words have me shaking my head. Collections? God no.

Despite living in half of the mansion, I've never stepped foot in his area. I have no idea what his place there looks like and Spikes knows this. This was one of the numerous questions they had asked me on our way up here this morning.

Kaarns had mentioned how odd that sounded, that I'd never had dinner in his kitchen, slept in his bed, but I shrugged it off. My relationship with Donny is anything but normal. It has always been my choice not to see what his space looks like. It's the space he shares with Alexius and I preferred to have our own place.

"Spikes, you need to see this," Kaarns' voice calls out from the living room.

His look asks me if I want to join him, but I quickly shake my head. Whatever they find has nothing to do with me.

And yet, I trail behind Spikes, staring straight in the middle of his shoulder blades, waiting for him to react before I do. When his shoulders bunch up, I look to what has caught his interest.

A UV light is on the pottery shards, illuminating a dark substance.

After everything I've seen, the whispers I've heard, without even asking what we're all looking at, I breathe out a single word.

"Blood."

Spikes glances at me over his shoulder, the look in his eyes confirming what I'd just said.

The UV light arches across the room, hitting other pottery items Donny has placed about on shelves and tables. Every piece reacts the same way.

Someone picks up one of the bowls set on a side table. "Margarite 1974."

I cover my lips with the palm of my hand as my throat tightens, squeezing all the air I need to breathe, away.

Spikes turns, but he doesn't say anything as he looks at me. He doesn't need to.

These are Donny's souvenirs. But not just Donny's. His father, grandfather, great-grandfather . . .

"Grab it all," Spikes orders the techs, "ever single piece, from every room. Catalog it by name and date and then start searching for the victims. The information you'll need is on the bottom of each piece."

He then looks to Kaarns. "The shed with the kiln, who's on it?"

"No one yet," she tells him. "They're waiting to get into the leather shed first."

"Have you been in there?" Nothing in his voice tells me now is the time to deflect or hesitate.

I shake my head. "There's nothing there. Just . . ." Just everything they need. All the containers of what I thought was red dye but instead is blood.

"He hunts," I say, my voice shaking. "Hunts animals and drains their blood for Alexius."

"I doubt this is animal blood, Starla," Spikes says.

I close my eyes, wishing I could hide, that I could rewind the past twenty-four hours.

"What did he tell you about the pottery? You must have asked him," Kaarns says.

I shrug but then drop my head. I'm living in a nightmare and there's no means of escape.

"They're for all the important women in their lives," I whisper.

"I'm sorry?" Spikes steps closer.

I can't look up, the weight of my words too heavy for me to bear. "He told me they're made only after the women they love die. It's a family tradition."

I stare at my hands. Hands that have held every single piece of pottery in this cabin, marveling over the hue of pink, thinking about the women each piece was dedicated to. Hands that need to be scrubbed raw just so I can feel clean.

"How many more are we going to find?" Kaarns' tone is low, distraught and I'm thankful that someone is able to put a voice to the question in my head.

How many bodies are there? Out there?

I swallow hard, force air into my lungs, remind my heart to keep beating at a normal rate while I think about all the days, evenings, weekends that I've been here, resting, walking, hiking. I've walked over graves. I've had sex with Donny on the grass. I've dreamed of a life with him, here, where we would grow old and gray.

"There's a rock," I find myself saying. When I look up, all eyes are on me. "There's a rock out past the yard. It's got them all on there."

"What do you mean by all?" Spikes' voice is deadpan straight.

I look him square in the eye, holding his gaze as the horror of what I'm about to say becomes real.

"Generations of Dixons have kept score of all the women they . . ." I want to say loved, but I know that's no longer the truth. "All the women they've killed. They're all on the rock."

I've been trying to prepare myself for this, ever since I got in Spikes' vehicle and closed my eyes to the scenery we drove past. In the back of my mind, I knew that my life would split down the seams until there was a before and after. Similar to the Old Starla and the New Starla. Except not the same at all.

I'm sleeping with a murderer. I'm entwined with a monster wearing the mask of a man and somehow his reality has become my nightmare.

37: THE PAIN OF TRUTH

Tuesday 7:40 p.m.

"Starla!" Mom is there, waiting for me, arms spread wide as my condo door swings open. I let myself fall against her, absorbing all the love, acceptance and willingness to be there for me.

"Where did you go?" She pulls me away from the door and directs me to the sofa. I crash with a groan. "I went to see you, to find out why they were holding you for so long, but they told me you'd gone out with those detectives."

She sits beside me, on an angle, as if ready to jump up and grab whatever I needed. I place my hand on her knee, lean my head back and close my eyes.

Which is a mistake. So many images are there, in the forefront. Images I can never erase.

"I took them to the cabin," I say. My eyes are swimming in unshed tears, but I'm not sure if it's from feeling so exhausted or horrified from all I've learned.

Mom doesn't say a word. She just holds onto my hand, her grip strong, her face stoic.

"He did it, Mom. He did it. I . . ." It's hard to swallow. "I didn't think he could, that he was a monster, but . . ." I stop. There's no excuses. Not for him, certainly not for me.

I had opportunity, ample opportunity to leave, to start over, to run as fast as I could, but I never did. Not when Mom begged me to, not when my own instincts shouted at me, not when the first glimmer of truth stared me in the face.

"This is not your fault, Starla Bishop. You hear me? He's the monster, not you."

The tears drip past my lashes and work their way down my cheeks until they hover on my chin. Mom wipes them away while all I can do is look at her for help.

"I'm the one who fell in love with him."

Her lips purse together. "You can't help what the heart wants. Don't you be taking that on."

I appreciate her advice, I really do, but it's still on me. It doesn't matter what she says, I know the truth.

I fell in love with a sick, twisted monster.

"What was at the cabin?" Her tone was soft, gentle. How could I tell her?

There were so many things I wanted to say, explain, but how could I explain everything that transpired at the cabin all day? There are no words.

Mom senses how I'm feeling. "Go sleep, love, I'll be here when you wake up."

My lips can barely lift into a sad smile. "But nothing will have changed, right?"

She gives me a hug. "Oh honey."

I know she wants more information, but I'm so drained, it needs to wait until I get some sleep.

"Starla, where is your ring?" She's tugging on my hand. I tug back.

"It's a fake." Even saying those three words, three simple, nondescript words, hurt.

I'd given the ring to Kaarns, told her to keep it for evidence, when I'd gotten dropped off. I obviously don't need it anymore.

"A . . . fake?" Mom's having just as hard a time processing that little tidbit of information as I had. Hopefully I covered my surprise better.

"You know, I was only kidding when I told you to get it appraised," she says, still staring at my bare finger. "What about the other stuff . . . the diamond earrings, the necklaces, bracelets . . . all that stuff you stashed away in the back of your closet?"

I straighten, caught off guard. "You snooped?" I'm not sure why I'm surprised — of course she snooped, she's not only a mother, but she's *my* mother. But there's a clash of cymbals going off all throughout my body, sirens screeching warning alarms and my heart pounds so hard against my chest that it begins to hurt.

"Of course, I did. You were hauled back into jail. What did you think I was going to do? Sit here and drink tea, waiting for the phone to ring?" She crosses her arms and glares.

It's hard to wipe everything off my face so she can't read me.

"Yes, I found everything," she says, which causes the panic already speeding through my body like a metro train to accelerate even faster.

She can't have found everything.

"Starla, I know you. I know where you hide your treasures, your secrets and those things you refuse to discuss. I know and still love you."

I run my nails through my scalp, not sure how to respond. 'Thank you' seems oddly inappropriate. 'I'm sorry' doesn't even begin to wash away all the lies I've told. 'Let me explain' doesn't even need to be said.

"You did what you needed to do." Mom holds up a hand, as if she knows I'm struggling to figure out what to say. "That's all I need to know."

"I . . ." My tongue unwrapped from its knot. "I thought I was protecting him," I finally say. The admission costs me. I try hard not to glance down at my now bare finger.

Mom stands and offers me her hands. "Now you're the one needing protection."

We walk to my room in silence. I curl on top of the covers and Mom throws a blanket on me, tucking me in like she used to once upon a time.

"It's going to be okay, Starla. I promise." She whispers her prayer as I close my eyes.

That is a mistake.

I see bare hands, deep red bowls full of blood and bare skin hanging from a hook. I hear the silent screams of women I've never met, their mouths open in agony. I watch as all those marks on the rock crawl off the hard surface and stand before me, morphing into human form, their arms outstretched.

Condemnation rolls over me until I curl into a ball, the bars holding back my emotions opening. Mom is here, her hand rubbing my back in circular motions until everything fades away and I'm alone and empty.

38: THE SECRET OF THE LEATHER

8:00 p.m.
DETECTIVE KAARNS

It's been one of the longest days in my life and it's still not over. Not by a long shot.

Spikes and I returned to town with a shrunken Bishop late in the evening. She'd barely said two words the whole drive back. We dropped her off at home with the promise she'd keep herself available. Considering her mom met us at the door, I wasn't too worried about Bishop sneaking away.

"You should go home and sleep," Spikes says as we pull up to the station.

That was the plan, until about fifteen minutes ago.

"I will, after I haul ass into the chief's office."

Spikes' brows raise at least two notches. "Burnard ratted you out?"

I shrug. "That's the only thing I can think of."

I stretch, my fingertips reaching as high as I can, releasing the creaks out of my spine the moment I step out of the vehicle. "You go home. You need your beauty sleep more than me."

I slap the hood of his vehicle twice before I climb the steps. After everything I've seen today, there's nothing left inside to prepare myself for whatever the chief wants to discuss.

"Let's get down to it," the chief says after he ushers me into his office and closes the door. He looks as bad as I feel, worn, torn and overwhelmed.

"This business with the Dixons, we need to be careful," he begins. He picks up a sheet of paper; his eyes scan the page before dropping it. "Her family is quite powerful and it's possible Alexius Dixon isn't involved in this mess."

"Mess?" My brows shoot up higher than a pole vault. He's calling these murders, the victims, a mess?

He rubs his face. "Poor choice of words," he mumbles.

"Got it. Glove hands with the wife, but what about Donald? He can't be off limits too. Everything points to him." I'm perched on the edge of the chair.

"Not off limits, just . . ." He gives his head a slight shake. "Be careful, that's all."

"Chief, I'm not sure I understand what you're trying to tell me." If I'm going to cross a line, I'd at least like to know where that line is located.

The chief clears his throat and pushes himself back against his chair. "The mess surrounding Dixon . . . it's going to get ugly, but we don't need that to spread onto those who don't deserve to be pulled in."

"This has to do with the Dixon Deals, doesn't it?"

I can tell he's not going to respond.

"You know, my mind goes crazy when I think about what everyone is hiding. Makes me wonder just how much dirt Dixon has on everyone." I share my thoughts verbally, watching my boss closely.

He doesn't move. Doesn't blink. He's a solid slate of marble.

"I have to go where the evidence leads," I say, parroting Spikes' earlier advice.

He nods, his agreement breaking through features that were blank earlier.

"Exactly."

"And discovering more about his Dixon Deals will help."

A scowl replaces the lift of his lips. "Leave those alone," he tells me. "Unless it's absolutely necessary."

I cock my head to the side. "You're not telling me to ignore evidence, are you?"

"What evidence?"

"That's what I'm trying to find out."

A knock sounds on the door and Spikes pops his head in before the chief has a chance to say hello.

"I need Kaarns," he says. "Look deeper into the dealership. Those keychains everyone carries around—" he looks directly at a set on the chief's desk — "that leather ain't animal and the binding . . ." His lips press tight together.

I push to my feet. "We need those tags. Every single one of them."

My boss remains seated, but he's got a 'this is going sideways fast' look on his face.

"Any final words?" Spikes asks.

He leans forward and grabs a pen from his desk, playing with it before he looks up.

"Tread softly. Do what needs to be done, but do it with discretion." He looks hard at me, as if trying to convey a message I can't read. "If you can."

I look to Spikes. He's shaking his head.

"There's no way to hide in the shitstorm that's about to erupt, you realize that, right?" I say the words we're all thinking.

"Play in shit long enough, eventually you end up covered in it too." Spikes holds the door for me.

We walk down the hall to the room where my team is set up.

"Is it really human skin?" The idea that Dixon would do such a thing and think he could get away with it . . .

"Results just came in. This is going to get messy."

My mind races with the ramifications of these keychains. Somehow, we're going to have to request people to drop theirs off. How much skin did he use?

A tremor sweeps over my body, forcing me to stop and lean on the wall for support.

"Try not to overthink it. Don't let your mind rest on images you don't need to see." Spikes stands beside me, holding onto my arm, offering support.

He opens the door and the first thing I notice about the war room is the depth of silence. No fingers pounding on keyboards, no one muttering to themselves, nothing.

A shoebox sits in the middle of the table and my team is staring at it.

It's half full of keychains.

I let my gaze sweep over the box and settle on something less . . . disturbing.

"Coroner's office has confirmed that large swatches of skin appear to be missing on the victims. Back, legs, chest," Danvers says, his voice sounding garbled as he tries to contain himself.

Photographs line the wall, images taken from Dixon's cabin. Images of the pottery, wheelbarrows full of body parts, the leather shed with skins hanging from hooks.

"Has anyone told the monster what we know?" Spikes had better give me the answer I'm looking for. God help me, but I want to be the one to tell him, to wipe that bastard's smirk from his face.

"Jordan's handling him," Spikes reminds me. "We've got Bishop and the evidence. Focus, Kaarns." He says this last part softly, his back to the team, so only I can hear.

Focus? Oh, I'm focused all right. Focused enough to hang that asshole's ass on a stake and let him rot. There is no way in hell Dixon is going to get away with this.

"No cutting corners. No mistakes. When this goes to trial, we need to be one hundred percent certain we've done all we could. If he gets off, it had better not be because we screwed up." Spikes takes my group to task, his voice solid and cemented.

"If?" Trina squeaks out.

"If we screw up, his lawyers will find a way to use that," Spikes reminds them. Reminds me.

If this screws up, it's on us as a team and we can't let that happen. I saw too many body pieces today out at Dixon's cabin for me to live with the knowledge he got away.

I cross my arms and look my team over. They're all exhausted. Dark circles shadow their eyes, their shoulders are bowed, their movements a little slower than normal.

"Go home," I tell them all. "Get some sleep. Back here in six hours, understand? That gives you enough time to eat something and climb into bed. Go."

Every single face is looking at me with a fish-gapping gaze. "I'm serious. Do what you need to do to secure everything here, then get some sleep."

When I look at my partner, he smiles at me. His approval means a lot, but I'm not going to tell him that.

"You too," I say to him, pointing toward the door.

"Only when you do." His arms cross his chest and he's got that 'don't mess with me, old man' look on his face.

"I want to talk to Burnard first," I tell him. I need to figure out what Dixon has on him. "Then I'll sleep."

"I'll wait." He's not going to budge and we both know it.

I struggle not to roll my eyes. As everyone piles out the room, their movements a little quicker, I give Spikes the eye. "Gonna join me then?"

He shrugs. "Figured I would."

We head toward Burnard's desk where I'd seen him working on his computer earlier.

He is still there, head down, fingers moving on the keyboard.

"Time to talk?" I stand directly in front of him and place my hands on the edge of his monitor. He looks up, blanches and gives a quick glance over his shoulder toward the chief's office.

"Can't hide behind him anymore, sorry." I try to place one of those 'I feel for you' kind of smiles on my face, but from the cough from Spikes, it didn't quite work out.

"Let's go talk somewhere a bit more . . . discreet," Spikes suggests.

Burnard nods as he pushes out his chair and slowly stands. He looks to be a bit shaky and all my internal buzzers go off.

Once we're in an empty office, Burnard lets out a long, haggard breath. I'm waiting for him to break down and cry, that's how stressed he looks right now.

"I'll tell you everything I know." The words come out in a rushed steady stream, like he's been waiting to spill.

Both Spikes and I lean back in our chairs at the same time.

"I . . . I handed in my keychain," Burnard says first. "When I heard . . . I just . . ." His gaze turns wild as he looks from me to Spikes and then to the floor. "I puked. Quite a few of us did," he admits.

I nod. "I get it," I admit.

"I've known Dixon for years." He shakes his head. "He's been here, under our noses . . . using us . . . how did we not know?"

I've been wondering the same thing.

"He's sick," Spikes says. "His brain is wired differently than ours."

My brows raise. Is that really the answer he's giving?

"His deals aren't something you'll find invoiced. He's like his own personal mob. He's created his own network of connections and spreads the wealth, *per se*."

I lean forward, elbows resting on the tables, sleeves of my jacket pulled up and prepare to listen. Spikes already has his notebook out, so I'm not concerned about taking notes.

"I know a guy who hands out permits. He's been known to turn a blind eye a few times to help others. Dixon . . ." His body shakes with a tremor. "Dixon needed things done without anyone looking at it too closely."

I don't need to look at Spikes to know his wheels are turning. He's told me stories of the mob in the city.

"But how did that benefit you? Why would you connect him to your permit-friendly friend?" I need more. We need more.

I'm not liking how long it takes for Burnard to look me cop-to-cop and tell me the truth. It makes me cagey. My earlier suspicions about him being a dirty cop come back, slapping me in the face as a reminder.

"I ran into some financial problems a few years ago," he finally admits. This doesn't surprise me. "Dixon bailed me out. Has bailed me out a few times. He forgives the loans, just asks for favors as needed." The more he tells, the lower his voice gets.

I see Spikes stop writing. I want to look at him, but I'm not going to take my focus off Burnard.

"What kind of favors?"

When he finally looks up at me, I see the steel of a man who once had the goal to be a good cop.

"Favors I never should have agreed to." The way he says this, it's enough for me to know that something inside him has changed. Maybe it was learning the truth about Dixon. Maybe it was realizing he'd been part of it. Or maybe his conscience finally decided to kick him where it hurts and the impact made enough of a dent.

"I already handed in my report."

I lean forward, but Spikes places his hand on my arm and I halt whatever words were about to spill out.

"The best time to change is now," Spikes says. "Dixon will go down, but we'll do what we can to ensure this department doesn't join the ride." He gets up to leave, but I'm stuck to my seat.

What the hell? Is he just swiping all the crap beneath the rug and calling it a day? A dirty cop is a dirty cop.

"Look below the surface," Spikes finally says to me when we're alone. "Mistakes were made and there'll be nowhere to hide after everything comes out, but we're a family here. Dysfunctional and all."

"I want to read that report." He can turn a blind eye, but I won't. The fact this happened in our town, on our watch . . . I can't stomach knowing Dixon could have been stopped if only we'd paid better attention.

"Go home. Sleep. We've got a long road ahead of us. He's in custody and we're only at the beginning. I need you rested," Spikes says. "Trust me on this, okay?" He's trying to tell me something, but I'm suddenly blind to his nonverbal cues.

"Dixon isn't going anywhere," I say, repeating what he'd said earlier.

Spikes nods. No other words are needed. He's right. I am exhausted, but let's be honest, no amount of sleep is going to fix this nightmare we're all in.

39: THE BIRTHDAY GIFT

Two Months Ago

Today was Alexius' birthday and Donny had nixed dinner with me to take her out to a place in the city. He'd asked me if I minded. I did. I tried not to, though.

Knowing they'd be gone for hours, I walked from my condo to the office with one goal in mind — to get caught up on paperwork.

Of course, my reasoning was paperwork. It wasn't because I wanted to know when Donny came home. If they came home. It wasn't because I felt insecure and this had been my first reaction. It certainly wasn't because I didn't trust my fiancé.

As I sat at my desk, I'd made two piles to work on. One pile for Soil and Springs and one pile for Donny. Little by little, I'd started taking over things for him. Property lists, registrations, legal filings, etc.

I was learning more about the man I was engaged to than he probably wanted me to know.

When I'd first come into the office, the door heading into their house had been left open. I didn't close it all the way, knowing it would lock if I did so. I wasn't sure if it'd been left open on purpose or not. Which is why, a few hours after being there, I overheard a discussion between Donny and Alexius I wasn't meant to hear.

When I first heard Donny's voice, I'd risen from my chair, wanting to go and say hi, surprised and happy that they'd come home so early, but nothing in his voice indicated I'd be welcomed if I'd made my presence known.

"I can't believe you're going to him, especially now," Donny said, his voice a level above a child's whine.

I winced, listening to the way he wallowed in Alexius' presence. What was it about her that affected him so much? In every other moment of his life, from what I'd witnessed, Donny was a strong, self-reliant, controlling and dominating beast. But at home, in front of the woman he'd divorced years ago, he reverted back to a ten-year-old boy who still needed his mommy's approval.

That wasn't the man I'd fallen in love with and to be quite honest, I was tired of it.

"Oh, grow up." Apparently, Alexius was tired of the ten-year-old version as well.

"But I took you out for dinner, to your favorite place," Donny continued. Nothing in his voice changed despite the sharpness of Alexius' tone.

"Yes, you did. And I loved it. As always, you know how to spoil me, Donny. Dinner was fabulous, but now I'm ready for a little piece of dessert and . . ." There was a pause which had me leaning forward, wanting to make sure I didn't miss a single word.

"And what?" The whining had left Donny's voice. Now he just sounded mad. Like a little boy about to have a tantrum.

"Well, quite honestly, the menu you're offering isn't quite what I had in mind."

My stomach dropped as the knife of truth she'd flung pierced my heart, tearing open an artery that would probably never heal.

If any other words had been spoken, I couldn't hear them from the roaring in my head. She wasn't serious, right?

He wouldn't have suggested . . . he couldn't have meant . . . she didn't think . . . I couldn't finish the thought, the words wouldn't form, thank goodness.

There was no way what she'd insinuated could be true. Donny wouldn't do that to me, to us.

"What do you see in him?" There was a slam of a glass on a counter that followed Donny's words.

At least he hadn't confirmed what I'd feared.

"He's fun. A distraction. Makes me feel sexy as hell. It's a nice feeling."

I couldn't see them, but I pictured a cat toying with a mouse, reeling in a string of cheese, little by little, until that poor mouse nibbled on the cheese directly beneath the cat's jaws.

I jumped at the crash of glass against tile.

"Really?" Disdain filled Alexius' voice. "Was that necessary?"

"Do you have to be so crass?" Donny all but yelled, his voice breaking at the very end.

That surprised me, that he would yell at Alexius. I'd heard them arguing before. Heard anger, fury, and rage in his voice, but his tone had always been controlled. He'd never yelled. Not like that.

I couldn't hear the next words being said, not even when I walked closer to the door and leaned against the wall.

"I don't trust Jordan."

I jumped at Donny's words, mainly because it sounded like he was on the other side of the wall. I hurried back to my chair, as quiet as I could, not wanting to be caught eavesdropping.

"Really?" Sarcasm dripped like a melting icicle. "Why ever not?"

"He's too nosy," Donny said. "Haven't you noticed all the questions he asks? There's something about him that doesn't sit right."

"He does what's asked and he does a damn good job of it. I, for one, am happy about all the questions."

I tried to stifle a snort. Like hell she was happy with it. She liked being asked questions just as much as Donny did.

"In fact, if it weren't for his endless questions . . ." Alexius paused and instinctively I knew she was about to drop a bomb. "I wouldn't have thought to have the blood you supply me tested," she continued.

I hunched over, ready for the detonation.

"You what?" A slam of a fist followed a litany of curse words. "Why would you do that? I tell you exactly what kind of blood I bring you. Why would you involve him?"

I had a sense of regret not being in that room with them. I wished I could see their bodies, read the words not being said, viewed the way they held themselves. Since I couldn't, I imagined how the scene was playing out.

Alexius held a glass of wine in hand, a coy smile on her face, enjoying the way she played her ex-husband.

My fiancé would be standing there, arms crossed, his shoulders hunched like a scolded schoolboy.

If anyone watched, Alexius would be declared the winner. "What are you hinting at, Alexius?" Donny asked.

"I think you know," she said.

"I want you to fire him."

"No."

"Why the fuck not?" I pictured Donny's fists clenched, his jaw tight, his anger in check, barely.

"Because I don't want to. Because he has his uses. Because I like having him around, for now." Alexius rattled off her reasoning in quick succession. She didn't want to be told what to do and she made sure Donny knew that.

It was a constant game of pull between the two. A battle of wills that I knew intoxicated Donny. It was one reason why he couldn't ever leave Alexius.

What drew him to me, what kept him with me, for now, was that I rarely played that game with him. If he wanted to be in control, if he wanted to call the shots, fine. I had no problem letting him take the lead as long as I wasn't expected to be completely docile.

"Calm down." Alexius reminded me of a mother calming her spoiled son. "I know how much you like to play games, push the boundaries. I noticed something odd about one of the samples, Jordan happened to be around, and offered to get it tested. He claims to have connections and I wanted to confirm what I knew."

I swallowed hard at the news. It wasn't what she said necessarily, but more how she said it.

I wondered if Donny had caught it too.

She might claim Donny liked to play games, but he wasn't the only one. What she'd done with Jordan had been a test and she already knew the answer.

"C . . . confirm?" I almost didn't catch the stutter.

"You can't play me, Donald. You thought I wouldn't notice? That I'd use the blood you brought and wouldn't test it first? I'm a scientist. I want to know all the variables." The unmistakable sound of a tired sigh followed her sentence.

"I don't know what you're talking about," Donny eventually said.

"No one else will believe that, will they? Not once they find out all I know." The sound of clinking glass, of heels on tile, of a drawer being open and then closed pulled me closer. If only I were a fly on that wall . . .

"What's with the knife, Alexius? Honestly, if you want . . ." Donny swallowed loudly. "If you want to spend the night with Jordan, by all means . . ." His voice stopped and all I imagined was her placing the edge of the knife against his throat.

My hands fisted, my stomach tumbled, and my nerves were electrified, waiting for me to move, to announce my presence, to protect Donny.

"I know what you're doing, Donny," Alexius' sly voice filled the balloon of silence after Donny's voice cut out. "I've known for a long time. The women you bring here, parade about me, trying to tempt me . . ."

"No, no." Donny found his voice. "That's not it, not what I'm doing—"

"Oh, shut up," Alexius says, a low growl to her voice. "Don't play me like you're playing her. I know you, Donald Dixon. I know you better than anyone." Her voice dropped until it was almost hard to hear.

She was talking about me. My toes curled, my muscles tensed and I knew that everything from the moment when I arrived in Bervie Springs, until now, had been a game. But who were the players? Not Donny. I couldn't believe that. I wouldn't.

Alexius was playing him. I've always known it, but now, she'd confirmed it.

I returned to my place by the door, my silent footsteps leading me closer to the two, the need to hear everything being said stronger than my desire to leave.

"I've always known this part of you, don't you realize that? It's what drew us together in the first place, remember? The hunt, the intoxicating draw of reeling in our prey, of outsmarting everyone around us?" The seductiveness of Alexius' voice slithered over my skin, the unwelcomed trail of pain sliding over my spine.

I pictured her pressed against Donny, chest to chest, hip to hip, the knife lowered to Alexius' side, her eyes tracing Donny's lips.

Everything inside me, all my dreams, the small windows of hope I'd allowed myself to build, was torn apart, one inch at a time, as I stood there.

"Why did you leave me then? If you knew? If you are okay with it?" Donny's voice splintered as he spoke, the questions he asked ending in hope, hope that destroyed me over and over again.

I closed my eyes, unable to accept the images I'd played out in my head. The words being spoken scribbled pictures I never wanted to see again.

"I left because you got sloppy. Because I got tired of having to clean up your mess, time and time again." The click of her heels forced my eyes open. With each step that took her away from my Donny, the tightness around my lungs eased.

Slightly.

But it was enough.

"I won't go down because of you." Alexius' voice was close to me now. On the other side of the wall, closer to the door. Would she open it? Walk in and find me?

"You think you're so smart, love. But when will you realize I'm the one pulling the strings?"

The door closed then. One small click and anything else Alexius said was gone, muffled behind wood, insulation and drywall.

My movements stifled, robotic and slow, I returned to my desk and gathered my things as quietly as I could. I waited, for what, I'm not sure. But I waited for what seemed like hours for someone to speak, for a sound to be made, for answers to the crazy number of questions swirling in my head. But all I got was silence.

I had two options. Go to the door and announce my presence. Pretend to be clueless to everything said earlier, or leave.

I opted to leave.

It was the cowardly act, the weak one, but I wasn't sure if I was ready to face the consequences of what I might have seen.

40: THE PROTECTED BECOMES THE PROTECTOR

The sun peeked over the clouds, painting the sky with a unicorn paintbrush.

"Is it as beautiful there as it is here?" Mom asked me over the phone.

"More so," I said into the speaker, phone perched on my lap. I held a cup of coffee in between my hands and didn't take my gaze off of the gorgeous canvas above me.

"What's wrong?"

A sad smile spread across my face. Even though she wasn't here, she knew. She was that kind of mother, the kind I never want to disappoint again.

Last night, I realized I was on a path that could lead to exactly that, and I knew a decision had to be made.

It was the decision that broke my heart today, that drew tears as I gazed upon the sunrise.

I walked a tight line on a narrow road with steep drops on either side of me. One misstep and I'd be skewered to death, impaled on the lies others have told and I couldn't let that happen.

I'd slept alone last night. I hadn't expected Donny to show up, not really, but if he had, it would have made so many things easier, clearer.

On my walk home, all I could think about was what I'd overheard. I expected to see Jordan's truck drive past me, on his way to give Alexius her birthday present, but when I walked past the apartment building where he lived, his truck was still there, the lights in his place off.

My heart sank even more than I thought possible. That could only mean one thing and I absolutely didn't want to think about that.

"Starla." Mom's voice broke through the haze of my pain. "Tell me what's going on."

"Just tired." The lie slipped off my tongue with too much ease.

"Donny didn't show up, did he?" She knew yesterday had been Alexius' birthday and she'd warned me, after finding out he took her into the city for dinner, that I might not like what followed.

I'd told her she was wrong, that Donny was going to come and spend the night. I'd made sure to exude confidence, even when I knew it wouldn't happen. I wasn't that naive.

I exhaled. "No, he didn't."

"Oh honey, I'm so sorry." Mom's voice brought even more tears to the surface, tears I quickly blinked away.

"It's all right, Mom. You were right, you've always been right. I haven't been careful with my heart when it came to Donny and it's my own fault." I swallowed the lump of broken dreams back down.

"What does that mean? Are you breaking up with him?"

I almost choked on the mouthful of coffee I'd sipped. "Oh God, no. It just means I'm going to slow things down, pivot from where we are to where I think we need to be. Alexius is playing him and he's blind to how close she is to destroying him." I wasn't sure if that made sense.

I wasn't ready to give up on my relationship with Donny. I just needed to . . . readjust my thinking.

Since arriving in Bervie Springs, he'd made it clear his goal was to protect me. Now it's my turn to be the protector.

"Pivot? Destroying him? Starla, what are you talking about?"

I drank the last bit of coffee and glanced at the time. "You were right about her, too."

"Alexius?" Mom swore beneath her breath. "I told you . . ." She didn't finish her sentence, but I pictured her shaking her head with that 'why do I even try' look on her face.

"Mom, you couldn't have warned me from this. I think . . ." I wasn't even sure how to describe last night's conversation I'd overheard. "She's trying to pin something on Donny that could destroy him." That sounded lame, even to my ears.

"Pin what? I know you think he's a good man, and I'm sure he is, but he's not only a politician, he sells used cars, Starla. Everyone knows you never trust men like him." The harsh judgement that came through her words, it bothered me more than I wanted to admit.

I didn't know what sick, twisted and perverted things Alexius was doing, but I knew she intended to dig a hole large enough for a person to be buried in it, and that person wasn't going to be her.

She was a black widow in the body of a gorgeous butterfly. It was time Donny saw past the mask, time I stepped up and stopped allowing her to be included in our relationship.

"The less you know, the better," I muttered, my mind still rolling through all the possibilities of what I'd heard. My mind wanted to go into the deep dark recess of what her words could mean, but that was only because of my past, because of the people I'd been surrounded by.

Perhaps Alexius was only playing Donny. Maybe last night had been some sick form of foreplay. I wasn't sure what I wanted it to be more: the dark truth that Alexius could be a killer or that my fiancé and his ex-wife were still sexually involved.

"Don't!" Mom shouted loud enough that the phone on my lap vibrated. "Don't you dare, Starla Bishop. Every single time you tell me something like that, you end up in prison."

Startled, I found myself staring at the phone screen, trying to recall what I'd said.

"The more I know, the better," Mom's tirade continued. "How can I help you if you don't tell me? God, girl, don't you get it yet? I can't . . . just don't do this to me again."

The call ended. She'd actually hung up on me, without giving me time to explain. My first instinct was to call back, to talk her down, to explain what I meant . . . but I stopped myself.

How could I explain my fears? I had no proof. I was basing everything on my gut and what I'd overheard last night. I could just possibly be a jealous girlfriend who was being played.

Played, not just by Alexius, but by Donny too. The idea had me bending over in agony. Why would he do that? What did he get out of playing me like that?

The messed-up rollercoaster I continued to ride needed to stop at some point. I was the foolish one to stay on the ride. My hurting heart was my own fault, no one else's. I'd known right from the beginning that I had to stay out of the drama that was the Dixons and I hadn't listened to myself.

No one was more at fault than me.

Like last night, I had two choices. Ignore everything I thought I knew and continue to pretend my life had changed, or do something about the mistakes I'd made since arriving.

Donny believed the Old Starla was gone, but I'd only put her to the side, shoved her into the back of the closet and covered her with old, discarded sweaters. I wasn't stupid. People changed because they wanted to, but the threads of their past life, of who they used to be, those characteristics always remained.

Old Starla needed to reappear. Not completely, but in sections, for situations. It was Old Starla that would take down Alexius once and for all. One way or another, I'd find a way to distance Donny from her.

41: DON'T MESS WITH THE MAMA BEAR

Wednesday 9:05 a.m.
DETECTIVE KAARNS

My team are back at the table, noses buried in paperwork, staring at a screen, or on their phones. Bright eyes welcome me as I open the door, my arms laden with trays of coffee and bags of pastries.

"Everyone okay? Get some sleep?" I wait for responses before I hand out the coffees. "We have a psychologist coming in today. I strongly encourage you all to make an appointment to talk about how this case is affecting you." The chief had made me repeat that phrase three times before he let me walk by him.

"Are you?" Danvers says.

"I'm the first name on the sheet," I tell them, keeping the sarcasm out of my voice. The chief almost made me sign up for a time slot. I made sure to add Spikes' name below mine, whether he wants to talk or not.

"Tell me where we're at?" I pull out a chair and sit, needing to be caught up.

Danvers stands. "We have drop boxes set up all over town. We have alerts going out on the radio, the news station, and in the paper today about handing in any Dixon keychains."

"Where are the boxes?" My one concern about retrieving all the keychains was mass hysteria. We needed people to understand how important it is to hand them in, but we don't want to tell them why. Not yet, at least. Eventually it'll come out that what they thought was leather was actual dried human skin and evidence.

"Grocery stores, gas stations, convenience stores, the bakery, town hall . . . basically anywhere and everywhere. We've already had a few phone calls of keychains being dropped off at locations without boxes." Trina pokes her head up from behind her laptop screen. "We have officers going around during shifts to pick them up."

I nod. We wouldn't get all of them, but we'd get a lot and hopefully they'll help us to identify Dixon's victims. "We need to go through cold cases, missing person's files. We want to look specifically for women, twenty, thirty or even fifty years back."

While everyone is taking notes, I twist to look at the board behind me. There's a whole list of things we need to do. As some get completed, more get added.

"We have a team going through all the invoices and mapping out possible burial locations," Trina continues.

This I know. More sites were added while I slept. I drove by a few of those locations.

"Where are we on the pottery?"

Trina looks up from the sheets she's been poring over since I arrived. "Dude used blood as a color additive," she said.

"Dixon." I wasn't fond of the term 'dude'.

"Yeah. Him. Anyways, all items were cataloged and then sent off to a lab in the city. I've got the names here and am tracking down information on them. We've got a few hits, missing persons and all that." She reaches for a notepad where she's been cataloging names and hands it to me.

There are eight on this list. Eight missing persons' files that we're able to close. Eight families that need to be contacted.

Eight out of how many? The nausea that came over me yesterday, it's here again. It's probably going to be here for a very long time.

"Chief is going to host a briefing in two hours," Spikes says, walking into the room.

I stand, the list falling to the table. I catch a slight stiffness to his shoulders. "What's going on?"

He's holding the door open. "Jordan's about to go back in. Thought you might be interested in watching."

I grab my coffee, my bag and bolt from the room.

Halfway down the hallway, I catch a glance of Caryn McCoy sitting on the couch, her purse clutched tight in her hands. I take two steps back and turn.

Spikes almost crashes into me.

"Did you know she was here?" I ask him, pointing to the room.

The frown of confusion tells me he's just as clueless as I am.

"Mrs. McCoy?" I retake those two steps and stand slightly in the door.

She heaves a hard sigh and rises to her feet. "Officer Kaarns, thank you for seeing me," she says in a rush, as if worried I'm about to disappear.

Spikes nudges me and when I look at him, he's handing me his coffee. "It's fresh," he grumbles. "I'll take notes. Join me when you can."

I watch him walk away and everything inside of me screams for him to wait, that I want to be there. Will Dixon finally admit to every disgusting, disgraceful and deranged thing he's done? God, I hope so.

"Here you go," I say instead, offering the coffee before taking my seat. "What can I do to help you?"

"Starla is sleeping and I . . ." She swallows, takes a sip of her drink and attempts a weak smile. "There's things you need to know, things I just discovered that will help clear Starla from all of this."

I don't tell her my focus has already left her daughter, that after yesterday, it was clear she was as much in the dark as any of us. She's going to carry the stain of being associated with Dixon for the rest of her life, but we're not going to add to it.

"What kind of things?" I lean forward, rest my elbows on my knees and force my attention to be on what she says and not what's happening a few rooms down from us.

Caryn sets the coffee cup down and within moments I see a complete transformation take over. Gone is the mother concerned for her daughter, worried that she'll be heading to jail again. Instead, there's a woman determined to see justice served and this is the kind of woman I can get behind.

Her eyes twinkle with vengeance, leaving me to wonder what happened since our last conversation.

"Donald transferred companies over to Starla, placing them in her name," she tells me. I think she's expecting me to react, but I don't. This isn't news, not to me, at least. "Not just one or two. But over ten different company titles. A few are for land, but the rest are properties with condos, apartment buildings and such. They're his wedding present," she says with a frown.

"A wedding present for a wedding that was never going to take place?" That doesn't make sense to me and up until now, Dixon rarely made financial decisions that didn't make sense — at least to him.

Caryn gives a slight shrug. "Starla told me about the ring this morning." A muscle in her jaw pulses with tension. She's got the whole Mama Bear vibe going on, which is great. I can use it to my advantage.

"What else did you find?" I lean in close, my interest in the games Dixon played with Bishop increasing.

"Jewelry. Keys. Lots of notes." She leans back and mirrors the smile I know is on my face.

A lot of those question marks on the board that my team are working on. Danvers might just have the answers for me.

"Did you happen to read the notes?"

"Of course." The way she says it, I realize it's the stupidest question I could ask. She pulls out her phone and scrolls through until showing me the screen.

"There's a few photos there of the notes." She hands me the phone and leans back in her seat, coffee cup in hand, satisfied Cheshire cat grin on her face.

It doesn't take me long to get the gist of what Dixon has done. It's similar to holding out a dog treat for a puppy, close but just out of reach.

All the holdings Dixon was handing over to Bishop would become official on an upcoming date — presumably, their wedding date. He's smart, to draw up something that didn't hold his signature or date.

Why would he do this? What's the benefit to him?

Then came the jewelry. As nice as the engagement ring and probably just as fake.

Did he really think Bishop to be that gullible? That naive?

She's not. Except for when it came to Dixon. Hopefully she sees the monster now. I really hope she's not one of those prison brides.

"He was playing her," Caryn says. "Drawing her in, making her believe they were a team, that she was important to him. And she believed him." A shudder runs through her body. "God help me, I don't know why, but she really loved him."

Those words, they sit between us. I have no answers. No response. Spikes believed Bishop from the beginning and slowly, I began to see why. I believe her too.

"It's a little sad, isn't it?" I say. "A con artist getting played by another? That must eat at her pride more than anything."

She shakes her head. "No. Her heart is broken and that's all she's focused on right now."

She stands and holds out her hand. I place her phone in her palm. "Does that help?" she asks.

"Everything helps," I tell her.

Spikes once told me to think of every case like a puzzle. Not every piece makes sense, and you might not understand how it fits until you start putting the pieces together.

Little by little, this puzzle is coming together and we're about to nail Dixon's ass to the board.

42: THE GAME CONTINUES

I close the door quietly behind me, nod toward the chief and stand beside Spikes.

The room is crowded, with every senior officer in the squad wedged in. The room smells of sweat and stale coffee and if I didn't need to be — no, scratch that, if I didn't want to be here bad enough, I'd go someplace else and watch the playback just to get away from the stench.

Spikes commandeers the middle area right in front of the mirror, leaving me enough room to squeeze in beside him.

I swear Dixon is staring at me, like he knows I'm there, listening in. He doesn't, but he knows he's being watched.

I stare back. What does Bishop see in him? What is there about him that appeals to her so much? How could she have been so caught up in *him* that she didn't see what was happening around her?

Guess I could ask myself that question too. Any of us in this room could.

"Why don't you just admit the truth, tell me what I need to hear." Jordan's leaning back in his chair. There's a mirror on the wall across from us, which lets me see Jordan's expression.

He's pretty calm, all things considered. His arms are loosely crossed, there's a twitch to his lips that is part sarcasm part indifference, and the look in his eyes conveys a feeling of boredom. Looks like he's playing Dixon and playing him well.

"I'm not telling you shit," Dixon spits the words so fast, saliva hangs from the corner of his mouth and I gag.

Spikes looks at me. I shrug.

"How about I tell you a story, then?" Jordan says. He looks up at the mirror and winks.

Spikes leans close. "This is going to be good. Up to now, Dixon thinks we have nothing on him, that it's all on Bishop," he says in a low whisper.

"A new family moved into town and bought one of the old estate homes that have sat empty on the west side. You know those homes, right, Donny? Correct me if I'm wrong, but I think one of your shell companies even bought several of them." Jordan's shoulders heave, like he's stretching the muscles. He leans to the side and looks behind, toward us, his fingers signing something.

One of the officers in the room gets up and leaves.

Dixon doesn't say a word. Just sits there, a look of challenge permanently etched on his face.

"The new family owned a dog who loved to dig. Imagine their surprise when he comes into the house one night after a long romp in the yard with a bone tight between its teeth." Jordan leans forward then. "That single bone, a femur, in case you were wondering, led us down a long and windy road. It took a little digging, pardon the pun, but we discovered that the gardens were originally built by Soils and Springs, a company you retain half ownership to." Jordan leans back. "Or did," he says with a smirk.

From Dixon's slight hiss, this seems to be news.

Everyone in the room with me leans forward, closer to the window, in anticipation.

Jordan taps a file on the table beside him. "Your ex-wife slash ex-business partner has been a real help, but then, anyone would be if they didn't want to face up to life in prison."

"I told you to leave Alexius out of this." The low growl in Dixon's voice rumbled throughout the interrogation room.

"Know who else has been a great help? Starla Bishop, your pseudo-fiancée," Jordan continues.

Dixon leans back in his chair, arms crossed over his massive chest and gives a shrug. "I'm sure she has. But why would you believe a crook like her?" He bares his teeth in what he might assume to be a smile, but in reality is a sneer.

"Our team," Jordan continues, "were out at your cabin yesterday. Bet you didn't think we'd ever find it, did you?"

A muscle twitches on Dixon's face but he goes mute.

"Back to our story." The pitch of Jordan's voice rises slightly, like he's enjoying this. "I'll cut right to the chase, since I know you have places to be. Between the ex-wife with a need to save her own skin and the pretend-fiancée who woke up and realized what kind of man you are . . ." He pauses, staring Dixon straight on. "We have enough on you to put you away for life."

"You have nothing," Dixon snaps. "If Starla gave you anything, it's all a stretch to stay out of prison." His eyes close for a moment before reopening. "If you think she's clean, think again. Whatever it is you think you have on me, it will all lead back to her."

Jordan pushes up from his seat and leans on the table. "You sure of that?"

I hear the challenge in Jordan's voice and want to rub my hands in anticipation.

Dixon nods. "From the moment she moved here, she's been all up in my business." He leans forward, looks up at Jordan, his fists hitting the table. "She's smarter than she looks. Whose names are on the property titles? Who owns all these shell companies you keep claiming are mine? I own nothing. They're all hers."

"Again, are you sure of that?" Jordan repeats his question, his voice very low.

The tension in the room I'm in, it's escalated, built up until one small admission from Dixon is all it's going to take for an explosion of pent-up anger to erupt. We're all waiting, watching, as Jordan tears apart every loophole Dixon thought he had.

Dixon's mouth gapes like a suffocating fish. "I've had enough," he finally says. "I've been nothing but nice, helpful, but you've . . ." He swallows hard as his mouth tries to form words.

"Damn it," someone behind me mutters.

"Here, I thought we had him," another says.

Spikes is looking down at me. We're both thinking the same thing. For a man who is obviously guilty, he's waited an awfully long time to do the smartest thing.

"I want my lawyer," Dixon mutters.

The moment he says the words, Jordan lets go of whatever control he held. He swipes up the unopened folder on the table, throws the chair against the wall and yanks open the door.

Everyone in the room with me groans. One by one we leave, trailing after each other down the hall, everyone thinking the same damn thing.

Why demand his lawyer now?

43: TAKING THE BAIT

One Month Ago

My phone buzzed beside me and with practiced patience, I give it a swift look only to see what I already know. What both Mom and I know. It's Donny, texting me for the tenth time.

Are you sure we're okay? You're okay?

I haven't answered the past nine texts and I wasn't going to answer this one. I'd had a long exhausting week and just wanted to decompress. It's why I drove to Mom's place, why I told Donny about not being around for the weekend while I was driving and why I haven't answered him now.

"He's going to keep texting, or God forbid, drive down here, if you don't respond," Mom said as she rose from the lounger out in her backyard. "It's getting cold out. Come into the house after you've told him you're alive and not to come here."

We'd been outside for at least two hours, enjoying the crisp breeze while wrapped in thick sweaters. Mom had wanted to go in for the past hour, but I haven't been ready to move from this spot. Not yet. Sure, my nose was red, cheeks just as bright, fingers had turned into icicles long ago, but the wonder of being out, able to experience this as a free person, it enveloped me like a warm hug and nothing else mattered.

I scrolled through all of Donny's messages. All ten of them. All wanting to know where I was, what was wrong, why didn't I trust him and how could I do that to him.

Do what? Leave town and visit Mom for the weekend? How did that affect him? And what about what he'd done to me?

Me: *I'm fine. At Mom's.*

Donny: *THANK GOD! I thought you were in an accident. Don't ignore me like that again.*

Me: *Not ignoring. Just . . . busy.*

Donny: *Why did you leave? I thought we had plans? When will you be back?*

Me: *Mom asked me to come visit, she sounded lonely. I'll be back sometime Sunday night.*

Mom didn't ask me to come but there was no underlying guilt for telling that lie.

Donny: Are WE okay? You didn't answer me.

I leaned my head back and groaned. I hated when he did this. It wasn't often he'd play these cards, the wounded partner in a relationship, but when he did, he tended to lay the guilt on thick.

Me: *We're fine. Don't read into it too much. Mom asked me to come and . . . I figured you could probably use a weekend away from me and catch up on work.*

Would he take the bait? Grab my excuse and use it as his own? He'd be smart if he did. The truth was, I just wanted time away from him, from the head games between him and Alexius, from the probing looks from Jordan.

I just wanted a break from it all.

Donny: *I never need a break from you.*

Me: *That's sweet. Enjoy it anyways. Gotta run. Talk to you Sunday.*

With one last deep breath in, I inhaled the brisk, sharp evening air into my lungs and pushed myself out of the chair, pocketing my phone with the intention to ignore it for the rest of the evening.

"Starla, you need to come see this!" Mom yelled from the kitchen window. She stood there, motioning me in with her hand, her movements as frantic as her voice.

I hurried into the house where she grabbed my arm and dragged me into the living room where the television was on pause.

She had the news on. A bright red banner was on the bottom of the screen with the words *UPDATE* in bold black.

Her hands shook as she held the remote and hit the wrong button. I took it from her, stopped the show from rewinding even more and brought it back to the moment she had paused.

Sassy Sedona, my favorite news anchor sat at her desk, her hands folded in front of her, wearing a black blazer with a soft pink blouse beneath it. Her hair was perfectly styled to rest on her shoulders as she shared the latest with her audience.

Normally her eyes sparkled with a hint of playfulness. I'd always enjoyed how she relayed the news, adding her own spin to the sometimes stark and boring updates.

Tonight, her eyes were full of sorrow. Her lipstick-matted lips were in a straight line with no hint of either a smile or a frown and I could only imagine the words she was about to say.

"We have an update on the latest victim discovered in Bervie Springs," she said with a somberness that had Mom inhaling with a sharp gasp. She grabbed my arm and held tight.

"It has been confirmed that the latest victim discovered earlier in the week is Merilee Bogetti, a second-year student from Columbia University who had been declared missing two months ago."

She paused.

We waited in that moment, Mom with her hand over her mouth, me suspended mid-breath.

"This is the third such victim to be found within Bervie Springs over the course of six months," Sedona continued. "A source has confirmed that police are considering all three deaths to be linked."

Mom gasped, her grip on my arm tighter than before. "What are they saying?" Her eyes rounded, a shot glass filled to the brim with tears. "You can't go back."

It's not a question, it's a demand.

"Of course I'm going back."

Three deaths over six months. That's a lot for a small town like this, but not enough to scare me away.

"It's not safe." Her hand dropped from my arm, and the frown that covered her face warned me she'd argue her point until I agreed not to return.

"I'm safe, Mom. All three were from somewhere else. Maybe Bervie Springs is a dumping ground," I suggested.

"A dumping ground? Why on earth . . . Oh Starla, please don't go back. Tell that man of yours you don't feel safe and until the police figure out what is happening, you're not going back."

I laughed. I couldn't help it.

"I have to go back." It really wasn't her choice. "I'm scheduled to volunteer at the pet shelter tomorrow afternoon."

She was about to say something but stopped, pressing the mute button on the television instead. "You're doing a lot of volunteer work," Mom said, her words coming out like a slow drip coffee press. "Did Donald set that up for you as well?"

I shook my head. "All me. This is probably the one I enjoy the most," I admitted. All of the others were picked by Donny. I had to admit, he'd been right, too. People were getting to know me, respect me — even if just a little. No one mentioned my past anymore; the rare questions I'd get about prison life were from those who'd been in my shoes and wanted to know if I knew so and so. Sometimes I'd say yes. Most of the time I'd say no, whether it was the truth or not.

I liked being known as the helper, not the criminal.

"Why don't we watch a movie?" I suggested, needing to get her mind off of me and onto something she liked. "There's still a lot on my list I haven't watched."

She took the bait, like I knew she would.

44: ICE QUEEN MEET THE REAL QUEEN

Wednesday 11:15 a.m.

The sun is shining, the birds are chirping and I have to remind myself that life still continues even when horrible things happen.

I heard Mom leave the condo earlier. I also heard her return. I might have had a solid hour of sleep, but the images that plague my thoughts wouldn't leave.

I don't know how I'm ever going to sleep again.

I'm standing on the steps leading into the police station. Mom is beside me, as is the lawyer Mom contacted on my behalf.

I'm here with one goal, one focus, one reason. To see Donny.

Mom thinks I'm being foolish. What she doesn't know won't hurt her. I need to do this. I need to close this door, end this chapter, prove to not only to myself but to Donny that I wasn't as naive as he thinks I am.

The doors open and Alexius steps out. Her face is pale, her hair a ratted mess, her shirt wrinkled beyond belief. She looks nothing like the woman I'm accustomed to seeing.

When she sees me, she startles.

We stare at each other. So many thoughts, so many things that need to be said but never will be.

We'd said all that needed to be said a long time ago.

I can't imagine what her life will be like now. Will she dissolve the company? Start from scratch? Start over? She's tarnished; as much as she might want to pretend she's not, she is.

Who will hire her now? Only the sick and twisted, those who want to know more, who crave being associated with the perverted truth.

I should feel for her but I don't.

She slowly steps down, making her way toward me.

Mom's hand is on my elbow and she's trying to get me to move, but I don't. I won't.

I want Alexius to come to me. I want to know if she'll break our pact.

When she's one step above me, she stops. We look at each other, gauge each other's reaction, see who will flinch first. "Starla," she finally says.

"Alexius."

Mom steps to the side, then climbs up until she's at least three steps above Alexius. She's staring at me; her eyes are burning two holes into my forehead.

I refuse to tear my attention from Alexius. There's something she needs to say, she's trying to say, but can't get the words out.

I slowly nod, letting her know I understand.

"They showed me photos," she finally manages to say. She tries to maintain a semblance of control, but I notice the slight changes. The way her hands shake. The way her lips tremble. The way she constantly swallows.

"I was there." Three words that tell her more than she wants. The lashes on her eyes rest against her cheek, she breathes in deep and straightens her shoulders.

"I'm so sorry," she whispers.

I nod again. I know she is. I also know why.

She could have warned me. She could have told me to run. She could have sheltered me from all of this, from him and everything he brought into my life.

But then she wouldn't be here, walking free while Donald Dixon is still behind bars.

It was a day similar to this one. The sun had shone bright, heating our backs as we stood in the middle of one of the gardens at Soils and Springs. It was midday and she'd sent everyone to a job site, leaving just us.

I hated when it was just us.

It was a few days following her birthday, after I'd listened in on the conversation between her and Donny. After realizing the careful world I'd created around me wasn't as perfect as I thought it was.

She'd handed me a glass of ice tea and told me to join her on a bench.

"I know you're not stupid, Starla, so I have to ask, why are you letting Donny use you?" She'd asked me this like my answer didn't matter, except I knew it did.

"Before you try to play dumb and tell me he's not, or ask me how, I think you need to be aware of something. I know you were there the other night."

I looked away, embarrassed to have been caught eavesdropping.

"Donny is an animal you don't want to mess with. It's too late for you to run, but you can protect yourself. He's going to get caught." She reached over and placed her hand on my arm. "He's going to get caught," she stressed the words again.

I heard her, if that's what she was worried about.

I wanted to stay in my own perfect little bubble, pretend everything was fine, that I was fine, that I'd changed and what she was asking of me was something I could say no to.

But I couldn't. I knew it. She knew it. Self-preservation always ended up winning.

"When?"

She lifted a shoulder in a shrug. "Soon. There's still enough time to untangle yourself. But you have to be careful."

Back then, when I'd looked Alexius in the eyes, I'd made the choice to make her pay too. That if Donny was going down, so was she.

But today, after everything I knew, after everything I'd seen . . . this was all on him.

"I owe you an apology," I say now.

Mom is waving her arms like crazy but I continue to ignore her.

"You thought I was involved, I know. I don't blame you. But I . . ." She stops, swallows, starts again. "I couldn't do that," she says. "Kill those women, skin them alive like that . . ." She shakes her head. "He's a monster and I'll never forgive myself for not seeing the truth earlier." She shudders. "It was always there, but I . . . I looked the other way. Until I couldn't anymore."

When I'd been in prison, a lot of the other inmates had to deal with this guilt, but from the other side. They struggled with the guilt of involving their loved ones. This was the first time I'd witnessed the horror of those innocently involved.

She probably wants me to tell her it's okay, that she'll be all right, but I'm not going to lie to her.

"He's the monster, not you," I finally manage to say. I try to tell her more, hoping she'll be able to read every word in my gaze, because I can't say anything else.

Not with my lawyer present.

I want to tell her that everything we'd discussed, everything we'd planned, it all worked out.

I want to tell her that I'll take care of making sure she's cleared, that even though I'd made a promise to myself to make sure she paid, I couldn't and wouldn't follow through with my promise. Not after everything I'd seen.

No matter what she says, she knew. Deep down, she knew the man he was, the man he is, and she did nothing to stop him. She turned a blind eye to all the homeless women he brought from the city, the women who disappeared without a trace. She'd even said it to him, that night after her birthday dinner, the night when I overheard too much.

There's so much I want to say.

But instead, I say nothing.

"I hope I never see you again," she says to me.

"Wishful thinking," I tell her. This story wasn't going to go away for a long time and we'll probably run into each other, in law offices, the court room . . . no matter how far I move from this town, it'll always be there. They will always be there.

I step to the side, but in a rare moment of emotion, Alexius wraps her arms around me in a hug.

"I'm sorry," she whispers into my ear. "I'm so sorry you stayed when you should have left. But you'll be okay, right?"

I give a subtle nod of my head and she detaches herself from me.

It's not until I'm in the front hall of the police station that Mom leans close.

"What did she say to you?" Mom asks.

"She wanted to make sure I'd be okay," I tell her. It's not the whole truth, but it's close enough.

My lawyer pulls me to the side. "For the record, I think this is a bad idea," she says.

"Noted." Her advice doesn't change my resolve. I'm here to see Donny. I'm here for one reason and one reason alone.

To let him know he's screwed.

45: ALL GLOVES ARE OFF

I'm not sure what my lawyer said to Spikes, but here I am.

The room is slightly different than the one I'd been in. This one has no windows, for one thing. Everything about this room gives off a claustrophobic vibe. The camera up in the corner is blinking red, warning me we're being recorded.

My lawyer managed to get me an audience with the monster himself. I'm not sure where Mom found her, but I like her already. Donny is at the table, his hands in cuffs, and I'm not sure how I feel seeing him like this.

I'm finding it hard to reconcile with the fact I was able to love a man like him. The man I thought he was, not the man he is, and how someone with my life experience managed to get sucked into his bullshit. I have to wrap my head around that, understand it, accept it.

My movements are hesitant and I know he can tell. What is he thinking? How is all of this affecting him? My fingers shake as I reach for the edge of the chair, pull it back.

I'm frozen, unable to move, to sit down, all I can do is stare at him, the man, the monster, the . . . lover. My heart breaks over and over until only slivered pieces are left and I'm not sure if I'll ever recover. It's not just him I've lost. I lost the woman who started to believe I was capable of loving someone else, of being loved in return. I lost the fairy-tale dream of being the princess, of living my happily-ever-after. I lost the chance to be loved the way I want, need, desire . . . I'll never trust again. Not after this.

I stare at Donny and it's hard to reconcile the man in front of me with the man he must truly be. I thought I knew him, understood him . . . how could I have been so wrong?

"Sit down, Starla," Donny's gruff, indifferent voice startles me. I sit, hands in my lap and stare. That's all I can do in this moment.

"God, you really are stupid, aren't you?" he says to me.

The indifference on his face, so different from the last time I saw him, slaps me in the face, the effect casting me out of my frozen state.

This man I see, the one with his hands clasped together, his hair all messed, with dark circles beneath his eyes, this is a man I've never known.

He thinks he's still playing me. I can see it, in the way he views me, in the tone of his voice. And that's fine. Let him think that, because eventually he'll know the truth and it's going to hurt.

My lips curl into a sarcastic smile but I remain silent.

"Why are you here? Did they send you in, hoping to get a confession out of me?" He turns his gaze toward the camera. "You really think she's going to make a difference? She's the one who should be here in cuffs, not me."

I set my purse down on the table between us and scoot my chair closer. "Really, Donald?"

His eyes shutter, his face goes blank. "Yes, Starla, really."

"I didn't kill those women," I say, hoping for a reaction. But there's nothing. "I didn't use pieces of their skin to create leather keychains and hand them out to everyone in town." This time a sly smile appears on his face. "I didn't use their blood in the pottery around your cabin or give their blood to Alexius for her plants." That one still bothers me more than I care to admit. I couldn't look at another head of lettuce from a farmer's market the same way again.

He just sits there, a sardonic grin on his face and it's all I can do not to smack it off him.

"I also wasn't the one stupid enough to make the pottery with the names and dates of victims. You practically handed the police everything they need," I continued, wanting, wishing, needing a reaction from him.

By now, he's got a full-blown smile stretched across his face.

"You're sick, you know that?" It feels like I've sat across from him for a lifetime and now I'm covered in slime.

He shrugs. "Takes one to know one."

"No." I shake my head. "I have no idea who you are. You've been playing me from the very beginning, haven't you? The only thing I can't figure out is why?"

He slowly rolls his head into a circle, the crack-craack-craaaack coming from his neck filling the room.

"Why would I play you, Starla?" He turns his steel gaze to me, but his voice is sticky sweet. "All I wanted to do was help you. From the very beginning, that's all I've tried to do. Help you become a better person, instead of a waste upon society like you were. Admit it, without me, you'd be back in prison, even now."

I give his suggestion some thought. Yes, it's true. If it hadn't been for him, I most likely would be back in prison. He did help shape me into this woman I am now.

"Who was I to know you were a truly bad seed. You were full of promise but I got blinded." He tsks, showing me his complete disappointment. "You were the one organizing trips into the city to pick up the homeless and the sluts. You got them situated in the apartments, and then you killed them, planting them in our customers' gardens. The question is why? Why would you try to hurt me and Alexius like that?"

"What are you talking about?" I never organized a single trip or kept records of who stayed where.

"I have paperwork that says otherwise." Donny's gaze slides to the camera and then it all makes sense.

He's trying to frame me.

"Give it up. They muted it for a few minutes, just so we can have a . . . heart-to-heart." This time I'm the one smiling while he frowns. Kaarns had stopped me on the way in and I'd asked her for some privacy. She gave me a knowing look and said something like the camera sound might accidentally be off, too bad we won't be able to record your conversation, followed by a couple of winks. I'm hoping it's true.

Or not . . . as long as he thinks it's true, that's what matters.

"Why are you here?" His voice is empty, stale, without a single ounce of feeling, completely opposite from a few moments earlier.

And so now we get to see the real image of the monster lurking behind the face of the man.

"Well?" he says with impatience. "Why are you here?"

Good question.

I have so many reasons for being here, but only one pops to mind.

"Why didn't you kill me too?"

This is going to haunt me for a very long time. Every victim found could have been me.

"Haven't you guessed it yet?"

Guessed it? What?

"You're a con artist that always gets caught. You screw the wrong people, it's just who you are. I'm not going down for any of this. Neither is Alexius. But you . . ." He rubs his fingers together. "You were the perfect mark."

The way his eyes light up, I see the excitement, feel it in the air between us, almost taste it. I recognize it, the build-up from knowing you're always straddling the line of getting away with something or getting caught.

But Donny is delusional if he thinks he's getting away with anything.

"A mark never knows the game being played, Donny," I remind him.

"Exactly."

"A mark never realizes they're in danger of losing everything," I continue.

"I know."

"A mark remains in the dark even after everything has happened." I give him a direct, in-your-face stare.

He nods. "I know." He lifts his hands, like he's about to point at me, then drops them, leans back and his face convulses into a symphony of shock as what I'm saying sinks in.

It's quite priceless to watch, and the realization that I'm enjoying his discomfort shocks me.

I'd once been told I should have been born into the mob, that with a little bit of teaching, coaching, guiding, I could make it a long way.

How this moment feels to me — how important it is to see the understanding dawn on his face — I can see the truth to those words. It's a little scary, I'm not going to lie.

"I wanted to protect you," I tell him.

He sneers.

"I was there, in the office, on Alexius' birthday," I say, giving my shoulder a shrug as if that night no longer affected me.

Lies.

"The things I overheard," I continue, "I thought you were the one who was in over his head, that you needed protection." I shake my head at myself, for my own naiveté. "I thought Alexius was the monster."

Outrage morphs over Donny at the mention of his ex-wife's name, surprising me. "You know nothing," he spits out at me. "Nothing!"

One thing Donny has never realized is that anger doesn't bother me. I've seen enough of it in my life, I'm immune.

"I know a lot more than you think I do." My voice remains calm, my face placid, my body posture composed. "You're the stupid one, Donny. You're the one who signed—" I lean forward and drop my voice to a whisper — "everything that means anything to you, in a gift-wrapped box, complete with the finances to take care of me and Mom for the rest of our lives."

I made sure to keep my face tilted slightly away from the camera in case anyone was attempting to lip read. I didn't want this information to be public.

It takes a minute, but he laughs at the news. Not a shocked, 'oh my god what have I done?' laugh, but more of a 'boy you are screwed' kind of laughter.

"You think I'm stupid enough to give you everything? I gave you nothing. NOTHING." He bangs his hands on the table hard enough that my purse moves on the surface.

"You gave me everything that mattered." I don't bother to hide my smile. Why would I? I know Mom found the planted documents and notes. I knew she'd look.

The real copies, the signed copies . . . they're safely locked away. The accounts, moved, the money . . . mine. All. Mine.

"Did you really think you could play me, Donald Dixon? Yes, for a moment, I softened. I wanted to believe you were different, that you really did love me. But your game plan was flawed, love." I tilt my head to the side, flutter my lashes and add a slight cooing to my voice. "You showed your hand."

He scoffs, casting me a look that is filled with part fear and part derision.

"Did you forget your ex-wife talks in her sleep? That she was sleeping with an undercover cop who convinced her he could protect her better than you could?"

The cuffs around Donald's wrists slap against the metal table. I knew that would get him.

A myriad of emotions, thoughts, and realizations play across his face as he grapples with everything.

I wait. I wait and I watch the man in front of me morph into someone I once knew.

"I wasn't playing you," Donny says, the hatred, vitriol and disgust gone from his voice. The man in front of me, this is the man I'd fallen in love with. He won't look me in the eye, which is smart, because no matter how much honey drips from his forked tongue, there's no masking the truth in his gaze.

"I was protecting you," he says, parroting my earlier words, leaning in close. "Alexius . . . she's . . ." He searches for the words he thinks I'll believe, his gaze tracking the room for help. "She's sick, Starla. I . . . I didn't want to tell you, I was ashamed to admit it, I guess." He lifts his hands off the table for a brief moment.

"She's the one who killed those women." It's like he can barely speak the words. He looks at me then, for one brief moment before he closes his eyes. "She killed them for her blood. I . . . I hid the bodies because I couldn't . . . I just couldn't turn her in."

I'd thought about this. Considered this. I honestly wanted this to be the truth.

But the pottery, the keychains . . . A man trying to protect a loved one doesn't do things like that. Hiding bodies in gardens, sure, that's plausible . . . maybe. But skinning women and handing out his trophies to everyone in town? That's just sadistic.

"I wish I could believe you." I lean forward and reach my hand out, as if I wanted to hold his hand, but the idea of him touching me . . . a shudder runs through me that I try to hide. "I wish I could believe you," I repeat, drawing the words out, feeling them on my tongue, realizing how empty and shallow they taste. "But I'm not stupid, Donny."

We both lean back at the same time. I see the costume he'd worn, the character he'd played . . . I see it all disappear into a pool of nothingness at our feet.

"Did you think I'd forget all about my survival instincts?" I say before he has the chance to open his mouth. "That I would stop looking over my shoulder and start trusting everything and everyone around me?" This time it's me that tsks. "All those late nights I spent at the office, I was doing surveillance. Almost every room in your house is bugged. My lawyer has all the recordings and is in the process of handing those over while I'm in here with you."

I watch the wheels turn as Donald replays all our conversations, all the times I said I was working late, my weekends away. I watch as it all hits him. I watch and I begin to laugh.

"You're the naive one, Donny." I grab for my purse, suddenly done with our conversation. "The careless one."

There's nothing else I need to say to him. Nothing that will soothe a broken heart. Nothing that will answer the endless questions that will plague me.

The bottom line is that I was played. Even though I caught on quickly or that I turned the table on Donny. I still let my heart get involved, believed that I, a convict, could be worthy of love.

"I do have one question," I say as I stand there, purse in hand. "Why would you turn over companies to me, and the money?"

"You realize what those shell companies are being used for, right?" he asks.

"Laundering money. I'm not stupid."

"You're stupid enough to let the money sit."

I laugh. First it begins as a giggle and I slap a hand over my mouth, stuffing that giggle back down to be contained. "Did you honestly think I'd be so blinded by love that I'd let that money sit to be confiscated by the police or the government?" My face is turned again, so no one can attempt to read my lips. "I worked for the mob once, you fool."

He jolts to his feet, half bent since his hands are contained by cuffs secured to a metal hook on the table.

"You bitch," he snarls at me.

I don't let his words affect me. He doesn't scare me, not when he's like this. I'd be more apt to be afraid if he was detached, calm, cold . . . then I'd be more afraid. But this? He's playing right into my hands.

"Give it up, Donald. If anyone is the fool, it's you, the ass who signed away companies and handed over bank accounts." I let my shoulders drop and smile. It's the type of smile you'd expect on a cat about to pounce on a mouse, the type of smile that tells Donald if anyone is getting played . . . it's him.

He begins to growl, which makes me laugh.

"What?" I say, stopping him from whatever tirade he's about to release on me. "Don't play me for an idiot. Did you think you'd be able to steal those documents back? Shred them with no one being the wiser? Come on, *Donny*" — I stress the familiarity of his name — "like I was going to let that happen."

"You bitch."

I shrug. "Yeah, you've already called me that. Don't try to blame all of this on me. You were the one who got sloppy, stopped being on guard and settled, thinking you were getting away with everything scot-free." I lean in close then, ready to sucker-punch the hell out of him.

"The only stupid thing I did was fall in love with you. I blame you for letting down your guard, but I did the same. That's probably why you became so careless around me. Thank God for Alexius, though." I give a slight nod, as if what I'm about to say is a revelation, even to myself.

"What has she got to do with this?" He stops me from continuing, his growl lower, dirtier than I'd expected, which tells me one thing. He's on the edge of what little control he has left.

"Everything, really," I say as a wicked smile, one I know angers him, grows on my face. I let the smile deepen. "She offered me a deal, one I couldn't pass up. To work together, clear our names, make sure neither one of us is covered by your slime." It's genius, if you ask me.

I've known for months how sick and twisted he is. I've known and plotted to do everything I could to keep myself out of jail — even to the point of pretending I knew nothing, claiming his innocence from the moment Detective Spikes sat across from me in the interrogation room.

I didn't know everything though. What I didn't know what how sick, how perverted, how twisted he really is. I didn't know he was a serial killer. I didn't understand how depraved he truly is. Alexius and I had both assumed he killed a few prostitutes . . . I had no idea about the truth. I'm not even sure Alexius did.

The look of pure hatred on Donny's face doesn't even faze me. It's funny how fast our hearts become immune once we build those walls, layer the protection around our core so that nothing can penetrate. That's how I'm feeling now. Numb, cold, restrained.

"I'm only the employee, since no one knew we were engaged, thanks to you," I say. "And Alexius, why, she's the poor ex-wife who had no idea the monster she'd married." I shake my head as if I feel pity for the woman. "But now we're both very wealthy, again, all thanks to you." I lean forward, as if I was going to place a kiss on his cheek, but instead I whisper a phrase that's run through my head on repeat since I walked into this room.

"Thanks for keeping your promise, Donald Dixon. You really did turn out to be my fairy godfather."

THE END

THE JOFFE BOOKS STORY

We began in 2014 when Jasper agreed to publish his mum's much-rejected romance novel and it became a bestseller.

Since then we've grown into the largest independent publisher in the UK. We're extremely proud to publish some of the very best writers in the world, including Joy Ellis, Faith Martin, Caro Ramsay, Helen Forrester, Simon Brett and Robert Goddard. Everyone at Joffe Books loves reading and we never forget that it all begins with the magic of an author telling a story.

We are proud to publish talented first-time authors, as well as established writers whose books we love introducing to a new generation of readers.

We won Trade Publisher of the Year at the Independent Publishing Awards in 2023. We have been shortlisted for Independent Publisher of the Year at the British Book Awards for the last four years, and were shortlisted for the Diversity and Inclusivity Award at the 2022 Independent Publishing Awards. In 2023 we were shortlisted for Publisher of the Year at the RNA Industry Awards.

We built this company with your help, and we love to hear from you, so please email us about absolutely anything bookish at feedback@joffebooks.com

If you want to receive free books every Friday and hear about all our new releases, join our mailing list: www.joffebooks.com/contact

And when you tell your friends about us, just remember: it's pronounced Joffe as in coffee or toffee!

ALSO BY STEENA HOLMES

BERVIE SPRINGS SERIES
Book 1: ENGAGED TO A SERIAL KILLER

STANDALONES
THE SISTER UNDER THE STAIRS

Printed in Dunstable, United Kingdom

72645293R00153